The Engagement of Ozma

Book Two in the Umbrella Man of Oz series

By

Charles Phipps

This book is a work of fiction. Places, events, and situations in this story are purely fictional. Any resemblance to actual persons, living or dead, is coincidental.

© 2001, 2003 by Charles Phipps. All rights reserved.

No part of this book may be reproduced, stored in a retrieval system, or transmitted by any means, electronic, mechanical, photocopying, recording, or otherwise, without written permission from the author.

ISBN: 1-4107-9010-X (e-book)
ISBN: 1-4107-9009-6 (Paperback)

Library of Congress Control Number: 2003097703

This book is printed on acid free paper.

Printed in the United States of America
Bloomington, IN

1stBooks - rev. 10/14/03

Table of Contents

Chapter 1 1

Chapter 2 13

Chapter 3 22

Chapter 4 31

Chapter 5 43

Chapter 6 56

Chapter 7 74

Chapter 8 88

Chapter 9 103

Chapter 10 122

Chapter 11 133

Chapter 12 151

Chapter 13 163

Chapter 14 179

Epilogue 187

About the Author 191

The Engagement of Ozma
Book Two in the Umbrella Man of Oz series

Chapter 1

The Merry Old Land of Oz you've probably read of before. Whether as a wonderful fairy land where Dorothy and her fantastic friends have been having adventures since 1900 or more recently Ozma and her new companion Milo falling in love.

If you haven't, or simply need a refresher course, then Oz is a wonderful country just this side of the sunrise (or sunset depending on where you are standing) in Fairy Country where most of the behind the scene work of our world goes on. Things like the creating of gems, rainbows, and true love is the part and parcel of this world.

In Oz animals can talk. In Oz beings can be made of straw or wood or anything really and be as alive as you or me. In Oz death is simply unknown with danger merely inconvenient and never any real threat.

In the heart of Oz there lies the Emerald City and in the heart of THAT, lies the Princess Ozma who is the Supreme Ruler of Fairy Kind in her lands, second only to Lurline herself. Ozma is both a Queen among the fey and also heir to the Throne of the Goodly Fey ruled by her mother, the above mentioned Lurline. She's not a Mrs. though and will not be until she marries (in a few years less than 900 right now) but she has many other charming qualities that should be respected.

Ozma has boundless compassion, energy, intelligence, and a not less than considerable set of good looks. Ozma has the complete approval of her subjects and recently has done something that has won her even more love and adulation by taking a young man named Milo Starling as her someday husband.

Milo is a decent young man from the Mortal World, the humdrum Planet Earth that you and I live on, whom had the fortune to land in Oz. He then proceeded to rescue it from an invasion and win the Princess's heart in a span of three days, something that makes the 900 year wait until their wedding somewhat more bearable. Currently, the Princess and her consort, a fancy way of saying boyfriend, were engaged in a spirited intellectual discussion inside the Palace Game Room.

"D-i-v-i-n-i-t-y! Ha! Double word score as well!" Milo said putting the little wooden tiles of the Scrozzle game on the board. The Palace Game Room was well stocked with all of the classics of Ozma's reign such as Share: A game about not hoarding wealth, Peace: The world's first non-violent war game, and Magic Mystery which was a rather nasty game about finding out who killed the wicked witch with what and where.

Ozma was sitting across from Milo at a table, which was actually just a gigantic emerald in the center of the Game Room, sipping a glass of emerald green Ozade. "Good for you Milo. Hmmmm…" Ozma said as she looked over her wooden tiles. After a moment she moved every last one of her letters onto the board. "There we go."

"Pyrzqxgl is not a word my Lady," Milo said looking at the word she put down and trying to figure out exactly how to even pronounce it. "Frankly may I point out it doesn't even have any vowels. It has a q without a u behind…"

"It's a magic word of transformation Milo," Ozma corrected causally.

Milo put his fingers to his eyes and sighed, knowing better than to question the intelligence let alone mystical know how of his bride to be.

"One of these days I'm going to buy a dictionary of these words so I can win a game of Scrozzle with you. What exactly does that make the final score?"

"You did much better this time, 175 to 1,470," Ozma said as she looked over her calculations. "And you aren't pronouncing it properly. You need more accent on the P and then the zqxgl but don't try it in here or you may turn me into an emerald cricket or something equally unpleasant."

"Perish the thought," Milo said looking quite astonished.

Dorothy Gale, a Princess of Oz and a person I'm sure you're quite familiar with by now, entered soon after the young hero and heroine of our story got up for bed. Dorothy was the Second Most Popular Person in Oz after Ozma. Milo (nor anyone else) couldn't hold a candle to the girl from Kansas in popularity, though aside from her heroism it also may be due to the fact she was now the most eligible bachelorette in Oz now that she had chosen to grow up some as well.

"Hello," the princess greeted her two friends.

"Good evening Miss Gale," Milo clicked his feet together and bowed which was quite strange since he wasn't German and there were no Germans in all of Oz.

"Milo we've known each other for years, you can call me Dorothy," Dorothy spoke as Ozma noticed a large gold and green scroll case covered in carvings of beautiful faeries in her hands.

"Oh I couldn't do that," Milo said with a smile. Excessive Politeness was an endearing trait of the man's, even as Dorothy's unlimited sweetness was hers.

"Do you have a letter for me Dorothy?" Ozma interrupted as she took a deep breath and gazed onto the scroll with barely held in delight. The scroll could only come from one woman and it was the woman that Ozma wanted more to speak to than any other in the world.

"Yes it arrived just a few minutes ago by delivery from a large bee," The Princess replied as she pointed back into the hall she had come from. There a foot tall yellow and black bee was hovering wearing a pair of sunglasses and a graduate's cap.

"I'mmmmmmmmmmm Silasssssssssss theeeee mmmmmmmmmmessangerbeeeeeeeeeeeeeee." The bee hummed. "A relativelllllllyyyyyy new pheeneeeeeemeonnnnnn in fairrrrrrry magiccccccccccc. We'reeeeeee relattteedddd to spelllllllingg beessss."

Ozma smiled and giggled slightly as she took the scroll and opened it in anticipation. Puns you see were Princess Ozma's favorite form of humor and she had actually prepared for a punning contest to be held very soon.

"I saw that pun coming a mile a way," Dorothy said shaking her head at the hovering bee.

"As did I," Milo agreed with the girl from Kansas.

Ozma looked at the silver silk parchment she had unveiled and read its contents anxiously. Once finished she clutched it to her chest and she wrapped Milo in a spinning hug that took him around the room. Ozma, despite her rather diminutive size, was as strong as an elephant when she wanted to be.

"I take it the letter is good news," Dorothy said looking quite pleased at her best friend.

"It's incredible news. It is a letter from my mother!" Ozma could barely contain her joy. Ozma, you must understand, is a fairy princess and while Oz is hers to rule by right, it is a right that stems from her adoption by the Good King Pastoria and his wife. It's a rather large pity that the King, who was now the Emerald City's finest tailor, never got to spend much time with Ozma thanks to the machinations of the Wicked Witch Mombi.

"Pastoria's wife?" Dorothy asked.

"I'm sure she's a very pleasant woman," Milo said in all honesty. Though given he'd never met her, he was simply basing this assumption on Ozma's own goodness.

"No, tis from Lurline." Ozma smiled as she spoke the name. Lurline was a name which impressed both mortals who had only heard of the Fairy Queen second and often fiftieth hand. Lurline, the Queen of the Faeries, Lurline the Mistress of all Seelie Fey, Lurline the magician who enchanted all of Oz and brought it into Fairy Country from the plain old Earth. You could say Lurline was a pretty important person to Oz and it came as quite a shock that Ozma was actually related until you realized that anyone as beautiful and wondrous as Ozma had to have a great mother.

"Lurline!" both Milo and Dorothy said at the same time.

"Good luck." Dorothy said to Milo giggling. It was considered good sport in Oz to give a good luck wish whenever someone said something at the exact same time you did.

"Let me read it aloud. 'My dearest daughter I know that we have not spoken for over a century since the day I brought you as a child to the noble King Pastoria but my faeries have always kept close eye on Oz and I am very proud of the things you have accomplished. A little bird, specifically a raven, has told me that you are engaged to a mortal recently and I would care to invite you, he, and whoever you so desire to accompany you to my home island of Avy-Lyon. I wish to meet them and hear first accounts of your adventures in accordance with the custom of Presenting.'" Ozma then looked up and said. "Oh my, how could I have forgotten about the custom of Presenting?" and

The Engagement of Ozma
Book Two in the Umbrella Man of Oz series

the fairy Princess put her hands to her head in an embarrassed headache.

"Your mother hasn't spoken with you for a century?" Dorothy asked quite shocked. Dorothy's own parents were dead but she had brought her Uncle Henry and Aunt Em into Oz and made sure she visited them all day at least once a week, usually on Sunday. Abandoning one's family for a century just struck the Kansas girl as negligent.

"Yes that does seem rather rude. Well at least providing she was aware you were transformed into a boy being raised by a horrible witch and your adopted parents had been usurped," Milo said lifting up his birthday gift from Ozma, a yellow and gold umbrella (whose wonders will hopefully be demonstrated later in this story) while shaking it to accentuate his point.

Ozma's look at Milo caused him to stop shaking it. The little queen of Oz could melt silver with her unhappy looks.

"Of course I'm sure she wasn't," Milo quickly corrected.

Ozma gave both of them a hug then looked at the Messenger bee hovering still by. "Thank you. This is joyous news and I can't wait to see my mother and show you off all to them."

"Wouldddddddddd youuuuuu likkeeeeee ttttoooooo seennnnndddddd a reeppplllyyyy asssss sweeeeet asssss honneeey or stinnninggggging?" the Messenger bee asked while lifting his stinger into the air.

"Simply tell me my mother that I am coming as soon as possible and look forward to her meeting them." Ozma replied before the Messenger Bee zoomed out the window to make the long trek across the lands of Imagination to the homeland of Lurline and her fairy band.

"Well that's wonderful Ozma but how are we supposed to get to her homeland?" Dorothy asked looking at her friend with a wrinkled brow. Navigating Fairy Country was a tricky task and no sailor fairy or mortal had ever succeeded mapping all of it.

"And where exactly is her homeland fair lady?" Milo questioned. His experiences regarding Fairy Land geography were rather mixed. He knew Oz existed "between the spaces" of his world but the spaces were awfully large as far as Milo could tell. This was one of the main reasons all the explorers had thus far failed. You could step over a gigantic kingdom if you weren't looking.

"My mother lives in the Sea of Immortality Milo. It is a land well past the Forests of Burzee and one of the oldest lands in Fairy Country. There among its' island chains are Avy-Lyon, Edenia, the Ellie-siums, and the Mountain of Thunder. My mother rules over Avy-Lyon which is the strongest and most beautiful of the Islands."

Milo blinked at the mentioning of such mythic names and shrugged it off, content that answers would come in time. At once this was both a very foolish and very wise attitude.

A note about Milo, since he is going to be one of the heroes in this story, is the fact he is a man who relies very much on the 'plain and common sense' of his upbringing and religion. While he was luckier than others who might have similar plain and common sense in their faith given he grew up in one of the most enchanted regions of Kentucky, he was often astounded by encountering many things which very few references were made to in his favorite book. The Umbrella man of Oz thus had to rely also on his feelings to tell him what was wicked, good, and absurd as often as not. Milo was sure the Supreme Master would take the correct him should he ever go astray.

Ozma continued on "Unfortunately, such a trip across our world is very long indeed and we'll need to take the Train of Thought to get across such vast distance in our own lifetime. It arrives in Oz at random intervals so we'll have to be prepared for when it arrives tomorrow."

Milo raised a finger to question the logic of her knowing the time when it arrived when it arrived randomly but recognized his feelings told him it was in this case better not to question Oz logic.

"I most worry about the Presentation," Ozma said as she shook her head and took a deep breath. Worry was a most uncommon state for the Queen of Oz and one that was characterized by her removing the poppies from her hair and fiddling with their petals.

"It's some kind of fairy custom I take it?" Dorothy asked looking at Milo then Ozma with a shrug.

Ozma put her poppies together and said. "It's an ancient custom indeed my closest friend. The Fey are an immortal race and an indestructible one as well save for the lowest among us. Thus marriages are taken seriously indeed for they are the eternal union of souls and bring hope of children. Thus any fairy who wishes to take a husband or bride must have her parent's permission up to and including the Supreme Master himself."

Milo put his front two fingers to his lips in an expression of astonishment. The Fairy system of law was a complex one and it made him slightly uncomfortable that it had such direct interventions by such powerful beings. Rather like if you were aware you were about to be reviewed by your teacher or boss.

"I would not worry my darling for the Fairies of the Immortal Isles have always had fondness for mortals, above even their own kind and are unlikely to find trouble with you or Dorothy who are certainly the most worthy mortals I have met," Ozma thought best not to mention the rather large menagerie of humans who had come to Oz to her mother beyond Milo and Dorothy. While they were equally worthy in Ozma's eyes, many fairies might object to so many mortals being allowed to stay in the immortal lands. As long as folk like the Shaggy Man, Captain Bill, Trot, Betsy, the Wizard, and others lived in Oz they would never die. Some fairies wrongly believed this wasn't the way things were supposed to go. Don't ask why, fairies find a lot to complain about in of their eternal lives.

"A worthy wife is her husband's joy and crown so I suspect the reverse would be true my Angel," Milo nodded towards Ozma and quoted again the Good Book, which was his favorite source for day-to-day wisdom. "I will do my best to impress your relatives properly."

Ozma smiled. "Just be yourself my friend." which is sound advice because you can never be as good as other people are at being themselves.

***

Meanwhile very, very, very, very, very (and I do mean very) far away in the depths of Avy-lyon's deepest cove; Ozma's conversation was being monitored by someone of a less that friendly will toward the Princess of Oz.

"Mmmmmmmm Princess Ozma is coming to Avy-lyon. Interesting," the man said in a high-pitched squeal of a voice. The Princess's face was shown along with many other important persons throughout the world on a variety of magical screens in a chamber that somewhat resembled a mix between an alchemist's workshop and a mad scientist's laboratory (which was actually what it was no less).

The only thing there that you wouldn't expect in the damp lab was the contents of the very large cage in the back. Inside the cave was a beautiful tigress whose sleek form had no place in the horrible room.

The evil man stared at Ozma's picture as he paced about the heart of the room. He was quite the contrast to the beautiful princess of Oz. Tall and thin like a rail, he had long white hair that dangled over his chest in wild and twisted tangles that stuck up in every direction. His skin was reddish-brown like leather that was blushing, and his teeth were sharp like knives. A white lab coat was draped over a chemical stained tweed sweater and he wore sensible but equally stained khaki pants. Evile Lackey was his name, and at one point he was one of the most feared men in Oz. That was before the wicked warlock and his entire family had been driven out of Oz by Glinda nearly a century earlier.

In case you couldn't guess, he's going to be the story's bad guy.

"Perhaps she's coming to destroy you Evile," The Tigress said to the Wizard with a sniff of her nose that showed her disdain.

"I don't think so Sita. Princess Ozma and her kind were always content to drive wicked folk like myself out of Oz or strip us of our magic rather than out and outright destroy us. When my mother was destroyed by that vile witch slayer Dorothy with a bucket of water, it was an accident. When my son Igor was turned into a tree just a few years past, that was the result of his own stupidity. No, she's no doubt here to visit the Fairy Queen Lurline which will provides an ample opportunity for revenge," Evile Lackey chuckled to himself. The Lackey Family of course is the most evil family in the world. It included such unpleasant folk as the Wicked Witch of the West and Igor Lackey whose fates have just been described. To

The Engagement of Ozma
Book Two in the Umbrella Man of Oz series

say the family tree produced bad apples would be an understatement, not even the worms would have them.

And worms like everybody.

"I thought you just said they didn't do anything to your relatives," Sita said.

"No I said that it was accidentally that my family was undone. However, if the Oz folk had been content to lie down be abused then neither of them would have ended up undone. Thus as the Greatest Mad Scientist/Warlock in the world, it is my duty to avenge my family by doing...very...unpleasant things to them," Evile let out a wheezing chuckle that sounded like he was a vacuum coughing.

Sita shook her head and put her paw to her face. Sita had once been the Princess of the Tigers in Oz but had been kidnapped as a cub by Evile Lackey along with her fiance the Prince of the Tigers Rama. They had both eventually escaped but Evile had found her again, just before her wedding to Rama, and he had put her in the cage she now occupied.

"It's almost a shame that there are only three of them that I can torment," Evile said as he began to power up a machine that looked vaguely like a very large gun mixed with a television camera. "My Phantomizer Image Creator or PIC for short should do the trick nicely. Anywhere in the world I can beam images of whatever I want into it. All I have to do is point it at the Oz Star and the beam will bounce of it to trail down on anyone I want."

Sita occasionally questioned whether Evile Lackey was very smart or very stupid. "Evile, why do you tell me such things when I am your enemy and will surely use your secrets against you?"

Evile continued to laugh before he started walking towards another room in his cave home. "Sita I have no one in my cave but you to talk to. If I didn't tell you about all of my dastardly inventions and evil plots then I'd be talking solely to myself and frankly I'm not a very pleasant person to talk to."

Evile Lackey then went to fetch some extension chord when Sita leaned out her paw from her cage onto the machine. With a flick of her furry digits, she turned on the strange device.

"Let us hope that your skill for once matches your boastings Evil One," Sita said as the Phantomizer shot a beam of golden green light through the caverns that reflected off the walls until it bounced towards the Oz star and settled downwards upon the Merry Old Land of Oz to the person most wanted to speak to by the Princess.

***

The Hungry Tiger was currently lying in the great jungle of the Lion's Forest. This just goes to show you that Oz geography is unlike any other countries in the world since Jungle is not normally found in forest.

The Hungry Tiger was having his favorite dream, a dream mostly about the eating of fat babies but it somehow not being wrong and hurtful to his conscience. If you are scandalized by a tiger dreaming about eating such things, please take heart that the Hungry Tiger never actually has done so. Even in his dreams he has never quite figured out how to do so.

"Rama!" a voice said in a shouting plea. Immediately the Hungry Tiger sprung into a crouch for an attack. The Hungry Tiger then looked around and scratched the top of his head with his claws, wondering who said the name he had not gone by for a long time. He had not been known as Rama since before he had fled the Magical Circus of Horrors.

"Rama it is I," the voice said to which the Hungry Tiger put his paw to his ear and listened hard.

"I am afraid I do not know anyone named I." The Hungry Tiger said, continuing to look around the jungle for the source of the voice and finally simply plopped himself down on a nearby log to listen. He knew many strange folk but thought he would remember an invisible person with such a short and easy to remember name.

"I do not have much time but it is your long lost love Sita," the voice said painfully.

The Hungry Tiger stopped for a moment to consider that the beautiful tigress he had loved even as a cub might have been turned invisible by some nefarious means but thinking was never his strong point on an empty stomach.

The Hungry Tiger simply spoke "Tell me where you are Sita and how I can be of aid."

The Engagement of Ozma
Book Two in the Umbrella Man of Oz series

Sita's voice was soft and cool like Rama remembered it but her words made him very angry. "I am once again the prisoner of Evile Lackey."

"Grrrrrr if my conscience ever did stop bothering me it would be eating him!" The Hungry Tiger growled.

"Patience my tiger. I fear it is many leagues beyond the sunset where I am for he has brought me by his magic to the land of the Mother of Oz," Sita purred and The Hungry Tiger wished he could curl up to her again. They had been raised brother and sister but Sita was a white tiger from a faraway kingdom and meant to be Rama's wife.

"I will ignore my all food and rest for as many years as it takes to reach you." The Hungry Tiger declared. The Tiger lifted himself up proud even as his tummy growled. Well, maybe he'd eat and sleep a little but just enough to keep going.

"You do not have to journey many years to find me Rama," Sita chided the Hungry Tiger.

"I don't? I'm glad to hear it. It might take me past some fat babies…" The Hungry Tiger then heard Sita groan.

"I was hoping you'd have overcome your fixation with such treats Rama."

Sita sighed.

"It's just the warlock described them as so tasty." The Tiger said with a sigh, salivating at the food that he had never tasted of nor, for all of his evil, had Evile Lackey.

"In any case, you must seek out Princess Ozma and her companions before they reach the Train of Thought for they are journeying to this land by it. On the train you'll be able to reach our land though I fear it will be perilous indeed because of the horrors Evile has wrought here," Sita replied before saying "Oh no he's returning! Good bye my Rama!"

The Hungry Tiger wasn't exactly sure what had happened there but after howling Sita's name in a few directions of his jungle, he decided that she was gone.

Charles Phipps

Wanting nothing more to do with his jungle while the tigeress he was most fond of was imprisoned, and deciding he wasn't too hungry, he began a bound for the Emerald City.

***

The Engagement of Ozma
Book Two in the Umbrella Man of Oz series

Chapter 2

Princess Ozma's preparations for her visit to her mother took up most of the morning with the installment of Trot, Button Bright, and Betsy as temporary ruling triad of Oz. Ozma didn't expect the unlikely Royalty of Oz to meet with any trouble while she was away but they were such a remarkable contrast in personalities that she was sure they could deal with anything that might imperil her kingdom.

Ozma prepared a packed lunch, packed a enchanted suitcase of clothes for all occasions, and got on a good pair of walking shoes for the trip down the Blue Brick road into Winkie Country.

Some of the palace residents were being slightly less than cheerful about her departure however, and confronted her in her bedroom during the last of her packing.

"You can't be seriously thinking of leaving Oz entirely!" The Sawhorse shouted. The wooden trotted around her as Eureka the Green Kitten sat on it's head and stared at her accusingly. The fact that to Ozma's knowledge the pair absolutely despised each other was a testament to just how strongly they felt about this.

"It's ridiculous. Preposterous. Unthinkable," Eureka said and showing that the green kitten had been listening to her best friend the Wogglebug a bit too much. The two got on so famously that Ozma was fairly sure that Eureka was listed as an alumni at the Athletic College, even though she couldn't swallow teaching pills. Ozma had even tried giving her a saucer of milk to wash them down to no avail.

"If any person in Oz would be glad to see me leave for awhile Eureka, I thought it would be you," Princess Ozma said. She had very nearly sentenced the tiny cat to obliteration in hopes of scaring her away from doing such monstrous acts like eating her fellow animals. Ozma had gradually given up on that idea because even trusted friends like the Cowardly Lion and Hungry Tiger couldn't understand why she didn't want them to eat their fellow animals. Even the most vulnerable like the Mice and their queen were content with the arrangement as what was 'natural'.

Eureka leaned in a rather lazy way on the top of the Sawhorse and looked Ozma square in the eyes. "I admit we have our differences Princess but, as much as I don't like to rely on human help, those nine piglets will be the death of me unless you are there to stop them! I still don't know how they keep dying my fur different colors every few months! First it was purple then it was pink then it was yellow and now green! If they have the nerve to do this while you're around, what will they do when you're in another country?"

"What if everyone in Oz starts to grow old and die without you!" The Sawhorse says. "I'm a hundred year old wood and don't think it's right to petrified!"

"You look pretty petrified to me," Eureka said as the cat's teasing got it summarily thrown from the Sawhorse's head. Thankfully, the cat landed with a bounce on the nearby bed.

"I've left Oz before for Ev and other kingdoms Sawhorse. I'm not going to be gone long either so I suspect your chances of turning into wood pulp are minimal," Ozma said. The Queen then gave her beloved steed a kiss on the top of its head. "Besides I'm going to visit Lurline for presentation and I can't marry Milo for 900 years if I don't get it."

"I never trusted that boy anyway. He's not wooden," The Sawhorse sulked.

Ozma scratched behind his ears to make him feel better.

"If Jack is willing to call him stepdad, Sawhorse you'll be able to be nice to him. Besides, he'll never replace you because he's not suitable to ride long distances and doesn't make a clapping noise when he walks..." Ozma neglected the times when Milo wore tap shoes but she thought that was beyond the point here.

The Sawhorse reluctantly nodded and Ozma put a spell on Eureka that she promised would protect the small cat from any physical harm. Ozma didn't have the heart to tell him that it was actually she who gave the piglets the coloration powder to help in Eureka's punishment for the cat's trying to eat them. It had gotten to the point where Ozma was already picking out colors for Eureka come Easter and Christmas.

"Now let's see when and wear the Train of Thought shows up." Ozma said exiting down the Royal Stairs to the Palace below. Ozma didn't know much about the Train of Thought but in her witchcraft studies under Glinda she had read that the mysterious fairy

The Engagement of Ozma
Book Two in the Umbrella Man of Oz series

vehicle could transverse the boundless Fairy Lands in a short time because it traveled the tracks left by human dreams. Oddly enough, the schedule listed the times 'Whenever you want' for all twenty-one hours of Oz's day and 'Wherever you want' for the Gates.

Jellia was meanwhile roller-skating down the steps with her feather duster and Ozma adverted her eyes to watching her chamberlain and maid crash in a most uncomfortable way. "Jellia are you alright?" Ozma called down to her maid, deciding it would be polite to ask.

"Just fine milady!" Jellia gave an A-O-K sign with her fingers before getting up and starting to roller-skate again, dusting everything in sight. Oddly the new footwear made her job twice as difficult but she was having a great deal of fun with them so Ozma decided not to take them away.

Ozma personally was wondering what it would be like to see Lurline again. Ozma remembered a thousand years of life before she was Tip and they had been spent on the strange and beautiful Island of Avy-Lyon. They were like a dream compared to the mere century she had spent in Oz however.

Ozma's memories of her mother were often contradictory at best and all she knew of her mother was that she had been as beautiful as any fairy could be and that she had loved her very much. It left Ozma with some unsettling questions however why it was she who was chosen to leave her homeland and rule Oz and not some other fairy.

"*Chomp* *Chew* *Gulp* *Burp*." a rather messy series of sounds was heard and Ozma looked to the side of the hall she was passing where the Kitchen staff were feeding large pieces of meat to the Hungry Tiger. Despite the Hungry Tiger was always a welcome guest in the Palace, it looked like several of the kitchen staff were counting their fingers every time they handed the wild beast his next helping.

"Enjoying yourself Hungry Tiger?" Ozma leaned over and saw the Tiger was just finished sucking the marrow out of a large bone. The Cowardly Lion had brought the Tiger Prince to Ozma many years before. Ozma had given him the name the Hungry Tiger since he was so uncomfortable with the one his family had given him, Ozma did not press why.

"Alas I am filling up my belly with as much food as I can though I know nothing can truly fill my aching tummy." The Hungry Tiger said. He seemed quite melancholy, more so than his usual tummy troubles made him. "However I must do the chore of eating as much as I can before I go on the great and terrible journey that I must undertake."

Ozma was quite taken aback by this. It was not often in Oz that people undertook terrible journeys. Well it was more often than in the mortal world but one could argue every journey taken there was great and terrible in its' own way. "What journey is that Hungry Tiger?" Ozma asked as she petted down the Tiger's backside.

"The one you are going to take me on Princess," the Hungry Tiger answered causally. He then began chewing on an extra-tough steak the cooking staff had provided him. The Garden of Meats was likely to run out Ozma guessed before they succeeded in feeding the Tiger full this time, Ozma usually had to stock a week in advance whenever the Hungry Tiger and Lion visited.

"Oh." Ozma muttered blinking. She supposed that her journey was great though she had been hoping to avoid terrible this time around.

"I was visited by the ghost of my dead tigress love Sita who said that she wasn't dead, wasn't a ghost, and that I needed to rescue her from the evil wizard who captured us both from our positions as rulers of the Tigers. She also said that you would lead me to it so here I am," The Hungry Tiger yawned and dabbed his mouth with a napkin the Winkie Cook Goody O'Plenty handed him. The plump yellow tinged woman was Ozma's favorite gourmet and had over forty children who had since all become gourmets in Ozma's service as well which lead to a very organized and very fractious kitchen.

"I see." Ozma blinked as she processed the Hungry Tiger's words. "I can assure you that I will do everything in my power to help you rescue your sweetheart and you are quite welcome to accompany us."

The Engagement of Ozma
Book Two in the Umbrella Man of Oz series

Aside from the disturbing fact that the tigress was held by an evil wizard, Ozma was delighted to hear that the Hungry Tiger had a girlfriend.

"That was most delicious goody. I shan't eat any of your children because it was so good, though I sorely tempted to," The Hungry Tiger said as he dipped his fingers in the bowl of water they had provided the Hungry Tiger with the drink but he used to clean off the sap from the barbecue tree stuck to his fur.

"Oh won't you?" Goody said with a joking sigh, before whacking her seventy-going-on-twelve year old son Jeremy's hand with a wooden spoon. The Winkie boy had been trying to sneak a cookie from Ozma's jar of rainbow nut flavored ones. The jar then stuck out its tongue at her.

The Hungry Tiger shook his head and followed after Ozma. The monarch of Oz led the Tiger down towards where she hoped soon they would begin their journey to the enchanted Sea of Immortality where the Fair Folk had first come to the World.

***

Dorothy Gale had packed a very large duffle bag on loan from Trot, who had in turn borrowed it from Captain Bill. The heavy green sailor's bag was filled with quite a bit including; a self brushing toothbrush, an extra-large bottle of toothpaste, several changes of clothes with everything from ball gowns to hiking gear (Thank Goodness King Pastoria knew how to make clothes wrinkle free), a new diary book for her adventure in Avy-lyon (at 112 years of age she had quite a bit written already in her journals), trail-mix because she just never went anywhere with out it, and a set of pictures of everyone so she wouldn't forget them (as if that were possible).

At apparently now seventeen years of age Dorothy was a very beautiful near-woman currently dressed in jeans and a plaid shirt. Her long blonde hair was done back in a pony-tail and she was waiting patiently for the arrival of Princess Ozma at the gates of the Emerald City.

"I'm telling you its' going to rain so would you please help me...no really I think we need to do it like...ack." Dorothy heard these words from a nearby pair. Dot was watching Milo working with the Soldier with Green Whiskers to try and open his magical umbrella. The magical artifact had been a gift from all the licensed magic users in Oz and specifically Ozma herself but Dorothy hadn't the heart to tell her that its owner had never actually figured out how to use it.

Milo was currently pulling on its' handle with both hands as Omby Amby pressed with his leg as hard as he could on the folds. Not unexpectedly the two ended up lying in a pile on the ground.

"You know maybe we should just wait for Ozma here. I don't think it's going to rain after all," Dorothy advised to the young man engaged to the Princess of Oz. Dorothy liked Milo a lot because he seemed to combine the best aspects of quite a few of her friends, always held the door and a chair for her (which was doing double duty with Ozma), and she'd even set her sights on finding a loved one if Ozma could. The young preacher was currently dressed in his Saturday best, identical to his Sunday through Friday best, and had packed a simple pair of matched luggage for the journey.

"Sorry, I'm just a little paranoid about rain," Milo said. It was a bit of an understatement. The last time Ozma's love had been rained on. It had catapulted him out of his world and nearly destroyed Oz. Milo put his umbrella away in his luggage's side before making an observation "Aren't you bringing Toto? I'm rather surprised he isn't showing up, you'd think he'd want to see the wonders of the Isles of Immortality. Thank you Omby Amby anyway."

The Soldier with Green Whiskers gave a salute and said "Always a pleasure to render any aid no matter how dangerous, destructive, or painful...which is what that umbrella is!" the seven foot tall guard sputtered at the green and gold umbrella. It had given him more bruises than a century of frequent invasion had.

Dorothy looked rather embarrassed at Milo's question. "Well actually Toto said he'd like to come but he was too busy with his campaigning."

Milo blinked a bit as Omby Amby returned to his guard position. "His what?"

The Engagement of Ozma
Book Two in the Umbrella Man of Oz series

"It turns out the previous Mayor of the Emerald City's eighty year term is ending and he's not going to seek re-election in order to grow Waltzing Turnips in Munchkin country."

Dorothy had very little desire to see that part of Oz. It made her uncomfortable enough about food with so many animal friends to see vegetables dance. "Toto decided that it would be a good idea to run for the position."

Milo had never heard of a dog running for government service before though he'd known quite a few in the police. Not sure how to react to the situation, he did the first thing that popped in his head and placed his arm on Dorothy's shoulder. "I'm so very sorry."

"I know," Dorothy accepted the sympathy and wondered what she'd done wrong to have her little dog enter politics. "What's worse is that he's running against the Wizard."

Milo then told "Well that's a pity. Toto has no chance then."

Milo Trustworthy Starling shrugged his shoulders and looked for Ozma around the area. It was unlike her to be late.

Dorothy looked up at Milo, a little surprised. "Why whatever do you mean?" She didn't entirely approve of Toto's career move but she was fairly proud of him with the organization he and his Animal Party had taken to winning the position.

"Well Toto is a…and the Wizard is a…and people um…" Milo realized he was treading on some fairly scandalous water here. The Good Book rather clearly said 'Love thy neighbor' and Milo's neighbors included a talking clam, his confident E. Bused the Toadman, and other less than human individuals. The preacher however knew greatly the Wizard's political skill. "I'm voting for your dog. Your right."

"That's better." Dorothy said, crossing her arms. It occasionally took a bit of prodding for new Ozites to adjust to the world even years afterwards.

Ozma stepped out of the gates dressed for her trip with a picnic basket over one shoulder though the Hungry Tiger had his hands inside the back of it and was chewing. Milo's heart was obviously skipping a few beats from the look he gave Ozma and made another one of his funny bows to her. It gave Dorothy a queer feeling and not an entirely pleasant one towards her best friend.

"Milady," Milo muttered kissing Ozma's hand.

"There's a slight change of plans in that the Hungry Tiger will be joining us on our picnic before the Train of Thought arrives," Ozma said in a clear tone and blushed slightly at Milo's romantic gesture.

Dorothy looked at the Hungry Tiger and said "I somewhat doubt there's much left for a picnic Ozma."

Dorothy was wondering what riding on a train of thought would be like. She'd ridden normal trains on a few times several years ago and wasn't sure how literal a train this was going to be.

Ozma frowned and Milo, Omby Amby, and Dorothy turned their backs on the Hungry Tiger. Ozma's glare was enough to melt stone and each of the three had felt the Princess of Oz's gaze of unhappiness before. "I had planned for a picnic with my friends Hungry Tiger, that was very selfish of you."

The words were worse than any of the three could have imagined.

The Hungry Tiger was reduced to tears seconds later and Ozma had to pet it to keep him from wailing as well. "Well I suppose now we'll just have to take the Train of Thought directly from the Emerald City," the Princess said, putting away the picnic basket in her bottomless luggage.

"Yea we're kind of wondering about that. Where is the Train of Thought going to come from? I've never heard of it before" Dorothy looked around, half expecting tracks to magically appear...and they did.

The train tracks moved behind Dorothy and continued moving on as they dipped down from the sky and back up into it. Dorothy also heard the whistle of an old time steam engine. The Train of Thought itself appeared around the corner not soon after. The Red locomotive had the numbers '00' emblazoned on the front of it and several lovely passenger cars from various eras following it.

"Well I suppose that answers that question," Milo said blinking.

Dorothy could only stare as a red skinned engineer with a stove pipe hat that poured smoke from the top of it leaned out from the engine's side. "All aboard who are coming aboard! Faeries,

The Engagement of Ozma
Book Two in the Umbrella Man of Oz series

Thoughts, Humans, and Animals welcome but no run on sentences! They have to ride in the caboose."

Ozma smiled and boarded the side of the car as her passengers soon followed.

"Apparently it comes whenever its wanted."

***

Chapter 3

Trot, Betsy Bobbin, and Button Bright looked around the throne room of Princess Ozma. They were trying to get a measure of what they were going to do now.

The three had dressed themselves in their Emerald City best for the part of ruling Oz. Two beautiful gowns for the girls and a fine tailored suit for young Button Bright in fact. All three of them felt extremely uncomfortable in the finery and looked like it too.

The throne room was empty for them and the Jester E. Bused, who was standing on his head while juggling flaming torches with his feet. Most of the Emerald Palace's staff was busy with preparations for the Emerald City elections. Toto had recruited practically all the children, animals, and sentient furniture in the building to help with his campaign while the Wizard had recruited most of the adults (most of whom had worked under him when he was still ruler of Oz). Thus Trot, Betsy, and Button were left more or less to their own devices.

"Well I suppose we had best figure out what to do first now," Trot said as her gown shimmered with the fiery rubies that adorned it.

"I think so too," Betsy said as her own gown glittered like the ocean thanks to the opals that covered it.

"Yeah," Button Bright said and looked up the throne that Princess Ozma's crown and royal scepter were resting on. Button crawled onto the top of the throne and put the crown on with the scepter across his lap. Button Bright looked less like a king than an eleven year old wearing a crown in a chair too big for him with a scepter across his lap and a hair crown on his head.

"Hey! You shouldn't be sitting in Princess Ozma's throne," Trot walked over and took away Princess Ozma's crown from Button Bright. The sea fairing girl had a pretty strong sense of her own worth and others and didn't feel that anyone should do too much in Ozma's absence. They weren't actually the rulers of Oz but were merely making sure nothing bad happened while she was gone. They were caretakers and nothing more.

"Well somebody should sit in it. That's what the chair is there for," Betsy said. The young girl pointed to it and poked it a bit. "I think we should take turns on the throne with the crown and specter."

"Now that's silly. We'd never get anything done that way," Button Bright replied. "Let's handle this like the Sultans of old. One of us will rule over the rest and they'll handle the things he doesn't."

Betsy looked displeased at Button-Bright. "What do you mean *he* doesn't?" she added accent to the very mannish word.

"Well the way the old sultans ran things the guy would be in charge," Button Bright said rather innocently but knew well better than to say such things at his age. Even were he were merely eleven and not a century or more older.

"Well I know how the Amazons would run it too. They'd kick the tar out of the sultans," Trot said appalled at Button for so clearly going against Princess Ozma's ruling. Trot had a particular affection for the warrior women since Captain Bill had told her about them and had been studying up on them in hopes she'd find a group in Oz somewhere.

Button Bright blushed and looked guilty but the mischievous twinkle in his eye told all. He wasn't giving up the throne without a fight.

Betsy spoke next "Well I think we should all do what will settle things best and easiest. Kingdoms don't run themselves you know."

Betsy Bobbin had grown up on a farm and that meant she was mainly settled to doing the things the fastest and smartest way she could.

"Ozma said we all had to rule things together and she didn't say anything about sitting in a throne, wearing her crown, or using her scepter," Trot retorted "Since that's the way she said things were going then that's the way things are going to be and to the Abyss with what you say."

Trot had grown up seaside and to respect what someone you respect says.

Button bright grew canny "Trot you remember when we were together on Sky Island and all how we worked together to make everything work out alright? You were a Queen there, why don't we work together and be King and Queen of Oz while Ozma is gone."

Button Bright deliberately left off Betsy Bobbin who while his friend had given his brown sugar collection to her mule Hank and which Button had not yet forgiven her for it.

"Are you ganging up on me?" Betsy looked appalled at the pair. To Trot's credit she was more shocked at Button Bright's suggestion than interested. "That's it, I don't care what you two say. I'm going to run this kingdom like Ozma would want and do her decisions like she'd want them."

Betsy wrestled the scepter out of Button Bright's hands and started to storm off.

"Captain Bill says a ship should never have it's first mate and captain argue!" Trot called back immediately to Betsy and walked up behind her. Betsy was Trot's best girlfriend along with Ozma and she didn't want to make her mad. She wished the Captain was here at present but he was off paying court to a mermaid in the Nonestic Ocean. Frankly it made Trot a little cross he'd choose now of all times to leave.

"What does Captain Bill know about ruling a country?" Betsy asked spinning around with a very sour look on her face.

"More than you!" Trot said defensively.

"Maybe you could all divide up responsibilities for running the Emerald City and Oz based on your areas of expertise. Button Bright could manage the courts, Betsy the Countryside, and Trot handling all the troubles from disaster and adventure with everyone getting what they want." E. Bused said. The Toadman then accidentally caught the tapestries in the throne room on fire and tried desperately to stamp them out while keeping the rest of his flaming torches in the air.

"Now that's just ridiculous," Betsy dismissed E. Bused suggestion and Trot nodded. Button Bright ignored the Toadman as he began drawing up proclamations about what people in the Emerald City would have to wear for "Button Bright Day". He'd also have to make some laws to break for "Pie in the Face punishments" in the town square.

The Engagement of Ozma
Book Two in the Umbrella Man of Oz series

The conversation got increasingly louder and more hostile before the doors to the Throne room burst open and the Scarecrow ran in. The Straw Man stopping only to back away in horror from the rather large fire that E. Bused was now running back and forth from the kitchen to get buckets of water to try and put out. "Your Majesty! Your Majesty...Ah!" the words rang out as Trot, Betsy, and Button noticed that the Scarecrow was fairly badly burned though not by E. Bused fire.

"What's wrong?" Trot asked before she grabbed a nearby vase, pulled out the plastic flowers, and poured its water on the fire. Plastic flowers don't really get thirsty but they appreciate the sentiment.

"It's terrible Your..." the Scarecrow stopped for a moment to take notice that Ozma wasn't anywhere to be found but was animated enough that he continued with his story "But the Illumi-nation has rebelled against the Crown! A radical splinter faction of the candle people are marching towards the Emerald City armed with hundreds of lighted wicks for the purpose of taking it over in order to force everyone to make candles for the rest of their lives! They already burned me while I was taking a nap and nearly got Scraps too!" the Scarecrow looked around frantically "Where is the Princess? She has to be told!"

Trot, Betsy, and Button exchanged nervous looks.

"She isn't here."

***

Evile Lackey looked at Sita through her cage bars with a large toothy grin. Evile was not the sort of warlock who brushed regularly so there were several gaps in his teeth and the teeth he had remaining were yellow and sharp. "That was very naughty of you Sita contacting the Hungry Tiger with my PIC. I'm going to have to punish you soon."

In truth the Wicked Wizard was actually very pleased that the Tigress had contacted the Hungry Tiger. Oz was not yet the hospitable and universally pleasant land that it is today and Evile had gained a great many gifts and trinkets by opening up his Magical Circus of Horrors. One of Evil's best attractions had been Rama the Baby Eating Tiger. The only problem was that no matter how hard Evil tried to make Rama eat babies the Tiger never went beyond licking them. When Glinda destroyed his Circus she had made sure Rama had escaped with his mate, it had taken Evile years to find Sita again. While he was no longer in showbiz thanks to losing his power to create monsters, Evile considered it the princible of the thing to get the Animal back.

"I somewhat doubt it Evile. Princess Ozma is a sorceress well beyond your piddling little powers." Sita licked her paw and looked at Evile with a heavy frown, secretly very afraid of what the warlock was up to.

"With my latest invention there won't be any need to actually face Princess Ozma or the infamous witch killer Dorothy," Evile chuckled.

Evil Lackey went over to a large square machine which had a crystal ball attached to it. The crystal ball was presently showing an image of Rama, Ozma, and Dorothy sitting in a train and silently chugging along towards New Avalon. "The PIC thought technology mixed with some variants on advanced quantum mechanics and ESP direction research has allowed me to create the…" Evile fumbled over a name.

"The Really Ugly Looking Machine For Doing More Senseless Pointless EvilTM?" Sita suggested the name that popped into her head as a drop of water dripped down on her nose from the stalagtite inside her cage.

"A very nice title but unfortunately one too long. This device will lock onto the Train of Thought that these noble heroes are presently riding on and act like a gigantic magnet in reverse. Once I have attached it to it I'll be able to throw them anywhere in Fairy Land or the Earth so that I will never have to deal with them again," Evile said to himself about the brilliance of this particular scheme. He then began punching in the location of the most unpleasant place on the planet he could think of.

The Engagement of Ozma
Book Two in the Umbrella Man of Oz series

"Oh no." Sita stared, the White Tigress now honestly afraid for her lover and his friends as she recognized the location Evile was going to send them by the numbers. Which Tigers are very good at.

The Really Ugly Looking Machine For Doing More Senseless Pointless EvilTM began to glow, sputter, and whirl with the numbers Evile punched in on its side. Lights flashed on the top of the device so that the cavern was treated to a display of ever color of the rainbow but it was not a pretty sight at all.

***

The inside of the Train of Thought was a curious sight to see even in the Land of Oz for the beings that were taking it held no allegiance to any particular time and place. The new comers aboard saw a man who looked startlingly like Abraham Lincoln, A man in a space suit reading a newspaper whose date was a few centuries in the future, A woman with a fish's head and a human woman's legs, and at least one person entirely made out of eyes.

Taking a row of seats by the window, Milo ended up sitting next to a fairly human looking man about sixteen years of age.

"Hello," Milo said as he strapped himself in.

"Oh hi. Pardon me do you know which way it is to Oz?" the young man asked, he was somewhat freckle faced and had a bit of a longing look to his face. A laptop computer was to his side and he was gazing outside the window of the Train of Thought in exactly the wrong direction to see the Emerald City. Worse the train was starting up again and it was too late for someone to get off.

Milo blanched so slightly. "My friend I don't exactly know how to tell you this but you just missed Oz."

The man looked at Milo and then cursed a very popular but extremely dirty word in Oz "Hippakloric!"

Milo supposed that any human being trying to get to Oz can't be all bad so he tried to cheer the man up by patting him on the back. "There, There my friend I'm sure you'll be able to get to Oz around the next bend." Milo of course had no idea whether or not this train made regular stops and if it did how long it would take to get back to Oz. Fairy Land existed between the nooks and cracks of his world, yet had a size all of it's own. A little girl could fall into a rabbit hole in England and find herself in a huge countryside twice the size of Wales but only a single rabbit hole's space was taken up. The wonders of Fairy Land were, in truth, so vast that Milo occasionally wondered if it was actually Fairy Land attached to his world or his world attached to Fairy Land.

"That's assuming I have any thoughts left by the time I reach the destination!" the young man said and clutched his computer protectively.

Dorothy looked over along with Ozma and Milo towards the man and his queer exclamation. The Hungry Tiger didn't take much notice as he stared rather longingly at a very fat baby in a business suit talking to a cell phone a few rows in front.

"Princess Ozma I don't know if this thing is entirely safe. Do you?" Dorothy asked Ozma with a rather concerned look.

"Thoughts please," A strange looking robot asked. It looked like a combination of a washing machine and a tricycle then began rolling down the center of the Train of Thought's center carpet. The outside view of the Train transformed into an image of Fairy Land countryside from thousands of feet up. It was very hard to look at it and not get sick however because the Fairy Lands sometimes repeated themselves, the Sun sometimes rose and set rapidly, and strange things such as window sills and clocks with wings passed by.

"I think that green and white shoes are ugly," the man composed out of eyes said. Curiously enough no sooner had the Eye man said this that a magical red ticket appeared in the man's hand and he gave it over to the Electronic Ticket master.

"I don't much care for people over the age of 1," the baby in a business suit said and a green ticket appeared.

"I'm afraid of heights," the Spaceman said and the process was repeated until the Electronic man rolled over in front of the Oz resident's row.

"Thoughts please," The Robot asked as it's eyes blinked rapidly.

"Ummm I don't understand what's going on." Ozma said even as that thought disappeared from her head and appeared into her hands as a red ticket. Suddenly the Princess actually did understand

The Engagement of Ozma
Book Two in the Umbrella Man of Oz series

what was going on as the thoughts that the passengers gave the Train of Thought allowed it to keep running. Ozma then handed over her ticket as the others looked at her and understood.

"The square root of nine is three." Dorothy said and blinked as the information disappeared from her head and appeared in her hand as a blue ticket in her hand.

"Now that was a very foolish thought to give up. You might need that information some day," Milo commented before a purple ticket appeared in his hand and he wondered what he was saying. The Ticket master removed the purple ticket from Milo's bewildered hand and moved on to the Hungry Tiger.

"I'm not sure what thought I want to give up. All I know is I'm hungry," the Hungry Tiger saw two tickets appear in his hand one yellow and one red. The Hungry Tiger gave up the yellow ticket to the Robot conductor then swallowed the red one in a rush in order to restore his appetite that he'd lost the moment he said he knew he was hungry.

Milo shrugged in his seat and looked over at Dorothy "Well now that we've paid our ticket. I wonder how long it will take for us to reach the Island of Avy-Lyon. Some of these fellows look like they've been waiting quite some time to reach their destination," Milo mentioned, pointing to a man with a five foot long white gray beard covered in spider webs that had been woven around him while he was asleep it seemed.

Ozma was about to answer when the Robot reached the front of the car and the Train of Thought came to an abrupt stop. "All leaving for New Avy-lyon please step out."

Dorothy looked at Milo and then Ozma as they both exchanged glances. "Well that answers that question."

However when the four departed out the side of the Train of Thought's door, the land they were located in looked nothing like Princess Ozma had described. The first thing to note was that the Sun completely black in the sky that you wouldn't even notice it at all save that there was a cold radiating from it just like our sun radiates warmth. All around was a black, drab, and worn down city with inhabitants that made the new arrivals very uncomfortable. Skeletons were walking around the City reading newspapers, carrying on conversations, and one driving up a cart to help carry their luggage. Among the skeletons were werewolves, mummies, vampires and other creatures that you might be hesitant to invite to a dinner party.

"Ozma I don't think we're in Oz anymore," Dorothy said to her friend beside her.

"I don't think we are either." Ozma answered and turned around to find that the Train of Thought had already left for its' new destination.

The Hungry Tiger then, in the height of rudeness, grabbed the leg bone from one of the skeletons and began to chew on it.

"YOU THERE!" A voice shouted at the top of it's...well not lungs but where lungs would be. It was a very large skeletal man dressed in armor, riding a skeleton horse that was munching on some sugar cubes. "Are you goblins, ghoulies, monsters, or otherwise not among the living?"

"I think I can vouch for everyone when I say we most certainly are not." Milo lifted up his umbrella in a salute and apologized to the Skeleton the Hungry Tiger had stolen the leg of. Milo as an added gesture pulled it from the Tiger's mouth to return to the angry dead man who took it with a sneer. Milo thought at least that it was a sneer. It was hard to tell.

"Then I'm afraid you'll have to come with me. Living people are forbidden in the Land of the Restless Dead." the Skelaton Guard commander's voice was most forbidding and filled with quite a bit of chattering since he didn't have any gums to soften the sound his teeth made when they talked.

Ozma looked at her friends, feeling very guilty about bringing them into another adventure.

***

Chapter 4

Milo, Dorothy, the Hungry Tiger, and Princess Ozma were marched by Captain Bones of the Royal Order of Mortis through the streets of the Kingdom of the Restless Dead.

It was strange because they seem to be as completely frightening and shocking to the citizens of the undead kingdom as they were to them. In fact they probably frightened them more so because by now most of them were used to at least the possibility of something so strange as a Kingdom of walking corpses.

Still the four were hardly calm as they walked past the bandage wrap stores, the coffin makers, and fountains of bright crimson where the inhabitants filled goblets to drink.

"That can't be very appetizing," Dorothy said watching one of the skeletons drink down one of the goblets. The red sticky fluid passed down their skulls and leak out over and through their ribs.

"I don't exactly think that these fellows are entirely that concerned about their health Dorothy," Milo said as he shook his head. Being a Good Book reading man, the idea of a Kingdom of the Dead existing without being a very happy looking place was very disconcerting to him.

"All of these bones and not a bit of meat on them. This is truly a terrible place," The Hungry Tiger bemoaned.

The group soon came on a black brick road towards a palace made entirely out of bones standing like a terrible overseer of the strange kingdom around them. Walking up a deserted craggy road, Captain Bones stopped them before the front door where two more skeletons stood guard.

"Private Femur, Private Tibia. We have prisoners to see the Illustrious King Sean the -21!" Captain Bones called up as the door of bones was opened.

"I wonder what they're going to do to us?" Dorothy asked aloud. The girl shivered slightly at the extremely creepy atmosphere before Milo took off his coat and put it around her.

"Well the worst they could do is kill us. Though I must admit if this is where we're going to be staying afterward I'd rather avoid the possibility," Milo muttered.

The minister looked around before starting the walk in, stopped by Captain Bones.

"His majesty is entertaining. You'll have to put these in your ears," The Captain handed out four balls of wax, seemingly conjured from nowhere.

"Why?" Princess Ozma asked looking at them and wondering if she should call the Train of Thought back or use her magic to enact an escape. Right now she thought it was best to observe the local customs of this kingdom but the presence of so much death around her very mortal friends didn't help her much.

"Don't worry. We Oz folk can't be killed and no meet or not I'd be glad to chew through them all if you but say the word," the Hungry Tiger answered. He pulled his ball of wax apart and put the two resulting pieces in his ears.

"It is the banshee. His Highness loves to be entertained by the fairy spirit of the dead but her cry is otherworldly and shrill that a mortal who hears it is bound to not survive the night," Captain Bones replied matter of factly.

"And I thought your singing was bad," Dorothy murmured to Milo.

"Thank you Dorothy. Thank you very much..." Milo said sarcastically not feeling at all in a humor filled mood.

"Your welcome," Dorothy said having forgotten what sarcasm was like.

Putting the remaining wax inside their ears, the group wandered through the Halls of the castle of King Sean the -21.

"So is King Sean a good ruler or a bad ruler?" Ozma asked in her new private motto question for visiting strange and bizarre kingdoms that seemed to frequently pop up every time she left the palace.

"Unfortunately I must say that King Sean the -21st is a very bad ruler. The -20 before him since we converted from a Kingdom of the Living to the Dead were full skeletons and even a few zombies but

The Engagement of Ozma
Book Two in the Umbrella Man of Oz series

King Sean is only a skull and thus spends all of his time leading us," Captain Bones said looking around.

Ozma looked surprised "Isn't that what a ruler is supposed to do?"

The Hungry Tiger frowned. "I was hoping the ruler would have some meat on him."

"We are the Kingdom of the *Restless* Dead lady. Hence we are never truly happy with our rulers. However those that try to rule we dislike even more. The people are nearly ready to try democracy," Captain Bones said with a sullen look to his…skull.

Ozma looked scandalized. "How horrid."

"AIYEEEEEEEEEEEEEEEEEEEEE!" a terrible shrill voice sounded. Everyone immediately covered their ears with even Captain Bones covering the holes in the side of his head. A skeletal cat on the ground screeched and a ghost in a nearby mirror put on earmuffs. The mirror unfortunately shattered into a dozen pieces which seemed to upset the ghost in it, quite a bit.

"I take it that was the banshee?" Ozma asked, knowing something about Death Faeries.

The skeleton guard nodded "You take it correctly. She's another reason that we don't like King Sean."

Captain Bones wobbled a bit from the sound and his left leg fell off before a skeletal dog, which was hiding in wait for the skeletal cat, snatched away with it.

"Oh curses," the undead captain shouted before resuming his march towards the audience hall.

Passing through the Hall Milo saw two figures from ancient lore that he recognized from book he'd read. One was a man in a dark cloak with a blonde mustache and burning coals for eyes dressed in a black shroud. The other was a handsome but foreboding man wearing a golden helmet. The two mythological beings were currently playing a game of chess where the pieces moved and had the appearance of awful monsters.

"Pardon me but is that Arawn and Hades I see over there?" Milo asked the captain. Both were powerful fairies that had required their worship as gods whenever they passed over a territory and brought much death and destruction.

"Yes, both of the immortals enjoy meeting here in the neutral territory here to relax," Captain Bones replied. He stopped hobbling when he noticed Milo walking over to the two figures infamous throughout mortal history as symbols of evil. To understand Milo's next action you'll have to remember that he is a reverend to be and takes matters to heart whenever a person of evil goes unpunished for his actions.

"SHAME ON YOU BOTH!" Milo then promptly swatted both immortals on the head with his umbrella and scattered the pieces of their chess game before rejoining the group. Leaving the two lords of the underworld so utterly confused that neither had the idea to punish the impudent mortal as they probably would have else wise.

"That was…direct." Dorothy muttered in shock.

"It had to be done Dorothy." Ozma defended her love. Hopefully both of them thought about contemplating their actions after someone had the nerve to finally stand up to them.

Captain Bones then proceeded to quickly lead them into the main audience chamber of King Sean. Inside the hall a wide assortment of the dead were in line to speak with the monarch. The throne room was like the rest of the palace and completely made of bones, which made it somewhat gruesome to walk through.

In the center of the room on an elevated platform there was a huge black iron throne that held a single red cushion. Upon it rested a skull with a golden crown around it. Even with no face it was doing an excellent job of looking bored. To the side of the king in a black sequin covered dress was a surprisingly pretty if pale woman with long blonde hair that the Ozites guessed was the banshee.

"Your Majesty, I bring prisoners! Living mortals who have broken your edict!" Captain Bones shouted at the top of…err his bones.

"You know, there sure are a lot of edicts we end up accidentally breaking," Dorothy observed. Thinking about all the insular communities in Oz that had repeatedly tried to kill her or friends for no other reason than being different. Oz was unique in the fact it was simultaneously the most tolerant and diverse kingdom in the world yet had the most incidents of people trying to destroy others for being different. Ozma had almost put a stop it but it was still a common problem amongst its fairy-kind. Ozma personally blamed the Wicked Witches who had set nearly every community against one another.

"Shhhh Dorothy," Ozma said to her companion beside her, though she privately agreed.

King Sean's reaction was rather strange as he shouted "Lackeys!" and two of his bone courtiers proceeded to toss him over the waiting line of undead towards Ozma's party. Lucky for him, Captain Bones had the foresight to catch the skull emperor before it crashed on the ground.

"Hello..." King Sean said to Ozma and the rest with a smile. "Everyone else...out!" the skull commanded and soon the throne room was all but empty.

Princess Ozma regained her composure and curtsied before the King, Dorothy followed suit, and Milo bowed. The Hungry Tiger merely wagged his tail, which is rather unsettling when you realize that is when Tigers are about to attack. Thankfully no one told the Hungry Tiger this and it just meant he was happy.

"So you living people thought that you could defy my edict against living people eh?" King Sean said with a sneer.

"Actually..." Ozma began.

"Shhhh!" King Sean shhhed.

"Very well," Ozma replied.

"I said Shhh!" King Sean cut her off.

"I was o..." Ozma put her hand to her head as the King shhhed her again.

The Skull looked at them. "The penalty is most severe for this crime."

The four were rather tired of this at this point and Ozma's patience while still strong for a fellow monarch was running thin as well.

"You must...take me with you." King Sean's eyes darted round the room.

Ozma blinked. "I beg your pardon."

"Hooray!" Captain Bones tossed King Sean in the air. "Ooops" and ran to catch him before the guard went tumbling some furniture thanks to having only one leg.

"Take you with us?" Ozma asked as Dorothy looked around, wondering if she had heard that right.

The Skull bounced from the captain's arms up to the mortal's feet.

"Absolutely! Have you any idea what it's like ruling a kingdom of the Restless Dead? Not only are they always restless but it's impossible to get these people to enjoy a good party! No matter how hard you try! It's despicable! Ah but to be alive again! You people really know how to have a good time!"

Princess Ozma looked down at the small skull and then at her companions.

"And if we don't want to take you with us?" Ozma gave a slight query, she didn't want to be rude but she knew very little about this person.

King Sean the -21st pointed to the Hallway. "I understand that people in Oz are immortal, correct?"

"Yes." Ozma didn't like the sound of this.

"I can make an excellent case that immortality it isn't a good thing with a pit of acid and some unpleasant looking pointy things made out of iron." King Sean gave her two eye sockets full of menace.

"Oh my, that doesn't sound very pleasant at all," Milo wincingly answered to that.

Dorothy just frowned and considered giving the skull a swift kick across the floor before summoning the Train of Thought.

"Very well King Sean we shall bring you along with us," Ozma said crossing her wand across her chest.

"Ozma," Dorothy looked at her friend in a bit of surprise.

"Now listen here King Sean. Realize once we take you with us, you're not going to be a King. You better behave yourself. That means no insulting people, threatening them, and...well forgive me if this sounds rude, but I doubt you'll be unable to avoid scaring people. Just don't intentionally try."

Milo suspected that the Restless Dead were in this kingdom for a reason and was very hesitant to remove any but he trusted his wife to be's judgment. Milo still wanted to make sure the skull didn't try anything funny though.

The Engagement of Ozma
Book Two in the Umbrella Man of Oz series

"Of course, anything! Oh I declare you King Bones the One legged." King Sean looked at Captain Bones then spun around so fast that the crown sailed off the skull's head and landed on the Skeleton's.

"But I want to start a democracy!" King Bones shouted and realized he would really have to get his leg back from the palace dog Chewy.

"Tough calcium," King Sean chuckled.

"You'll have to get everyone's opinion on that. They may not want a democracy and elect you King," Dorothy said to the new King with a pat on his arm.

Ozma closed her eyes and in a few moments a large tunnel appeared in two ends of the throne room. A large metal-train soon came rolling through the tunnel and though it was different from the first Train of Thought an identical engineer leaned out and shouted. "All aboard who are coming aboard! Faeries, Thoughts, Humans, and Animals welcome but no run on sentences! They have to ride in the caboose!"

King Sean looked at the strange thing for a moment then bounced up the side into the passenger carriers.

"Pardon me sir but what exactly is your policy for the undead?" Milo asked the Engineer as he helped Dorothy onto the train.

"No eating fellow passengers and no using run-on sentences. We really hate that," the Engineer replied to the minister to be.

"The good man finds life, the evil man death." Milo sighed looking around the Kingdom of the Restless Dead before shaking his head as he helped Ozma onto the train "I must have done something rather unpleasant this week."

"Captain Bones, remember if everyone wants to be part of this democracy idea that you must make sure that the people who want a monarchy have one too!" Ozma said waving to the captain as she went up the train's steps. Ozma wasn't actually against democracy but she hated to see monarchies deposed because that meant someone was unhappy or not doing their job right.

***

Evile Lackey cursed up a blue streak as he saw the Oz band escape his trap for them in the Kingdom of the Restless Dead. It had been of course his magical device which had detoured the train of thought and nearly gotten them into a GRAAAVE situation. Hehehe sorry, even authors need to do puns once in a while.

"You might have made sure that they never summon the Train again," Sita commented languidly in her cage.

"Blast! I was hoping the undead would have torn them to pieces! I mean that's what they're supposed to do! What's the world coming to when you can't rely on the dead to act in a generally unpleasant manner!?" The wizard tugged at his hair and pulled large clumps of the gray out by the roots asking this question.

It should be noted most dead people are quite content with their life, after all you don't hear from them often do you?

"What do you intend to do now? Dump in the middle of the Ocean or a volcano?" Sita immediately regretted the words because the wizard probably would do that now. True to her worst fears Evile Lackey looked very intrigued by the prospect for a moment. Pacing about his foul cavern Evil stopped and shook his head "No they're suspicious now and Lurline will no doubt be expecting Princess Ozma's arrival soon. I dare not arise her wroth n…wrait…wroth wrath w…" the warlock stumbled over the next few words.

"You dare not arouse her wrath now," Sita corrected Evile and enunciated very slowly for his benefit.

"Don't correct me!" Evil Lackey whacked the bars of her cage with a nearby metal rod.

"I repeat myself Evile that you are doomed," Sita said simply and the White Tigress stuck her tongue out most rudely.

"Oh be silent White Tigress! I shall have to make preparations so that after Lurline's welcome…they receive one equally fitting from me," Evile Lackey sniffed. Rubbing his hands together, Evile licked his lips menacingly. Doing nasty things was much like eating to Evile, he needed it to survive.

Despite her bold words, Sita was actually rather worried about his plotting. Evile Lackey indeed had managed to survive on the

The Engagement of Ozma
Book Two in the Umbrella Man of Oz series

island of Avy-Lyon with trickery that would make him very dangerous to Rama and the tiny princess of Oz.

As if reading her mind, Evile continued "I've been living here in Avy-Lyon for more than a century Sita. Ever since that rather detestable altercation with King Zo on the Sky island of Zo had me dumped in the Nonestic Sea. I floated for several months through the brine til I washed up on these shores. I have dreamed about proving myself the most powerful wizard that has ever existed ever since. Of course proving yourself to be the most powerful wizard in the world requires a great deal Sita…"

Evile Lackey then put on a pair of spectacles, as he began preparing the potion that would be the key to his plans to destroy the Ozites on a nearby table.

"Including an ounce of magical ability beyond parlor tricks?" Sita asked, deliberately baiting the wizard. Tormenting him was one of the few ways to disrupt his concentration. For while Evile Lackey wasn't a very powerful warlock as warlocks go he was very clever in making sure that what magic he had was used to great effect.

"Bah! I may need great big machines where other wizards and fey need just wands and words but the effects are the same! Hmmm a little mugwort and crushed bubble bear berry juice." Evile Lackey poured the ingredients through a huge computer of his own design's funnel. The machine separated the various strange chemicals and mixtures through glass tubes into a single magical potion that glowed bright pink.

Sita shook her head and roared a lament for her mate Rama and hoped that he would not fall for the Wizard's newest scheme.

***

Trot, Betsy, and Button Bright had put aside their differences in ruling long enough to make a decision to deal with the invading army of the Illuminati.

Specifically, the decision to get Jellia Jamb to override any decisions they made. With the chamberlain's advice, the monarchs of Oz summoned the Wizard from his campaigning for Mayor to handle this crisis.

Presently, a council was being held in the throne room with the group and the royal advisors. The Illumi-nati had agreed to send an ambassador to negotiate for a peaceful resolution.

Unfortunately the noble loyalists of Ozma were deeply divided by issues between them yet still.

"I still say you're a stinking cheat." The Wizard looked down at Toto with a crinkled nose and the Dog frowned up with him.

"It's not my fault that we're doing a hand count election. If the polls say I'm winning that's because I have more votes." Toto sniffed up to the wizard. Around his collar was a silver medal that said "Toto/Billena 2001."

"Octopus shouldn't count because they don't hands. Paws shouldn't count because you get four to my two. AND I don't know where you get off courting the chair vote," The Wizard practically hissed.

"We're both four legged. I understand their problems better than you," Toto replied raising his nose in the air.

"That's courting specism! Just plain and simple!" The Wizard shouted and if he wasn't a good Omaha territory man he would have given the dog a good swift kick in the fanny.

Trot, Jellia, Button, and Betsy watched the altercation between the would-be-mayors of the Emerald City with some degree of amusement. It was Trot who finally decided to interrupt. "Pardon me but do you think we could get back on track to dealing with this whole invasion threat?"

"Well I say we just get a horde of people having their birthdays and resolve the issue toot sweet," Button Bright offered his explanation. "Plus everyone would get oodles of wishes."

"I still say that's pretty ridiculous." Betsy said to Button Bright with a frown. Being blowhards wasn't going to resolve the candle crisis.

"Actually I kinda like it. Though I still say a big river could be diverted like Hercules did to clean out the stables. That would end the Illumi-nati threat real quick," Trot said, having always admired Hercules.

"Yeah well if you find a river to divert in a country surrounded by desert I'd be glad to help," Betsy said sharply. She

The Engagement of Ozma
Book Two in the Umbrella Man of Oz series

really hoped Ozma would be back soon because this rulership deal was really ruining their friendship. Trot wondered how Ozma kept herself so nice to everyone.

"Dunno," Button Bright shrugged and adjusted his fanny slightly on the emerald throne. The Wizard was about to respond when Jellia walked in and cleared her throat.

Jellia in her new role as advisor was dressed in a delightfully sumptuous royal gown and a crown on her head with a J. Neither Trot, Betsy, or Button liked the concept of Queen Jellia but she was an excellent arbitrator. "Ahem the ambassador from the Illuminati has arrived!"

Jellia opened the door and a golden candelabra bounced his way in. The figure had a small angelic figure engraved on it but the figure's eyes were shifty and frankly looked paranoid.

"I demand to speak to Ozma of Oz!" the candelabra swaggered around and looked at everyone haughtily. "I am General Wicker of the Wax Legion of the Illumi-nati and I've come to state our demands."

Trot, Betsy, and Button had trouble keeping from bursting out laughing at the site of the figure. Queen Jellia would not approve however so it was Trot who spoke up first, getting glares from Button and Betsy.

"Very well General what exactly are your demands?" the sea-girl looked down at the candle and blinked a few times to make sure she didn't laugh.

"For years the Illumi-nation has labored under the faulty assumption that every candle in the world came from our domiciles. Recently however, a freak encounter has shown that not only are there other places where candles may be made but Oz has actually not arrested these people threatening our monopoly! And after having had an account for the selling of our people for Princess Ozma for decades no less!" the candle spoke, trembling with rage.

Jellia looked down at the candelabra "Ozma has an account? Oz doesn't even have money!"

"Of course Oz doesn't have money! We have something better! Credit!" The Candle looked up at Jellia. "Not to mention credibility! Of course Princess Ozma in her illustrious wisdom has decided not to ever pick up any of her credit bills at our bank which of course has resulted in numerous taxes and fees that have eliminated the account in question several times over." The General looked around "I'm afraid we're going to have to confiscate the Castle in back taxes and someone called Dorothy."

"She probably didn't even know she had an account!" Betsy frowned and if the candle had been a man she'd probably have socked him one.

"That doesn't matter I fear," The General simply wagged his candle flames a bit.

"Listen," Trot decided to be diplomatic. "What if we put a stop to your people being shipped off to be people's candles?"

Slavery was an abomination and Ozma had put a stop to it wherever she could.

"Good Lord why would we want that?" General Wicker said shocked. "We want compensation for our monopoly and copyright violation fee. In return our courts, which have already found you guilty, are promising legal action in the form of hot foots and burning everything to the ground unless you comply."

The rulers of Oz exchanged glances and it was Button Bright who made the decision. "Jellia. Make it so."

Button pointed at the candle and made a flick of his front finger.

"Gotcha Your Majesty." Queen Jellia went to the side of the room and got her mop water bucket. The maid of Oz then poured the contents the bucket then on the General who slumped to the floor, down and out.

"I suppose this means war," Trot said to Betsy.

"Well you could have been a bit less direct in summarizing your response but yes.putting out the diplomat is a declaration I think," The Wizard summed up his feelings quite handily.

***

Chapter 5

The Train of Thought arrived at the Isles of Immortality much sooner than any of the five expected, which was to say at all. The group had lost all of its confidence in the Train of Thought as a method of transportation but of course that is when it actually does work. In fairy country of course nothing is what you expect which is why it occasionally is what you expect to throw you off guard. The Train let the couple off on the top of the highest cliff in Avy-lyon which surveyed the landscape for miles and miles.

"Oh my," was all Milo could say as he saw the Sea of Immortality that was made of liquid silver and stretched off for an eternity.

"They didn't even offer an in-flight meal," the Hungry Tiger complained. The furry beast felt his chest lightly with his paw, he was all empty inside.

"Oh bleah! Always complaining about you and your stomach! I'll have you know that I haven't eaten anything in a century! Do I miss it? No! Why because I know that anything I eat will just get caught in my jaws and have to be removed!" Sean shouted annoyed.

"Well my jaws are a bit better and I can taste it with my tongue," The Hungry Tiger pointed out to the skull, not offended in the slightest.

"There you go again! Just because you have all these extra organs and body parts you act like your more alive than I am," Sean huffed. He hated discrimination against the respiratory challenged.

"I am," The Tiger murmured but the Skull just hissed at him.

"Now be nice. The Isles of Immortality are where I grew up Milo…you see that Isle there is the Land of the Summerlands or Tir-na-og." Ozma pointed to a beautiful island where Milo could make out a giant beautiful people inhabiting the shores.

"Sounds like a drink," Dorothy said, remembering Uncle Henri's favorite Christmas concoction.

Actually Tir Na Nog was quite fascinating to Milo since his ancestry included many great fairy heroes and enchanted mortals. Long ago places like Ireland, Scotland, Wales, and England were home to many regular visits by the fey. They are still there today, of course, but they tend to keep a lower profile to avoid things like autographs and dissection. Tir Na Nog is the island those particular fairies have their ancestry from. Rather like Dorothy being Irish and Milo Scottish despite both being American.

"Fascinating…and that one?" Milo said and looked at a lovely mountain Island that seemed to extend into the sky and past with huge Greek style architecture.

"That's Mount Olympus though no one's lived there for years. No one actually knows if the Myths came first that somehow Fairyland made real or whether or not all the legends lived here and inspired man or somewhere in-between," Ozma explained about the mysterious isles. In a manner that was no explanation at all.

Truth be told she often wondered if Milo would ever be disheartened in his worldview by all the strange things he saw. Oddly though it was the plain minded like Milo and Dorothy who reacted best to fairyland. They simply accepted what was about them and went on, to trust one's senses both outer and inner was a trait Ozma greatly admired. It was foolish to judge things simply by what one was told.

"The truth is usually somewhere in the middle Princess Ozma. Why is the Sea all silver?" Milo asked looking at the beautiful waves.

"Oh that's because this is where the moon was made." Ozma said. "Long ago the Nomes were building the moon out of silver entirely but they grew so jealous and greedy about the precious metal they hid all the silver they were using here. Thus the Moon was built out of rock."

Milo and Dorothy looked at Ozma with a little bit of a blink as they tried to decipher if that were myth or actual truth. As hard as it was to believe it seemed as if Ozma were being perfectly serious. Another wonder of Fairy Country it would have to seem.

"Well I like the moon anyway as it is. I'm glad they didn't build it out of silver. Otherwise men might be spending all their time up their trying to mine it all away," Dorothy replied. She took that moment to give a good long gaze at the moon, wishing she could build a ladder to visit it.

The Engagement of Ozma
Book Two in the Umbrella Man of Oz series

Milo was about to reply he'd prefer silver to green cheese because the smell would be horrendous but he stopped to notice that King Sean and the Hungry Tiger were both missing from their little band.

"HELP MURDER!" The shrill ex-King of the Restless Dead shouted at the top of his...well the top of nothing but it was as loud as he could shout.

The trio ran down the high cliff they were on into a beautiful grassy gnoll covered in flowers of every color imaginable (and some you likely never have) toward it. There the Hungry Tiger was chewing on the skull-monarch and trying apparently to swallow it.

"TIGER!" Ozma pulled out her wand and with a spell off her lips, pulled the skull away from his mouth.

The Hungry Tiger looked at Ozma with a sigh. "I'm sorry but now that I'm on the Isle...it's been so long since I've eaten anything...I need to keep up my strength to find Sita."

"That's no excuse!" Ozma said completely shocked and more than a little angry with her friend as she dusted off the skull king.

"Well you'd think you'd want someone with a little more meat on him," Milo said blinking.

"Milo," Dorothy gave him a slight nudge to remind him that such things were not entirely appropriate conversation.

"Well I couldn't eat any of you. My conscience would bother me too much. He's already dead so I figured..." The Hungry Tiger began with a rather sour frown before being rudely interrupted by an irate skull.

"Excuse me but I am SOME dead not all dead. Undead as in 'not' dead, which is very much alive. I can't do anything to you since I am outside the Kingdom of the Dead, though if we were in my kingdom I'd have you made into a carpet! Or a lamp! Though we'd first have to find appropriate electrical wiring and quite a bit of cleani..." Sean the Skull ranted with rude indignation but trailed off into technical details about what he was going to do that would be very unsettling to read.

The skies then began to thunder a bit as Milo unfolded his umbrella above Ozma and Dorothy with little difficulty.

"What the Devil?" Milo said looking at his umbrella oddly.

"Yes?" Sean asked blinking before realizing no one was talking to him. The former King had been a rather vicious tyrant and the words Devil, Bad Person, Evil Dictator, and Skull with no Brain, Heart, or Courage (which was true) were often used to describe him.

"What? Your umbrella only unfolds when it's needed," Ozma said matter of factly.

Thunderous peels of lightning and rainbow prisms of countless colors started then to fill the air. The sight was so frightening that both Milo and Dot jumped into each other's arms for comfort.

"Tehehehe. Don't worry those are just my twelve sisters," Ozma explained.

In Fairy Country it was not uncommon for immortals to have a dozen, two dozen or even a hundred or more siblings. Large families made sure that every day was someone's birthday or some other special occasion and while a pain to send all the cards one needed for so many occasions, that was what magic was for. Better, no one was ever without gifts (unless you gave away yours and that's good housecleaning).

The fact that Ozma had sisters was quite shocking to Dorothy and Milo since she'd never mentioned her family beyond her mother and occasionally her father. The air seemed to then explode in a host of colors that were brilliant in their rainbows of colors.

Twelve figures appeared that glowed with majestic light and regality. They shined in gowns of moonlight, sun, wind, and the heart of the ocean among other natural elements. Each one of the figures was a woman every bit as beautiful as Ozma with long wonderful crystalline wings that made them seem half-butterfly as well as human. Their glow and loveliness made it impossible to mistake them for mortals even if they didn't have their wings, they were simply too wondrous.

"What? Mortals in the Isle of Avy-lyon? How gauche." the first of the Fairy Princesses said. Her name was Morgan and she was Ozma's eldest sister. She was severe in her manner and as dark as her raven hair in temper but never unfair in her words…save when it came to humans.

The Engagement of Ozma
Book Two in the Umbrella Man of Oz series

"How droll," the second teased with a smile. Her name was Gliterria and she was blessed with a fabulous gown of the stars which glowed like her hair that made her certainly the most eye catching of Lurline's band.

"How very true. Our sister has come to visit us and she has brought her friends," a third fluttered around them. Her name was Sparksia and she had the oddest microchip earrings. Her love of all things electrical included having lightning bolts tatooed on her cheeks.

"So this is our sister's lover? He's so…human," A fourth, Oceania with shining blue wings pinched his cheek. It seemed mildly insulting to Milo though the woman's tone was clearly not intending to be. She was married to Triton and had skin as blue as water yet eyes as lovely as pearls.

"Don't worry Milo, they're just trying to be nice." Dorothy consoled though she felt very small in comparison to the Shining Ladies and was shocked to see Ozma looked uncomfortable too. They were kind of talking like Aunt Em had talked about Toto as a puppy when Uncle Henri and her had brought him home.

Aunt Em had quickly warmed to her little dog though and Dorothy was sure that these folk would too in time.

"He is the one I am to marry," Ozma took Milo's hand protectively to accent this pronouncement.

"There are many troubles with mortal friendships let alone marriages to one of the human lands. The placing of immortality already is a great gift but are they yet ready for the maturity of true eternal companionship, let alone love?" The tallest, eldest, and most regal of the twelve sisters said. Morgan tapped her wand on the nose of Ozma. Her words carried considerable disapproval in them that made Ozma slightly cross with her eldest sibling.

You must not judge the sisters of Ozma too harshly for being skeptical of Milo's good intentions though. Though they were unjustly suspicious of the good man from Kentucky, they had personally seen many other mortals try and court fairy brides or husbands…only to disappoint them in the long run. Thankfully many fairy tales show quite a few ended up happily ever after as well. The most famous case being Ozma's mother Lurline and the mortal King David of Oz.

It is not well known but Ozma of Oz herself is actually a half-fairy and the only daughter of Lurline with mortal blood in her veins. All twelve of her sisters had been created by magic while Ozma was a product of love. King David had long ago gone to live with Lurline in Avy-Lyon and had given the throne of Oz to his brother whose line went on to eventually sire King Pastoria who adopted Ozma. The reasons for this are confusing but the ways of adults don't often make sense.

Ozma got a rather pained look across her face as she said "You will never find more truer beings whether mortal or fairy. Is my mother coming?"

The sisters exchanged looks that were a mixture of frowns, concern, and a bit of a mischievous smirk. When faeries smirked it usually meant something unpleasant was in the works.

"Unfortunately mother is not coming to meet you but she is anxious to wait...you." Morgana the words carried a slightly hinted at statement that was not at all good The slight didn't go over Dorothy or Milo. The other eleven sisters of Ozma looked various unpleasant looks of sympathy, sadness, and concern which made Ozma wonder what in Ozroar's beard was going on really.

"Will there be much to eat? I have to find my lady love Sita in this place here somewhere and I can't do so on an empty stomach," The Hungry Tiger asked, rubbing his belly lightly with his paw.

"Yes, please give the man something to eat! I also need some buffing for teeth marks," Sean said with a good deal of urgency.

"Certainly we do and you shall find nowhere in all of Fairy Land where the food is greater. In Avy-lyon the house spirits tend to every need, the plates produce water you wish, and the goblets never empty. The water falls run here as the finest of wine, the trees of Oz that produce all manner of confections were first grown here, and the seasonings make all food delicious yet never to make one obese." Glitteria smiled at the Tiger who licked his lips hungrily. He was salivating strongly to her description of Avy-lyon's treats.

"I daresay Dorothy the fish must be a rather drunken lot," Milo whispered before the Princess from Kansas gave the minister a

The Engagement of Ozma
Book Two in the Umbrella Man of Oz series

mild nudge with her elbow. There were some things that Dorothy and her fellow mortal from Kentucky shared that even Ozma did not know about, mostly in the realm of mischief.

Ozma however was thinking on weighty matters.

"I do not know why mother would not come to meet us." Ozma looked at her companions with a very puzzled and slightly worried grin. It was not very often that the Fairy ruler of an entire kingdom got married, let alone the daughter of the Queen of the Seelie Faeries. It was not a very good sign to Ozma that her mother would not want to be there for her the moment they arrived. Was she sick? Was she troubled by affairs of the state? Ozma didn't want to think of the one other option, that she had somehow offended her nearly omnipotent mother.

"Then lead the way to the Capital of Fairy Country Morgana. If my mother will not come and see where we arrive then we shall come and see her with all pomp and ceremony due my station…as her daughter," Ozma's voice tried to be commanding but there was hurt located inside of it that none who could call themselves her friend could ignore.

Ozma of course very much wanted to impress her mother and was worried that their reconciliation was not going to be as joyous as she hoped.

Kessily the Middle Most sister then spoke "Very well then most noble mortals and half-mortal sister, we shall spirit you Caer Eternity in the heights of the sky above Avy-Lyon by our magics. Unless you have grown your wings finally sister Ozma and will have no need of such things…tee hee hee."

Kessily was the most spirited of Ozma's sisters and prone to teasing her sister. It was good natured but astoo common of siblings, it hurtful nonthless. Kessily and the rest could clearly see Ozma had no wings, nor would ever develop them after a thousand and one hundred years of life. It was an expectation common enough to fey but one wholly inappropriate for a woman who embodied the best of both worlds at the price of a few of it's lesser luxuries.

The band gathered around Princess Ozma somewhat protectively as the twelve sisters pointed each their wands at the ground and chanting a song of aching beauty. The magic of the music called the mists at the edge of Avy-Lyon to form into a lovely cloud, which formed underneath their feet and lifted the five into the air towards the sky.

"Oh my," Dorothy said staring down at the country of Lurline which moved at incredible below them.

To describe how fast they were going in miles would be a bit inaccurate because while they traveled faster than any airplane the cloud had enough magic about it that they could see all the wonders below without it being blurry. Below herds of wild Gryphons flew across the plains and sky where they continually ended up fighting with the great unicorns but of which neither was ever seriously hurt, the Gigantic Ants of the Mormor valley built their great cities of sand, and the Metal People of Metallurgia passed by their shining lives.

"Hmm perhaps we should tell the Tin Woodsman about these people, he may want to visit his cousins here," Milo said.

The minister looked down as he adjusted his seating to comfortable. Unfortunately this actually caused him to fall through the cloud's soft exterior.

Thankfully Princess Kessily caught him from below and placed him back properly on the top of the cloud. She was after all the best of Ozma's sister in athletics, she'd once outwrestled a titan. Of course she'd cheated by using tickling on the poor thing but victory is victory.

"I somewhat doubt it Milo. The metal people of Metallurgia are notoriously stuck up and to associate with a man of tin would likely be beneath their dignity." Ozma said, relieved her love was alright.

"Well that's just silly, he has a heart much better than gold," Dorothy answered.

The young woman from Kansas adjusted herself and was careful to avoid pressing herself too hard against the cloud like Milo.

"...and a will better than steel." the Hungry Tiger commented and looked down with a frown at a passing kingdom of pig people. The Tin Woodsman was very admired amongst the animals for killing all the terrible beasts who had served the Wicked Witch of the West.

"Ah so this is life! I smell the air rushing down my nostrils! It sends tingles down my spine into my toes! Truly this is the greatest

The Engagement of Ozma
Book Two in the Umbrella Man of Oz series

merit to escaping the ghastly realm there is! I cannot wait to taste the wine of your mother's kingdom Princess Ozma and kiss the hand of the Queen who rules this realm!" Sean said as the skull bounced back on the cloud. Soaking in the rays of the sun.

Everyone on the cloud was of course too polite to point out Sean was still very much dead and unable to do any of those things. Ozma had invited him along so she hoped to reduce the suffering he might bring upon them that they'd have to tolerate, it just wouldn't be proper to tell a guest to be quiet. Also, the Skull King might have spent the day threatening them for interrupting his monologue.

It was then that the group came close to the Castle Eternity that twins Dawn and Dusk speed forward with their fluttering wings to announce their arrival.

The Castle was entirely made of glass but the substance was hardened by Skeedle Nostril blower craftsman into something much finer than rock. It glittered and sparkled with the colors that made up the daughters that to compare it and the Emerald Palace was to compare a rainbow with the greatest of gems and ask which was more lovely.

The Castle of Queen Lurline was also the headquarters of the Seelie Fey worldwide. All fairies everywhere who served the cause of good came to the Isle of Avy-lyon to visit her Majesty and seek her council on matters both great and small. Lurline had a reputation much like Ozma for fairness and compassion that made her much beloved by all beings great and small. Unlike Ozma though, Lurline also had inherited some of her mother Titania's temper and haughtiness that could make situations gravely worse. Still, such situations were few and far between so most respected her rulings above all others.

"Oh my Ozma! It's beautiful! Is this really where you grew up?" Dorothy put her hand to her chest and breathed in something heavy. Even the air of Avy-Lyon was different than normal air and somehow more fresher and more clean than anything she had ever tasted. It made you want to climb up on the top of your feet and shout out a joyous noise to simply be breathing.

To bad for Sean he didn't.

"Yes, when I was a mere girl I remember traveling with my father and mother across the Fairy Lands of Avy-lyon and learning my first lessons in magic from my mother from the towers of Caer Eternity. I remember making daisy chains and a childhood measured in centuries. I was the first child of the Queen of the Seelie court to have human blood within me which meant I received allot of attention…though it also meant I'm likely never going to have wings," Ozma replied to her friend. It was punctuated with a wistful look at her shoulders.

"He spreads his wings over them even as an eagle overspreads their young. Worry not Ozma if your destiny is to have wings it shall be…besides it might be difficult to hug you if you got them," Milo wrapped an arm around her even as they began their arrival.

"I think you look fine Ozma. You'd just be equally fine, no worse, no better if you got wings," Dorothy said as she stepped off the cloud into the beautiful crystal palace.

"Bow down and bend your knee before the most righteous omnipotent Lord of Life! All hail King Sean of the Kingdom of the Restless Dead and quake with terror!" The Skull bounced off and said with a terrifying gale.

"Ummm you're not a King anymore I thought," the Hungry Tiger mentioned.

"QUIET! I need to make good first impressions if I'm going to be satisfied with this whole life thing," The Skull replied with a maniacal laugh following his words.

A series of golden trumpets rose through the air carried by Poogies. Poogies are for those unfamiliar with Avy-Lyon magical creatures are guardian faeries that that resembled small fat babies with wings. We often get them confused with cherubs and Valentine's day would not be the same without them.

"Oh no!" The Hungry Tiger said as he stared at the chorus of nearly a hundred of the small yummy delectables flying through the air.

"Her Majesty Lurline, Best and Highest of the Fairy Nobility, High Lady of the Light Elves, Commander and Chief of the Order of the White Wand, High Queen of the Seelie Court which rules all of Fairydom from Spring til Fall, and Creator of Oz." the Chief

The Engagement of Ozma
Book Two in the Umbrella Man of Oz series

commander of the Poogie, General Boots said as his wings fluttered. He was a particularly attractive and fat baby that fluttered directly in front of the tiger whom he wished to prove his courage by confronting. The Poogie pulled them out his trumpet and blared it as high as he could into the face of the Tiger before fluttering off.

"How rude," Dorothy blinked and wishing silently she'd gotten the Hungry Tiger a pacifier to suck on while they were here.

Queen Lurline was someone that Milo sucked his breath in looking upon even as the others looked upon her in awe. She was much like Ozma with long black hair (though Ozma occasionally turned her hair ruddy gold, pure red, and even green) but there was a stately dignity to her that only came to women who were fully mature. Her dress was a sparkling blue that shown the light against the wild blue of her eyes. Behind her the wings that fluttered were a lovely shade that seemed to depict all the fairylands that Lurline had enchanted in a living map.

Dorothy felt very meek and wished she'd dressed more for the occasion in the presence of the great woman but she'd have been surprised that even Ozma felt a little homely in the presence of her family. Milo of course would have been the first one to tell her that some prefer a softer beauty to the living flame of her mother and sisters, himself of course being one, but he was right now too busy looking upon his love's mother in awe.

"Michael the Supreme Sorcerer of Avy-lyon! Formerly Supreme Sorcerer of the Kingdom of Ix, Formerly Supreme Sorcerer of the Silver Islanders, Formerly Supreme Sorcerer of the Land of Amazonia, Formerly Supreme Sorcerer of the Sunken Continent of Atlantis, Formerly Not So Supreme Sorcerer of the Not-So-Sunken Continent of Atlantis, Formerly Pot Boy of the Red Wizard of Atlantis Jigglegoo." the Poogie trumpeter said "I bet he's a good wizard." Dorothy said as she elbowed Milo, shaking him from the sight of Lurline.

"Mayhaps Dorothy. At least we know he travels a lot." the would-be-husband of Ozma said as he stuck his hands into his pockets. There was something decidedly unsettling about the way the woman's eyes refused to face her daughters or look upon him, staring directly at Dorothy or her other daughters. There was a sadness that both he and Ozma could see in her face.

Ironically it was Milo who had been around fairies the least in his life that recognized what exactly this look meant. His mother had taught him that mothers who don't approve of choices of spouse their daughter make, never look them in the eye. Wilimena Starling also had told Milo that was actually the rightful King of Scotland so you might take her opinions with a grain of salt though.

Michael the Wizard came out just a few moments later and he was indeed a sight to see. Six and a half feet tall he was dressed in a white pair of pants and shirt that was wrapped by a golden belt. A long flowing white cape fluttered around his side with a huge red M scribbled on it's back. He had long golden hair, a curved face, and pointed ears which marked him as at least partially of the fey if not totally one of them. There was a bored and rather snooty expression to his face as he twirled a staff not quite as large as he in his left hand.

"Mother..." Ozma walked forward to wrap the Queen in a hug when Lurline raised her hand to stop her.

"My dear daughter I fear you will not want to embrace me in a moment so I will spare you the feeling." Lurline's voice was cold as a snowstorm.

Ozma blinked and looked at her mother feeling somewhat ridiculous at the whole thing. Why should she not want to embrace her mother after a hundred years? Furthermore why was the Court Wizard Michael here and not her father David? Was there some reason her mother had to disapprove of Milo? Was it something to do with her ruler-ship of Oz or bringing Dorothy? Ozma's mind couldn't fathomn the reason. "I think you had better explain."

"I have watched your courtship by the mortal in my magic crystal so do not think my daughter that I think ill of him for any actions of his own. He is one of the most excellent of mortals but that is indeed what he is and that is indeed why I must forbid my permission to the marriage. I have come to regret my actions one thousand years ago and thus you must be the first of whom to know. I intend to break the enchantments I have woven around the kingdom of Oz and restore it to its natural state as a human country. No longer will be mortals be immortal when they live there, no longer will animals talk, and no longer will magic work," Lurline's words sounded rehearsed and the very words cracked in her throat like she was breaking.

Ozma could only stare in shock at her mother as she took a step back and tried to hold back her eyes from welling in tears of horror. What was supposed to be a joyous had become a nightmare. Dorothy could think of nothing to say and her reaction was only slightly less than Ozmas. The Hungry Tiger thought it a horrid thing and worried terribly that he might lose his conscience if disenchanted, even if he would have been fairly happy as a normal tiger with Sita. Milo was first shocked by the words that his suite was being forbid to the Lady Ozma but next felt the horror at the innocent people in Oz who would be as good as dead should this happen. King Sean, well King Sean nodded enthusiastically because the highest ranking person in the room had said it.

"Father would never stand for this," Ozma said wondering whether a wicked spell had overtaken her mother or this was some joke in very poor taste.

"Your father my dearest of daughters is no more. He is as dead," Lurline said lowering head in sadness.

Yes as reunions go, this one would go down in history as a disaster of one. On the other hand, it certainly does make for a much more interesting book than a happy one now doesn't it?

***

Chapter 6

The air around the Crystal Palace of Lurline went utterly still with the Queen of the Seelie fey's words. No bird chirpped, no wind blew, and no being spoke until the Princess of Oz spoke. Princess Ozma put her hand above her heart and stared in complete and utter horror at the words of her beloved mother. "Dead? But that is impossible! In fairy country no one should need fear the cold and dark hand of death!"

"I beg your pardon! Yes you should!" King Sean said offended. He then noticed everyone giving him a cross look and lowered his eye sockets in difference. In matters of someone finding out their family is now suddenly one man less it is always best to let the family do the talking.

Lurline the High Queen of the Faeries looked upon the Princess that was her youngest child with a mixture of pity, sadness, and reserved love. It was easy to see where Ozma got her sense of compassionate beauty from yet the Fairy Queen refrained from embracing the girl she loved with all her immortal heart. Her next words were painful and against everything the lady believed in her heart, yet said they were. "There are ways you must realize my daughter for the terrible lords of death to reach their cold hands into the hearts of even joyous realms of life. It was a mistake to interrupt the natural cycles with our magic and halt mortals from their inevitable rest."

Such conversation made Dorothy and Milo extremely uncomfortable though more so the Princess of Oz rather than the Kentuckian. Dorothy had lived a century and had long since passed the time she would normally have passed on to the realms beyond Faerie had not Lurline cast a spell upon Oz to keep those who dwelled in it from aging. If she had started to regret her decision, would she revoke the magic?

Ozma was shocked beyond words and cried out "Mother! You cannot mean it! What possible evil could come from the sparing of mortals the hand of the time, merciless disease, and accident? If not for your marriage to a mortal man thus enchanted I never would

The Engagement of Ozma
Book Two in the Umbrella Man of Oz series

have been blessed with my life! Milo my love do tell my Lady Lurline how much you enjoy being kept from the twilight!"

Milo looked extremely guilty. "Errr Princess I am afraid I cannot."

Ozma blinked at her lover, surprised at his words.

"I do not personally fear the transformation from this crude matter to the state of divine you and your sisters share. Indeed I would welcome it as the fulfillment of natural purpose for all mortal beings. Yes the hand of Death is painful but it is the chrysalis to new life…not a Good Book quote but a good one nonetheless." Milo gestured to the cornucopia of beautiful women gathered around him.

"Well ppppppht," Ozma said blinking. She doubted many in Oz would share his enlightened thinking, much as in our world.

Dot added her own thoughts "Umm Ozma if it's any consolation I personally am very happy with being immortal."

Dorothy twiddled her thumbs and felt very small around the many sisters of great Princess Ozma and her very lovely but stern seeming parent. Still, she would gladly fight to the bitter end for the Land of Oz she had so often protected before.

"Trust me. Death is not all that it's cracked up to be…sure I only know what it's like to restless dead but if it's anything like it then I have to say I'd prefer to be a beautiful breathing wonderful living being like I am now," King Sean said as the skull rocked back and forth like he was dancing.

"Your mortal lover Princess Ozma is surprisingly wise for his short lifespan. I have dwelled since the dawn of time however amongst mortals and though I loved them fiercely it was wrong to bond my soul to them even as it was wrong to make a realm in-between man and fairy. I have summoned you young Princess Ozma not to celebrate your choice of becoming one with a mortal man doomed to die but to tell you that no longer is your presence as the ruler of Oz needed. The preparations now be made to undo the magic of Oz and restore it to its state as a county of humans. The Enchantment of Oz for one hundred years is to be broken," Lurline's words shocked all of Ozma's sisters even as they left the Ozites stunned beyond all measure. It was the causal ending of all they worked for.

Charles Phipps

Do not think for one moment Oz was enchanted solely by the Fairy Queen Lurline but all of her Band helped do so, specifically Ozma and her sisters.

"But you can't mother! We worked for *ages* on the enchantment of Oz!" Sparksia said as the chestnut haired Princess of Fairydom chewed on a strand of her locks in stress as little lightning flowed through her teeth. The Queen of all Technology faeries was especially fond of mortals and her CPU slyphs had hoped to add a internet-server hookup to Oz within the month.

"What of all the people who aren't mortal men! It's not fair to force them to die too!" Rebecca the Jokester of Ozma's sisters pouted as she thought of all the wonderful living puns throughout Oz. She had long blonde hair whom loved every last one of the bread, china, and stuffed bear people she had brought to life.

"The Queen Lurline can do whatever she likes! I the Supreme Sorcerer and a mortal man enchanted to live himself recognize the necessity. The Mistress of all Goodly fey has spoken her command and there shall be no changing of her will! Let silence thus reign as preparations are made for you all to join in the Enchantment's breaking," Michael the Supreme Sorcererof Avy-Lyon said in a commanding voice that made him tower over the faeries thousands of years older and only slightly less strong in wizardry.

No one dared speak. Even Morgan the Eldest of Lurline's band however, who was older than mankind and always wondered what the fuss her sisters made of them, was not happy with the callous decision of her mother regarding Oz. Faeries rarely changed their mind and few times so drastically. All the sisters of Ozma had known Lurline was not approving of the marriage but this had come entirely from the space beyond time (also known as left field) as far as they could tell.

"I have something to say," The Hungry Tiger lifted up his paw as the group once again turned to him.

"Can we eat?" Milo guessed what the Hungry Tiger was feeling. He also wanted to lighten the mood since people who were in pain tended to make poor choices and better choices were obviously needed.

The Engagement of Ozma
Book Two in the Umbrella Man of Oz series

"Of course not! I was going to ask if the great sorcerer Michael could help me find my long lost love Sita. Of course since you've suggested it I have no particular objections either," The Hungry Tiger objected.

The Tiger began to twiddle his paws and looked at Ozma pleadingly. He wasn't exceptionally happy about Oz being turned back into a plain old country where he'd be a Tiger without a conscience but the Hungry Tiger wanted to handle one problem at a time.

"I will not let you do this mother. I will convince you this is wrong," The Princess said firmly. Lurline shook her head and departed back into her home's crystal hallways. It was a strong a condemnation one could make to the Queen of all Good Faeries without being rude.

When Ozma's tears hit the ground they grew beautiful poppies even in the middle of the crystal floor.

Glitteria who loved Oz for all of its many beautiful things took her sister by the hand. "Do not cry sister. You have been absent from our beloved castle for over a century and we have missed you terribly. Many things have changed in your absence and our stepfather's death is not the least of them. Let us take you to your chambers and your friends like to the banquet. I'm sure there we can discover a way to change mother's mind but only if you look pretty."

Ozma looked at herself and wondered if she was pretty. "Have you ever considered cosmetic magical wing implants?" Glitteria said taking her sister by the hand as she fluttered her own.

"Oh sister." Ozma rolled her eyes and the group began its walk. Despite the broaching of the uncomfortable wing subject, she was glad for her siblings support in this time of crisis.

"Does this mean we're going to eat?" The Hungry Tiger asked. Let no one say that the Prince of the Tigers wasn't a animal keenly aware of what he wanted in the world and knowledgeable about how to get it.

Following the Princesses of Avy-Lyon down the hallways of the Crystal Palace they saw many wonderful sights and strange creatures that were much greater in size, diversity, and power than the inhabitants of Oz. Still there was a disturbing lack of warmth in the magnificent structure that made sure that everyone who had visited Oz if forced to choose between the two would definately choose the Kingdom of Ozma the Good.

It had not always been like this and the Crystal Palace had once been a place just as friendly if not more so than the enchanted Kingdom but recent events had made everyone slightly suspicious in the castle.

Strange sounds could be heard all around the Castle at even the darkest hours of the morning while weird magical lights flew from what could only be the most arcane magical experimentation. Lurline had stopped acting in quite the same just manner that she had normally been when she even bothered to give judgment at all. No parties were held in Avy-Lyon and the missing presence of good King David, her Majesty's consort, was felt by all who lived on the island.

"We'll make sure that you don't starve." Ozma said with a weak smile as the memories flooded the young woman princess's mind.

Walking down the hall conjured memories of her hide-and-go-seek which she always lost because her winged sisters hid in places that could only be flown to, being tossed from the top of the Castle battlements in the winged faeries version of 'catch', and the fairy-games that required wings she couldn't play like 'flutter ball' and 'swoop croquet'. Those oddly were some of Ozma's happiest memories because every time she went home crying because of her lack of wings, it was her father David who comforted her and made her proud to be half human.

"I always feel like I'm starving even when I've eaten a whole pantry. Though all the metal made me sick the last time I did. I guess that I must be lacking some vitamin that is only found in Fat Babies. Of course I'd never eat something like that nor have I ever but I'm sure it's a great sacrifice on my part." The Hungry Tiger illustrated.

The tiger began cleaning his coat with his tongue when the Skull King Sean tapped him on the leg.

"Pssssst! This way." the undead Skull gestured to a hall nearby. The former King of the Restless Dead had a plan that required the utmost secrecy and a very large jawed tiger.

The Engagement of Ozma
Book Two in the Umbrella Man of Oz series

***

Acting-Queen Jellia Jamb and Chamber Maid of War (it much like Chamberlain of war only female) looked over the walls of the Emerald City with her telescope toward the distant horizon.

Looking through the large end in order to make sure she got a very magnified picture of the advancing army of candles Jellia unfortunately couldn't see much.

Jellia was dressed in her emerald armored Maid's outfit this day. She had her feather duster specifically coated with their most flame resistant and ticklish feathers for the upcoming conflict and was ready for the battle. Not that Jellia intended to get hurt or hurt anyone herself but metal was surprisingly stylish. Jellia had discovered this after last years Tin designer dresses were the smash hit of Ozma's birthday ball.

"Never has so little been risked for so much by so few," Jellia sucked her gut with a heavy breath and stuck out her chest for the picture the Camera-Man of Photocopia was taking.

The man who was little more than a lens, film case, and flash on legs had suggested that for truly inspirational photos they might do a bathing suit edition for the papers but Jellia would wait until later on that. Oz had only one newspaper in the Ozmapolitan and very few read it due to the generally depressing news of constant invasion and Ozma's refusal to be photographed. Jellia reasoned her beautiful face would probably triple readership. If that didn't work she could just make it a royal decree to have everyone in Oz pick up a copy of the issue that featured her. It was good to be queen.

"Love it girl! Flutter those eyelashes! Beautiful! Now where's the beach ball?" The Camera-man, Shutterbug, tossed in a Oz color scheme inflatable ball that Jellia caught for the next picture. Shutterbug had been a photographer literally his entire life and rare was an exclusive on the mysterious and beautiful maid of Oz, at least mysterious since he'd written that down for her headline.

Trot meanwhile was wearing Yellow metal armor from Winkie Country with depictions of mermaids on it. She walked up to Jellia and tapped her on the shoulder. It had been the Wizard of Oz's idea to contact the Tin Woodsman and the Winkies in order to begin working on their planned weapon to defeat the oncoming invaders of the Illumi-nati.

"Uh Jellia?" Princess Trot sighed as Jellia flashed her teeth for the camera, a sparkle to her ivories.

"Not now Trot. Can't you see I'm inspiring those under my command?" Jellia tuffed up her hair slightly. She'd considered adding a web-cam for the Oz citizens to watch her dusting and polls said she'd get at least 50% of all computer users in Oz to watch which was admittedly the Emerald Court out of the Emerald Court and the Wogglebug. It was occasionally hard to drag Ozma away from online Oz lists. Of course Sparksia had been planning to add access next month but the Wizard had invented Ozonet ahead of her plans.

"AHEM," Trot said with a bit more force as Jellia looked over to the Camera-Man, Shutterbug.

"Take five Shutter. Yes Trot?" Jellia blinked as she wore her crown most regally.

"The Army of the Illumi-nation is coming," Trot pointed out towards the forests which had been evacuated by Toto of all animals. Trees that had minds were evacuated by Uncle Henri, to the considerable complaint Emerald Garden soil was 'too rich for their sap'.

"That's ridiculous Trot. I sent Button Bright out on the sawhorse to make sure that the Illumi-nati army would be warned of our coming well before they arrived," Jellia chided.

Seconds later Button Bright's voice rang out through the city streets. "The Candles are coming! The Candles are coming!"

Jellia checked her watch "And it's only noon."

"Look! There they are! Probably thinking they're all tough for torching everything in sight! Oooo I can't wait to give them a knuckle sandwich!" Betsy Bobbin dressed in her own Munchkin Blue Armor said as she slapped her mailed gauntlet fist into the palm of her other hand.

Betsy was usually quite passive but if you could get the farm girl riled up, she could be quite dangerous.

"Now now Betsy you'd only end up burning your hand. We have our own method of dealing with these flicker may come invaders," Jellia Jamb smirks even as the smoke from the forest

The Engagement of Ozma
Book Two in the Umbrella Man of Oz series

burned upwards and the sight of ten thousand candlesticks and lamps came forward to Oz's heart.

"I only hope the Wizard has our secret weapon ready in time." Trot looked over to the huge device that was still being tinkered with by the candidate for the Mayor of the Emerald City.

The secret weapon was covered by a huge emerald colored sheet that hid it from the Illumi-nati's sight. It stood three stories tall and it was the largest project the Wizard had ever worked on.

Frankly Trot was a little suspicious whether he had the knowledge to make his thing work. He was in fact the best Wizard in all of Oz but Trot hadn't taken it as a good sign that the old man spent most of his time mumbling campaign promises and memorizing his acceptance speech for when he was elected Mayor of the Emerald City rather than working on it.

"Um Trot have you any idea what were gonna do if this rinkey-dink the Wizard is working on doesn't work?" Betsy Bobbin asked Trot as the Princess of Oz echoed Trot's thoughts.

"Well then I think we just hope Ozma comes back real soon," Trot said simply.

Betsy mouthed the letter O before looking at the on-coming army of candles. "If they do end up burning down the Emerald City I don't think that Ozma will ever let us serve as re-gents while she's gone again."

"Now that's silly Betsy. When the chips were down and the first crisis to Oz occurred beyond who got what in the throne room we had the wisdom to pass the throne down to Jellia so we'd quit arguing. That has to count for something doesn't it?" Trot said before looking at Jellia giggling with her beach ball.

"Ozma is never going to let us be regents again." Betsy sighed.

"I think she may demote us from Princesses of Oz as well." Trot said as she put her metal glove over her face. Oh well being a Duchess or Countess of Oz wouldn't be so bad though it would kill her to be the same rank as a certain little half-fey dress-maker. Trot sighed and walked down the steps to go talk to Button Bright about his getting a rank as Oz's knight.

***

Queen Lurline the Grand, Queen Lurline the Beautiful, Queen Lurline the Wondrous could not help but cry her eyes out inside her throne room. Having sent away her cherubic guardians in the Fairy Poogies she was alone save for her ever faithful court Wizard Michael.

The Throne Room of Lurline was a peculiar place for such sorrow because it was quite possibly the most grand building in all the world with moving tapestries of all the great forests and fairyland sites hanging from the walls with pictures of her glorious family gazing smilingly at the Fairy Queen. Treasures from the Holy Grail to the Magical Armor of Mo decorated the lovely room and her weeping on the chair of Diamond was just wrong.

"Your Majesty do not cry your eyes out. It is wrong for one so beautiful as you to red such delightful orbs with tears and by the Winter Court's reign. Look what the gardeners will have to do to all these flowers your creating!" Michael the Wizard said, gesturing his magic staff toward the small group of lilies that had appeared where Lurline's tears fell. With a stamp of his foot the wizard smashed as many of them as he could.

"Oh how can I be so cruel to my own child friend Michael? For a thousand years, blink of an eyelash that is to me, King David was my husband. It was for my love of him that I enchanted Oz and yet I love him still. Oh curse cruel, cruel fate for depriving me of him! Why must I deprive my daughter of such love however as well? Is it not better that she loves for a time rather than a lifetime of not?" Lurline took a silk handkerchief from underneath Michael's sleeve and pulled out with a trail of a few hundred more.

Michael sensed the Queen's wavering dedication and placed his hand on hers. "My dearest Lurline you must think about this logically. If faeries and man were meant to be together then logically they would have been born both faeries and men instead of one and the other," of course even Michael realized that there was little logic behind this. Truth be told he had an idea of courting Lurline himself but hypocrisy was always best in hindsight.

The Engagement of Ozma
Book Two in the Umbrella Man of Oz series

"But to be so cruel as to use the methods you have suggested to break up the pair!" Lurline stared into the floor before her and saw her sad heartbroken expression.

"Tut tut Your Majesty. In a few thousand years, when she's had the time to think about it, your youngest daughter will recognize that it was all in her best interests and thank you for it," Michael the Wizard had been a sailor who had crash landed on the shores of Avylyon after the fall of Atlantis. He had been very cross and unpleasant to the fairies himself but eventually had come to appreciate their company and become renowned for his wisdom among them.

"I suppose your right but I do not believe that we should so callously destroy Oz!" Lurline rose up from her throne and lifted her wand in the air, filling the room with light.

Michael placed his fingers together and considered his next words carefully. "You heard her fiancé Lurline. The young man finds death neither scary nor corrodible. Obviously, it is only his love for your daughter which is keeping from fulfilling the Supreme Master's way. Oz in general is likely much the same land over. Pride and your misguided love for King David of Oz led its enchantment,"

Lurline was hesitant to believe such an odious lie but the mortal wizard tossed some grayish powder into the Fairy Queen's face that lowered her resistance to his words. It was a powerful wizard that could alter the opinions of a Fairy Queen but Michael was just such the man.

"Yes, yes you're right. Make ready what you must so my daughter's feelings may be spared and my sin in enchanting Oz may be undone," Lurline said as some part of her heart broke. She knew someplace inside her that she was telling herself a lie and only the Wizards magic kept her from rethinking her plan.

Lurline no matter how much she tried could not forget that in her heart she would always love her husband David and could never believe evil could come of loving a mortal as she had done.

Furthermore, Oz had been a creation of her love for mortality and that was a love no less powerful than the one that she had for her husband who had been lost to freak accident. While true love always melted magic that sought to place itself against such a force in

Lurline's case Michael was able to prey upon the one emotion that undermined the nobliest of emotions-self doubt.

Lurline who was the nobliest of faeries was fair to all things great and small but herself and one could only love another as much as one chose to love oneself. With her husband's 'death' she loved herself very little indeed.

Guilt is a funny thing that way.

"I will begin making preparations immediately for the tests of Princess Ozma and her intended's devotion. You can have my assurance that no matter what they feel for one another it will be exposed as the lie that it is," Michael's words held surprising bitterness. The Wizard of Avy-Lyon had a reputation for gruffness but never in his lifetime had he expressed doubt towards the emotion of love itself.

Quite the contrary, among the Atlanteans it was the most beloved feeling of all and any man who hated love hated himself and all things. It might have been poetic to say that Michael had been betrayed in his youth or secretly held his heart for someone whom he had lost but the man who wore said wizard's skin was in no way poetic.

He had never loved nor ever would because he held nothing but hate in his soul and naked desire.

That was the true reason that he would see Oz stripped of all of its glorious magic and forced to die.

Thankfully we know THAT's not going to happen, I hope.

***

"I'm really sorry about your father Ozma. I hope it wasn't painful," Dorothy said as the group of fairy women and their mortal companions walked through the halls of the Crystal Palace.

Dorothy had never really gotten to know her parents, who had died in a sea wreck, but she could sympathize with the loss. While Ozma still had her adoptive father Pastoria, it had to be painful to lose any parent just like Uncle Henri while grand wouldn't be as good as Uncle Henri and her Dad.

The Engagement of Ozma
Book Two in the Umbrella Man of Oz series

"I'm not sure that is something that can possibly be hoped for Dorothy. The Enchantment on Oz is much like the natural effects of the food, air, and water of Avy-Lyon. It is through no mortal means that my father has perished of that I am sure," Ozma said, hoping that her sisters would fill her in on what exactly had occurred.

"Either way my love be content that I am sure he is in a better place than even this palace of wondrous splendor," Milo said even as he got a rather nasty look from Ozma for reasons that he simply could not fathom.

"Dorothy is right Little Sis that daddy-kins didn't die from something painful. It was only sad chance that resulted in his doom," Kessily said frowning. King David Ozroar was the best friend she'd growing up and shown her all sorts of interesting sports as they emerged on Earth. Running, javelin tossing, discus, basketball, cheerleading and later television snack getting were all sports she'd loved.

"Indeed Noble King David had the misfortune to wander into the Forrest of Misfortune and came across one of the dreaded Cocky-Trace," Tasb the ninth daughter of Lurline said, she was the most mysterious of Ozma's sisters and resembled Morgan closely. She was said to be the most powerful witch in the Universe after Lurline and only Michael eclipsed them both.

"You mean Cockatrice," Milo said remembering his mythology.

"I mean Cocky-Trace," Morgan looked at Milo Starling like he had no idea what he was talking about.

"But why would my father wander to such a terrible place! He had never shown such poor judgement in all the centuries that I knew him and it was from him that I learned all my wisdom," Ozma looked appalled, knowing what a terrible power Cocky-Trace's had.

"Nevertheless he was found turned to stone by the small chicken-shaped birds. Despite the best efforts of even Michael the most powerful Wizard of all Avy-Lyon he could not be restored to his natural state of flesh. Thus the Queen in her grief placed his form at the top of the highest tower and warded it with her strongest spells. It is her grief now that has resulted no doubt in her forbidding your marriage to the mortal Milo and perhaps soon the doom of Oz,"

Morgan said in a forbidding tone. While the human king had been strange to her, she could recognize Ozroar's good heart and how happy he had made her mother.

"She can't really turn Oz to a...normal...kingdom can she?" Dorothy asked as she put her hand over her heart. Oz was beautiful because it accepted everything and everyone because of their differences and the idea of turning everyone into plain old humans horrified her more than the thought of everyone dying afterwards.

"I am afraid she can Princess Dorothy of Oz. Oz was once a normal human land ruled by the Poet-King David called Ozroar barely a thousand years past. His songs so lovely and his desire for peace and joy for her people were strong enough to attract the Queen of all Good to his side. Because of the love they shared it was Lurline's idea to bring Oz into Fairy Country and surround with the Deadly Sands in order to protect it from invaders," Morgan said as the eldest lead them up stairs made of a metal stronger than steel but prettier than silver.

"It just sort of went from there. I mean we saw these wonderful but stupid folk named Flatheads so we decided to give them brains..." Sparksia the Tinker said smiling, Ozma's elder sister only by a year.

All the other fairy sisters had been born of the Four Elements and Magic with no father which among other things made them quite a bit more strange than Ozma.

"I thought a town of Bread People would be delicious," Rebecca chuckled at her words. She was Ozma's favorite sister in some ways.

"I love the color Yellow so I made all the section I worked on that shade," Sparksia smirled happily.

"The same for me and Red," Kessily smirked. The Athletic girl had painted the entire Quadling country in just a month with a paintbrush she was proud of saying.

"I like Blue," Oceania fluttered her eyelashes.

"...and Purple is the color of nobility," Morgan reached Ozma's apartments which were at the next highest tower.

"I always liked Green," Ozma blinked as she remembered all of her family's fun enchanting Oz so many centuries past.

The Engagement of Ozma
Book Two in the Umbrella Man of Oz series

Amazing how some of the things we take for granted about Oz came to pass because of these wonderful ladies, huh?

"All of the Goodly Magic we did was done in Lurline's name though. If she orders us to do so as Good Fey we must obey," Tasb frowned as her magical robes fluttered about her. They changed color with her mood and were right now deepest black.

"It just wouldn't be proper to disobey one's mother," Morgan cast open the doors to Ozma's apartment and all the travellers from Oz were shocked by what was inside. Instead of the beautiful apartments that they had expected they were greeted instead by the sight of a laboratory with huge machines, piping, tubing, and electrical charges flowing to and fro.

"Ozma! I didn't know you were an inventor," Dorothy exclaimed at the sight of a robotic eagle flying through the lab.

"I'm not," Ozma turned her gaze toward Sparksia who looked sheepishly at her sister.

"Sorry but after you left my laboratory got a little full with my Tinker-Creatures and Tik-toks so I decided to uhhhh make use of the space you left behind. It's all very nice stuff! Certified Tinker and Smith Compatible!" Sparksia lowered her head then fluttered herself up a few feet in the air.

"Fix it," Ozma commanded and the little fairy sprite zoomed into the royal apartments.

"I'll help!" Kessily shouted who was always anxious to do something to help. The middle-most sister had outraced Hermes on occasion with her Fairland Flight record setting rushes.

Like a lightning bolt the Fairy Princesses began zipping the toys and equipment to other places through the palace as their family watched on.

"Milo may I ask you a personal question?" Ozma asked tugging at her dress nervously.

"Milady I love you unconditionally with all my heart. You may do anything you desire," Milo said in all honestly though he trusted she wouldn't turn him into a toad-man or anything.

Not that he expected her to but Milo had been in a pretty awful relationship before meeting up with Ozma.

"If death means so much to you then why don't you ask to age?" Ozma thought about his words quite clearly. Everyone could age in Oz if they wanted to but the vast majority chose to stay young and healthy.

"I do not hold any fear of death Ozma and recognize it for the gift that is meant to be. However for all that I feel a greater gift is to be with you," Milo said then looked rather bashful, the would be preacher wasn't prone to making such statements.

Ozma wrapped him in a long and warm kiss as she took his hands in comfort.

"Sigh," Dorothy looked at her two friends in contentment.

"Finished!" Sparksia called and Ozma was most pleased to see her room transformed back into a semblance of what it once was. Beautiful emerald fountains, a lovely gold bed with emerald shaded covers, emerald birds made from her favorite gem and brought to life. The room was very familiar to Ozma and she longed to visit her personal zoo, gymnasium, pool, four floor library, observatory, and theme park again.

"Wow," Dorothy stared in shock, it made the Emerald Palace look small.

"I hope you don't mind but I'd like you both to stay in my room with me tonight. I don't really feel right sleeping here alone. Besides these towers are about as big as Oz. One time I was lost for three weeks in the bathroom trying to find my way out until the Poogies rescued me. It was quite embarrassing," Ozma said looking around as she thought of ways she might convince her mother what course she took was madness.

"Ummm Ozma do you think that's entirely proper?" Milo asked in a voice that was rather hushed. It became considerably less so when all twelve of her sisters looked at him with mischievous and knowing gazes.

"Whatever do you mean Milo...Oh," Ozma blushed as she realized what he might be worried about.

You who don't get it can ask your parents.

"Don't worry Milo I don't think..." Dorothy tried to reassure her friend but burst out laughing at the thought of it as the peacher's son became red as an apple. Dorothy Gale found the thought just wonderful that he'd be so gentlemanly and hilarious too.

"Oh dear we seemed to have lost the Hungry Tiger and King Sean again," Ozma said, changing the subject as the young woman ruler of Oz noticed their conspicuous absence.

***

King Sean looked the Hungry Tiger square in the eye as they stood in the corner of one of the Crystal Palace's many magical hallways, far from Ozma and her sisters. The undead former King of the Dead had a very curious plan that he wanted to share with the Hungry Tiger who was more interested in snagging a Poogie for consumption than listening to the half crazed cranium.

"If I don't miss what my nose for intrigue tells me…" The King began before the Tiger decided now of all times to pay attention.

"You don't have a nose," Rama the Tiger pointed out with a claw to the two slits below his eye sockets.

"I'm aware of that! Though I suspect any moment now the magic of being free from the Kingdom of the Restless Dead will kick in and transform me into a full human, preferably a good looking one," King Sean said confidently. The dead couldn't exist outside of the realm of the dead so he had to be alive. He was just at present rather ugly.

"Okay," the Hungry Tiger muttered.

The Hungry Tiger sat up and yawned a mild roar that nevertheless echoed through the palace.

"DO KEEP QUIET!" King Sean yelled as the little ball of calcium lept up and down.

"Sure," The Hungry Tiger began sniffing the air for food but all that was on his mind was thoughts of his love Sita and the smell that a Poogie might give off if roasted gently for a few hours above a fire.

"If I don't miss my nose for intrigue then I suspect that the Wizard Michael is secretly manipulating the Queen Lurline into forbidding her daughter's marriage to the *BLECH* mortal…" the Undead then stopped for a moment "Which is what I aspire to be of course. I also believe he's probably behind the desire to undo your lands magical enchantment. In all likelihood it is because of some deep seated grudge of his having to do with his family being kicked out of Oz by a Good witch and being deprived of one of his precious animals...probably a Tiger which has blostered into a evil desire for revenge. Due to the difficulties of such a man finding his way into the service of one like Lurline so quickly it's also my opinion that he's somehow replaced the actual Wizard Michael and is some sort of wicked warlock," King Sean reiterated his theory that he developed from two minutes in the man's presence.

"That's amazing," The Hungry Tiger blinked down at the skull.

"When your King of the Restless dead for a century you develop the ability to put your finger on these sorts of things," The King said smiling. It was quite terrifying to look upon.

"You don't have..." The Hungry Tiger began before the skull started sputtering.

"I know I don't have a finger! The fact is that he is probably just the sort of person that a Royal like Lurline or Ozma would be grateful to for exposing and undoing all the evil enchantments of. If I don't miss my guess then also he's holding your love Sita captive as well. All we have to do is find him and you'll use your intimidating Tiger presence to force him to confess! Then no doubt Ozma and Lurline will reward me with a living kingdom to rule hehehe," King Sean plotted out. He would have rubbed his hands together greedily if he had hands.

"Well we're already halfway there," The Hungry Tiger said lifting a claw up and pointing to the form of the Grand Wizard Michael who was standing behind Sean.

Recognizing the smell of Evile Lackey on him despite the perfumes and silk, the Tiger roared menacingly at his age old foe. The Wicked Lackey Family Patriarch had cast an illusion on himself that even the great lords of the fey couldn't pierce but Rama was not fooled. Which just goes to show you a Tiger's nose can't be beat, unless you wave food under it.

"Oh do be silent Tiger." Evile lifted up his staff and said the words "Shrinktus psyxhalll calamari!"

The Engagement of Ozma
Book Two in the Umbrella Man of Oz series

With an explosion of white light the Hungry Tiger was now a Hungry Kitten and King Sean was little more than the size of a thimble. Wrapping them both up in his arms the Warlock put the pair in one of the many leather spell pouches around his belt and chuckled as he journeyed down to his hidden cave base, far below the palace. Everything was going exactly according to plan.

Well no, not really but Evile pretended it was.

***

Chapter 7

"This is a highly revolting development. And will you please quit sneezing!" King Sean said as he sat in the bottom of Evile Lackey's spell pouch. Beside him the Hungry Tiger who was waist deep in bat guano, caterpillars, and sprigs of poppies was sneezing up a storm. It had not been the Not-So-Wicked-Anymore-Royals plan to be captured by the Warlock and certainly not before he had received his rightful reward for unmasking him.

"I'm surry! I can't...ACHOO! I'm allergic to wogglepillars." The Hungry Tiger said with his eyes watering.

"We're not so terribly fond of you either," The first of the wogglepillars looked up at the pair and frowned. It was a male voice though quite immature, like a boy not quite fourteen.

"It's not like we asked to be to be put into this spell-pouch to be used in some vile enchantment. Both my cousin and me were just minding our business when that awful wizard picked us off our flowers and dumped us in this bag. We were about to weave our chrysalises too!" the second wogglepillar said with a voice that was distinctly feminine, and just as young.

"If I wanted your life story bugs, I would have asked for it!" The Skull said with a sneer and tried to figure out a way to break free of his current predicament.

"We're not bugs!" the male caterpillar seemed quite offended.

"We're Woggleptera! I'm Cindy and this is Ralph. Sorry, Princess Christine named us so we're not very Woggleptera style named." the female said waving her many legs.

King Sean sniffed, which was quite the accomplishment with no nostrils. "I'll have you know child that I was the King of Oz in life!"

The Hungry Tiger looked at the skull. "No you weren't."

"Okay your right on that. Middle Earth?" Sean suggested an alternate kingdom.

"No," The Hungry Tiger spoke out, frowning.

"Narnia?" Sean's eye sockets did a passable imitation of a blink.

The Engagement of Ozma
Book Two in the Umbrella Man of Oz series

"I don't think so," The Hungry Tiger muttered while leaned back against the folds of the pouch and yawned.

"Alright! Your right! I was a used car salesman from Boise!" the Skull ounced up and down on the six leaf clovers that were directly under him. It was a humiliating revelation, though this should not be meant as an insult to any used car salesman from Boise reading this.

"Being Woggleptera is much better than that." Cindy said wiggling her several dozen legs.

"What's a Woggleptera anyway?" The Hungry Tiger asked, scratching his head.

"We are!" Cindy replied.

"We're Wogglebugs which haven't become full Wogglebugs yet. Our Highly Magnified Thoroughly Educated uncle sponsored our internship on Avy-Lyon until Princess Ozma changes the rules at the Athletics school!" Ralph frowned.

"It's discriminatory! We can't do any of the athletic sports and we'll complain until we can!" Cindy leapt up a bit as she frowned her wogglepillar face.

Before King Sean could come up with a suitably nasty remark regarding her preferring to be a short insect instead of just becoming a bigger one, the group of all four found themselves being shook out of their hiding place into a glass jar.

The jar was in the middle of Evile Lackey's laboratory far beneath the Kingdom of Avy-Lyon's palace and well far away from Princess Ozma and her friends.

Dropping his disguise, Evil Lackey clasped his hands together and laughed manically. It's just sort of the thing you do in a situation like this.

"Lackey you fiend! For this I will eat you! Even it takes…weeks." the Hungry Tiger said shouting his tiny little voice from the jar up to the giant wizard. He had been about to say a hundred years but even in his shrunken state he was awfully hungry and the giant wizard didn't look like he could satisfy such a big ache in his tummy for very long. In retrospect his conscience made him feel awfully sick about eating the Wizard anyway and truth be told, Warlocks always give one heartburn.

75

"Foolish little Rama! I am the greatest evil wizard that has ever walked fairy-dom! I have lain waste to kingdoms! Turned great warriors and beasts alike to mounds of jelly and dust! I have held back the hands of time and made Philosopher's Stones into paperweights with my alchemical skill! Does thou really think anything you can could possibly stop me?" Evil Lackey gloated with sadistic glee. The son of the Wicked Witch of the West and a Phanfasm had produced a truly malignant mind in Evile with great magic indeed.

The Hungry Tiger thought about that for a second, thinking wasn't his strong suit on an empty stomach but after a few moments of deliberation gave his answer. "Yes."

"Listen Evile Baby. You see it's like this, we're working for Princess Ozma and we're very powerful individuals. In fact I'm a former king of an undead nation and in the interests of Good/Evil Relations I don't think you should be treating us quite so nastily. You wouldn't want to end up a cactus now would you?" King Sean gave a stare at Evil Lackey as the tiny ball of calcium hoped to intimidate the full sized Wicked Warlock.

Evil Lackey looked down into his jar as he put one hand on the top of it and used it to shake it merrily, watching with glee the four inhabitants shaken up with his spell components. "Soon. Very soon Oz will be destroyed and not just in any simple way like fire from the sky or dumping the population into the Deadly Desert...no I hate you all much too much for that. Everyone and everything in Oz will be destroyed by the sands of time and old age! Forced to watch beauty destroyed by wrinkles, backaches, rust, and rot that inflicts all the normal countries. People will complain about their not being enough time to do anything and children won't understand their elders. All the living objects will be silent and ignored by man and even the toys that children know to be alive will eventually be forgotten by the adults and disposed of. The Unicorns, Dryads, and Fair Folk will be forced to leave or become as men or objects...HAHAHAAHA...it will be glorious."

This evil rant was brought to you by Evile Lackey Inc. Maker of unpleasant insane inventions since 1875.

The Engagement of Ozma
Book Two in the Umbrella Man of Oz series

Despite being highly dizzy for their experience King Sean and the Hungry Tiger understood what the evil magician said well enough and didn't think it was glorious at all.

"That's not right!" Cindy shouted as the wogglepillar looked up at the wizard who kidnapped them.

"Christine told us all about her sister's adventures! Oz never did anything to you!" Ralph frowned as mean as he could. Sadly unless Evile had a magnifying glass in his eye it was unlikely he'd notice just how ugly an expression the wogglepillar was giving him. Even then it was unlikely he'd care. The Wicked Witch of the West had not been the nicest parent in the world after all, even if she was all Evile had.

"Well Dorothy did my kill my mother and aunt. Princess Ozma turned my son into a tree and his girlfriend. Glinda banished me and all my fellow Lackeys. I don't even want to tell you about my poor second cousin Glegg. Finally, do you know how difficult it is to find material components now that Ozma and her friends have virtually eliminated it everywhere in and around Oz with the neighboring kingdom's following suite? It's gone well beyond finding a fellow necromancer for poker night, it's a threat to the very evil wizard way of life!" Evile Lackey said with a shout as he counted off on his fingers the abuses that the people have Oz had heaped upon his companions.

It was the nature of evil not to be able to perceive irony so you'll forgive Evile lackey for not understanding the concept justice as it applied to people who were like him.

Ralph blinked his eyes at Evile Lackey "Well, there is that I suppose."

Evile Lackey was no longer paying attention as he slid the glass jar into Sita's cage and walked over to his machinery. "You must realize that this isn't just personal. This is VERY personal. Destroying Oz will not be enough to make me the greatest evil wizard in the eyes of the Dark Faeries of the world. Any man can destroy a country of the fey if he puts enough nasty spite into it but I intend to do an action which will show truly that I am the wickedest warlock of them all! I will destroy Princess Ozma's love for a mortal!" That single action was much more insidious than the mere destruction of a people, it required a heart that was blacker than black.

"You can't destroy true love! That's the most inviolate thing in all of Fairy-dom and the world of Man!" Cindy said, repeating what she knew of magic from Christine as well as from her heart.

Evil Lackey put up his 'Deception-O-Beam Faciliator' in his hands which resembled something of a cross between a Christmas tree, a rifle, and a toaster oven. "Just watch me."

***

Princess Ozma's thoughts were far away from such things as evil Wizards kidnapping her friends. Standing in her sitting room with Princesses Glitteria, Morgan, Flutter, Kiiri, Kessily, Christine, and Spaksia. She was being fitted for the banquet that was to be held in her honor. Her other eight sisters were helping Dorothy and Milo in other parts of her chambers.

Personally Ozma didn't know if she entirely trusted the rather man hungry Dawn around her fiancé but she trusted Milo was strong enough to fight off her advances. Besides she knew her sisters loved her and would never betray her in such a fashion.

"So Ozma do you think you might be willing to share your mortals?" Kessily smiled at Ozma with a mischievous grin.

"I beg your pardon?" Ozma looked down as they prepared her rainbow dress which would have put Polychrome, an actual rainbow, to shame.

"Well since you aren't going to be married to Milo it seems only fair you introduce him to others of your family. Even without wings he's awfully cute!" Rebecca chuckled as she tried on a Jester's hat "I remember one time in 1207 that…"

"Rebecca!" Morgan said with a look that was a highly offended.

"Thank you Morgan." Ozma said with a sigh, it wasn't a very nice question. Milo was her fiancé and that was that, she'd share almost anything with her sisters but there was a limit to some things.

The Engagement of Ozma
Book Two in the Umbrella Man of Oz series

"I mean really you two. He is a mortal! That's like breaking nine or ten promises that we made to our mother!" Morgan was very keen on keeping the promises to her mother.

"Morgan!" Ozma said even more highly offended than Morgan had been.

"Well it's not like I have anything against the poor lad. I must admit even without wings he is extremely cute little thing but then again so are flowers and puppies yet I would not join myself to one forever more," Morgan said with a sigh.

Morgan just hadn't met the right human you must understand.

"I like him! He taught me how to properly use an umbrella when one needed it for rain, sleet, or disarming an wand wielding opponent," Christina said. She was a thousand years older than Ozma but she'd matured allot slower and instead took the form of a little girl of eight.

"I admit he seems like a pleasant fellow but I really can't respect any mortal who doesn't dress in furs or leaves. It's been a long time since you really saw a mortal who could like in nature in Fairy-dom it sometimes seems," Kirri sighed. Ozma's eleventh sister was a bit of a wild child who enjoyed living in jungles and artic more than comfy castles.

"Does he have good luck?" Flutter asked. Flutter resembled nothing so much as a Leprechaun lass with wings yet she was conversely probably the most unlucky fairy princess in Avy-Lyon. Ozma alone approached her in the number of times she'd been kidnapped or transformed by some unpleasant wizard. All because early in her life she'd been born under a ladder, took her first step on a black cats tail, and managed to somehow break a mirror every seven years. To avoid all the problems on the ground Flutter constantly batted her wings to keep her off the ground which was how she'd got name, she even slept flying.

"Well he found me and survived an invasion. I like to think so." Ozma said smiling.

"Oh wonderful. Maybe I'll rub his head." Flutter said as she picked up her pet Centibunny Harvey. The cute little thing had a hundred rabbit's feet which was one of the many reasons she kept it by her. Unfortunately though, when it got going, it was VERY difficult to catch.

"Please don't." Ozma said blinking as she remembered when she'd rubbed her head for good luck and Ozma had ended up turned into Tip for most of her second adolescence.

Ozma then saw the room get rather quiet as the light of the Queen of the Light Faeries filled the room. Lurline and her Poogie guards soon filled the chamber as a crew of tiny sylphs (hoping for promotion to full fairies) pulled up her dress's train.

Lurline had taken the position as Queen of the Fey from her own mother Titania and someday one of her children would hold the throne of all good fey. Ozma didn't like to think it would be her since she was quite happy as the ruler of Oz but each of her sisters had a flaw that kept them from being truly in all things of the fey from snobbish Morgan to unable to be serious Rebecca.

It was for this very reason that Lurline had intended to make Ozma her heir just between you and me. As her daughter of love and part mortal, Ozma was able to relate more to the increasingly mortal filled worlds of our time. Plus she was a wiser woman Lurline recognized in her good moments, which were many, than even she. Now though, Lurline and Ozma were at cross purposes and only one could succeed in their goal.

Each of Ozma's sisters all bowed their heads and curtsied before their mother as Ozma reluctantly did the same, she did after all think it proper to be respectful to her Queen let alone the person who'd given her life.

"We were just setting up Ozma's dress for tonight's banquet mother. May I speak with you regarding the business of Oz..." Kirri said, she had done her best to fill Oz with talking animals and beautiful woodlands and had no desire to see any of it destroyed. If animals couldn't speak then how would they be able to tell humans not to eat them or turn them into coats, it was a horrible thought all around.

"No my daughter you may not," Lurline said calmly.

"Well actually I have a few objections regarding it myself!" Kessily said raising her own hand as Christine nodded, followed by Flutter, and even Morgan who devoted her entire life to following in

The Engagement of Ozma
Book Two in the Umbrella Man of Oz series

her mother's footsteps. Had Ozma's other sisters been in the room they would too have added their objections.

"We all do mother! What is given cannot be taken back save as a gift from the very people given to. It's very disrespectful of kingdom sovereignty and..." Morgan prepared a wonderful speech that she had been working on all day. She'd chosen the very brightest and nicest of mortals to fill Oz with kings and queens and occasionally still looked in on their descendants.

"I would care that you leave my youngest child and me alone for a time Morgan. That goes for all of us," Lurline's voice left no room for argument.

Each of the Fairy Princesses left the room quietly with only a slight disturbance from Flutter as the door closed directly on her face before she managed to get out. Opening it with a look of embarrassment soon she too was gone from the dressing room of the Queen of Oz.

Lurline's sylphs and Poogie guards were allowed to stay but they were completely loyal to the Fairy Queen and were unlikely to disagree with what she had to say.

"I have come to speak with you regarding your fiancé and kingdom," Lurline said with a maternal look of sadness on her face.

"I can only hope to say that you have changed your mind!" Ozma crossed her arms as she looked at her mother and tried once again to figure out who had put such awful idea in her head. She'd lived a thousand years before she'd met Milo yet now the thought of being unable to marry him was enough that she worried about dying from it. She could barely even think of her mother's proclamation she would break the enchantment of Oz because that was a betrayal on a level she couldn't even think on.

"I'm afraid not. Please lower your voice as well. Did not your husband say to honor thy mother and father in my observations of him?" Lurline chided as she waved her wand.

"Yes he did. But he did not say to necessarily agree with them," Ozma said, nevertheless lowering her tone. She was not angry at her mother but she was confused, hurt, and worried.

"He should have then. I know you feel strongly about my decisions but you must understand that it is at heart in your best interests," Lurline sadly believed this despite it being a product of the spell of the Warlock Evil Lackey. His magical dust of confusion was an especially strong creation of the Wicked Witch of the West's before she died. It caused normal people to become extremely vulnerable to the stupid ideas that even immortals get in their heads every day.

Maybe quite a few of our leaders and other authority figures have been hit with it on occasion?

"Mother my dear I love you with all my heart but I cannot causally sit back and watch you destroy the lives that so many have made in Oz. My people are peaceful and content and they deserve not to have such a radical change thrust on them. Furthermore I believe that love is the highest aspiration that either Fey or Mortals can strive for. If that means I must oppose you with my own magic and go against your wishes to be with my love I will in fact do so as much as it pains me," Ozma said as she took a long deep breath and held up her wand. The emerald thing glowed brightly as a symbol of her defiance.

Lurline shook her head as she removed her own wand of diamond that quickly caused the magic of Ozma's own wand to fade and disappear. "I fear my daughter that you have no chance against the power of your true Fairy Queen in direct confrontation. All magic flows from the Supreme Master and I am his representative to the goodly fey…thus yours, Glinda's, the Wizard's, all good magic can be snuffed by mine. However you are the Queen of Oz and that I will not begrudge you your right to protect your kingdom. I will also not begrudge you your right as a Lady to love a Lord. Thus I come to you with an offer."

Lurline's heart was not so affected by the power of Evile Lackey's dust that she had lost all of her essential goodness. Though pained immeasurably by the loss of her Husband King David Ozroar the Fifth and wishing to spare Ozma the pain she thought was solely the product of marrying a human, she wished at heart to be proven wrong in this conclusion. Thus destiny had struck with an idea that would test the love of Ozma and Milo to it's strongest.

"I cannot say I will agree to it but I will hear you out," Ozma said as she tried to cover up the desperation in her voice.

The Engagement of Ozma
Book Two in the Umbrella Man of Oz series

Because she had created Oz, Lurline was ironically perhaps the greatest threat it had yet faced.

"Very well my daughter. There are many great and noble fairy princes in the world and many wonderful mortal women for men. Love is a thing meant to be eternal and forever but the hearts of man have proven time and time again that such things last not. Thus if you may prove your love forever for this man and he for you then Oz I shall keep eternal. It will show that man and Fairy can live together as one." Lurline lowered her face down as she struggled with saying such a thing to her daughter.

"I am proof enough as it is that mortal and fey can make wonders. However if you must make this beastly challenge then I accept and I'm sure Milo will as well!" Ozma said with a pout, her mother's words hurt her deeply. She after all was half human and saying that man and faeries couldn't mix was saying that she shouldn't be. If there is a worse thing to imply to your child please don't tell me about it.

Lurline resisted the urge to embrace her daughter, tell her she was sorry, and say that they would arrange a marriage ceremony tomorrow. Evile Lackey's wicked dust had done its work well and it was all too easy to stick by a foolish thing than say you were wrong.

"Very well then my daughter we shall begin immediately." Lurline gave a smile that worried Ozma a great deal.

***

Dorothy was not the type to wait around while other people did things. After a very quick time picking out a dress for tonight's banquet the Princess of Oz had begun her investigation around the Palace of Eternity to figure out if there was something afoot that the regular folk around here didn't notice.

Dorothy went through all the possibilities in her mind about what might have made Ozma's mother go bad including a Mimic taking her place, that'd they'd gone into a parallel Ozziverse, and even Lurline's heart being frozen but thus far she couldn't find anything that indicated it. It was also very hard walking around the

Castle because allot of the rooms didn't have any stairs leading up to them and she had to ask faeries passing her by to ferry her up.

It was then that Dorothy found herself tapped on the shoulders by a magic wand as fairy-dust (which is the equivalent of sweat to faeries since they exercise so much with their wings but don't let that spoil how pretty you might think it is) fell about her. Looking up Dorothy saw two of Ozma's sisters whom she remembered being introduced Dawn and Dusk. Dawn was the most energetic, good dispositional, and positive of the thirteen fairy princesses of Lurline's band. Dusk was a bit more the realist with calm, rational, and occasionally pessimistic views. Dawn with her long golden hair streaming about was smiling broadly while Dusk with her dark black hair in curls and glasses adjusted was frowning concerned.

"Ah Princess Dorothy we've been looking everywhere for you! You're practically family and on such a lovely day as this we shouldn't be separated," Dawn chuckled as Dorothy blinked at her in surprise. The Princess of Oz hadn't thought it was a very lovely day since she found out Ozma and Milo's marriage might well be off and Oz was about ready to be destroyed…again.

"We were hoping that you might assist us in a little bit of mischief that hopefully will help save the Oz that we helped create." Dusk said adjusting her glasses. While as extraordinarily beautiful as the rest of Ozma's sisters there was a distinct frumpiness about Dusk's dress that made Dorothy think of a kindly librarian she once knew.

"Yes anything!" Dorothy said with a blink. This was the answer to everything that needed to get done if they could pull it off.

"We figure the reason that mumsey-dearest is about ready to destroy Oz has something to do with our daddy-kins Ozroar being turned into stone. Frankly I don't think that nit Michael has been half the wizard he used to be since David's disappearance and couldn't turn milk into butter let alone cure daddy," Dawn said with a bit of a pout as she flew upside down beside Dorothy and gave her a bit of a tickle from behind.

"If our mother's joy is restored at seeing her husband's return to a natural state then it is my calculated opinion that she will give up her desire to break the enchantment on Oz. Furthermore, our father was a hopeless romantic at heart and I'm sure that he'd be willing to support Ozma's marriage to that lovely young human your traveling with. He had the most fascinating thoughts on spore-mold growth when we talk..." Dusk was interrupted then by Dawn who smiled at Dorothy.

"Yeah and we figure you will be a great help in fixing it!" the Fairy said returning to her normal upright fluttering lest her skirt become un-Fairy princess like.

Dorothy blinked and said "Very well but why do you think I'd be a great help?"

"We've tried everything else. Wishes, Potions, Transformations, and nothing works to make him human again. You've done the impossible on numerous occasions before Ms. Gale so we figure that if anyone could fix Ozroar, it'd be you." Dusk said with a nod and tapped Dorothy's nose with her tweed comforted wand.

"Priddy, priddy, priddy, priddy please with mountains of sugar on top?" Dawn got really close in Dorothy's face which caused the poor girl from Kansas to sneeze from all the fairy dust. It was so strong that it ended up sending the poor likeable fairy tumbling into a suit of armor across the hall. Thankfully,there was no one else in the long crystal corridors that Dorothy could see save a few poogies a hundred feet up and a group of sylphs polishing the glass of the walls.

"Oh dear! I'm so sorry!" Dorothy cried. She put her hands to her face in the most dreadful look of embarrassment. These kind of things did not often happen to the very experienced adventurer that she had become over the past century.

"We don't have time to think about such things right now Dorothy! To the Statue room!" Dusk said even as the three of them disappeared in a flash of light accompanied by a crack of Thunder. Faeries absolutely love their dramatics when they disappear you know.

The next place Dorothy found herself in was the Forgotten Tower of Castle Eternia. It was called the Forgotten Tower because Lurline had cast a spell upon it that sealed it away from any being entering it or remembering its location if they somehow reached it.

Dusk was the only one unaffected because she had stolen away some of the anti-magical dust of Michael's lab so that she could remember it and get past the spell. In any case it was a rather foreboding place because it was the highest tower in the Castle and as such you could see the entire edge of the world from it.

The Forgotten Tower might have been beautiful were it brightly lit but the place was dark but for the light of the sun reflecting off Earth. Dust was everywhere and covering all the old furnishings that must have been for when this place was used as a place of recreation and fun.

"Oh my," Dorothy muttered looking about until she stopped and stared at the centerpiece of the Forgotten Tower.

Standing in the middle of the room was a tall man in a long kingly robe that hung around him rather informally like a trench coat. He had a small crown causally on his head which titled to one side and bore the sign of Oz's Royal House. His face was marked by a small goatee that covered a very youthful face. He also had Ozma's cute nose or more precisely he had his. He looked quite happy except for the fact he was turned into stone.

"King David Ozroar. He was such a nice guy, except for the tickling," Dawn said with a slightly longing sigh even as she wrinkled her nose at the last part. King David Ozroar was infamous about fairy-land for his tickling.

"When the Nome King transformed the Royal Family of Ev into objects, all you had to do was put your hand on them and say the name of the kingdom," Dorothy offered, looking at the man and feeling a wave of sympathy.

Lurline might be threatening to remove the enchantment of Oz but no one deserved to be have someone they loved turned into stone.

"Unfortunately it's not so easy. The Wishing Belt was made by the Wicked King of the Nobalds and his transformations always were made to be breakable by someone knowing the truth of the person. I'm afraid the only sure fire way of breaking a Cocky-Trace's transformation is his tears." Dusk sighed as she shook her head.

"What is a Cocky-Trace? Why haven't you tried getting some?" Dorothy finally got up the nerve to ask. It sounded like a type of chicken or a really arrogant sort as much as she could tell.

The Engagement of Ozma
Book Two in the Umbrella Man of Oz series

The Princess of Oz whapped her hands against King David to test to see if he was maybe just frozen by a stone outside and not really transformed at all. Unfortunately he was rock solid as near Dorothy could tell.

"It's a type of rooster that is part dinosaur. They're said to be extremely vain creatures and mostly spend their time admiring their own looks. It's one of the reasons that so few people have been turned to stone looking at them is because they are so hard to find. I tried looking for one with some magic glasses Tasb made but I found nada, nothing, zero, zilch, not a thing…" Dawn said as she started naming off synonyms for not finding a Cocky-Trace.

"Well I don't know much about your creature which turns people into stone but I know allot about roosters. I think I can find him for you," Dorothy answered with as much hope as she could muster. It just had to work.

After all it was the first available answer and those always seemed to work back in Oz.

***

Chapter 8

Milo T. Starling was sitting on the edge of the largest cliff face in Avy-Lyon which was so large that one could fit the entire kingdom of Oz along the edge of its size.

The Kentuckian King-consort of Ozma (which meant he was royalty because he and Ozma were engaged but not really supposed to rule anything) was so down in his face that several of Lurline's clouds went by him to ask what was wrong. Being a polite young man and not wanting to trouble the cumulus fellows with his worries, he told them he had to be alone with his thoughts and listened to their advice about the best way to brighten up one's day was to find someone washing their car and let all the tears fall on them. When the clouds left Milo shook his head and pulled out the lunch he'd packed for the trip and sat down to chew on the peanut Butter and jelly sandwich with grits on the side.

"This is a most disturbing development." Milo said to no one in particular as he chewed down on his meal and drank from his thermos of 2% fat milk. The Good Book was open on his lap and he was currently paging through it as he tried to find a relevant passage to his predicament. Unfortunately he couldn't find anything about what to do when a parent was wrong in forbidding a relationship.

It was however much easier to find useful information about why to not destroy Oz. Milo had no idea who had put this awful idea in the woman's head but he would at the night's banquet make a speech that would talk about the benefits mortals had received from being immortal. He would mention they had a better chance to learn good manners and pass them on, he'd mention that they seemed to enjoy their lives considerably more, and that Oz had proven a substantial boon to the behavior of outside kingdoms.

He'd then talk in a hopefully moving manner about how he himself had fallen in love with Princess Ozma that would melt Lurline's heart, metaphorically unlike some other incidents in Oz's history, and convince her to approve of his marriage to her.

He would have felt better if he had something to do or say if he failed to convince her with his speech but Milo contented himself with the knowledge good would always triumph over evil even if there was an unpleasant period in-between. You should really thank Milo's mother for all this honesty and decency because she was the one mostly responsible though his father did teach him how to balance a checkbook amongst other practical knowledge that is of no use in Oz.

Unfortunately, Milo was not particularly aware of the evil gaze of Evile Lackey who was watching from nearly a mile away with his left eye as he kept his right eye shut. Igor had inherited his mother the Wicked Witch of the West's powerful eye and while he usually had to wear a contact so he could see what was going on close to him, he right now was putting his eye to very good effect spying on the love of Ozma.

Firing up his 'Deception-O-Beam Faciliator' Evile took aim with the device's long range fire and prepared to shoot the poor lad with one of his most powerful science-magic spells. Still disguised as the Arch-Wizard Michael Evile Lackey did his best immitation of the Sorcerer's voice and shouted.

"Hail foolish Mortal! It is I Michael the grand Sorcerer of Avy-lyon and I have come to tell thee of a terrible time of testing upon thee!" Evile said with a chuckle. His father's blood allowed him to transform into virtually anything and the impersonation of Michael always gave him such a thrill. Evile was a powerful wizard tis true but he was nowhere near the most powerful sorcerer in the world Michael.

"Oh bother." Milo got up and checked his clothes out to see if he was presentable. Clearing his throat, the young man said "Yes, very well what is the test most High Dingy Doo of Wizards here?"

He wasn't sure this was the proper term of respect for a man of Michael's power, he had heard the term from a group of nice kids he had known back in Kentucky. They solved mysteries with their dog.

Evile couldn't for the life of him figure out whether the young man was mocking him or showing the proper fearful respect by those words "You are to be cast under a magical spell which will conjure forth in your mind untold doubles of your love. By magical law if you choose the right one then Lurline's opinion of your love will grow stronger. If you choose incorrectly then I will use one of the magical wishes in my pills to wish you to never see your lover again!" Evile of course could have wished the poor man away from his love anyway and it would have been deeply satisfying to the inhuman warlock. However, it was more satisfying knowing that if Milo failed to overcome his machine that he'd be wracked for the rest of his life with guilt.

"Well, ahem. I suppose I must say that I am ready and willing to face all tests for my love. I would rather do nothing more than defend our romance against your worst." Milo said nearly at the top of his lungs. He after the fact realized that wasn't strictly true however. Milo would prefer personally to be back at the Emerald City completely unaware of any of this and playing billiards with Ojo. Truth be told he'd even rather be home in Kentucky watching his Doctor Who videos eating popcorn than have this called into question but there was nothing he could do. Milo was like all men in love, stuck with it.

"Oh I can assure you Mister Starling that what you are about to experience is a far cry from my worst. That I will tell you is something I am saving for later. Hehehehe," Evile let out a wicked laugh as his telescopic eye focused on the man's uncertain and unhappy face.

Firing the Deception-O-Beam-Facilitator Milo was hit by the wicked kaleidoscope of lights that instantly put him under the full effects of the illusion. Popping into existence all around Milo's vision were hundreds of duplicates of his Princess Ozma drawn from his memories and the magic of the spell. Each was almost a perfect representation of the Princess but Milo could detect tiny flaws in their posture and stance that showed him the truth. None of them possessed the vital spark of life that had drawn Milo to his Princess Ozma.

"Well this will be easier than I thought!" Milo exclaimed. Evile had absolutely no understanding of the intimate language that lovers have between another. That and Evile was an absolutely terrible magical artist too lazy to modify his own work to be any prettier than it was.

The Engagement of Ozma
Book Two in the Umbrella Man of Oz series

The story might not have changed significantly if not for the fact that atop another nearby cliff three of Ozma's sisters in Young Christine, Savy-Sparksia, and Unlucky Flutter were watching the cruel action by their court magician on the mortal whom their fairy sister and sister in blood was so fond of.

"What an awful horrible, cruel man! I never liked Michael because he always liked the traditional way of doing magic best!" Sparksia stamped her foot and frowned nastily at the false Court Wizard. In truth, before Evile had replaced Michael as the court magician Sparksia and he had quite a few wonderful conversations on how to improve sorcery with science. The Court Wizard had considered her much like a daughter and she him a father. Sadly, these past few years he had been a complete bore unwilling to talk to her about anything.

"I would be very sad if he were wished away and he might have bad eyesight. We should help," Christine said flying up to her sister's head in height. Mortals often were subjected to magical tests when they tried to wed faeries but all of the sisters were well aware that almost none managed to pass them. King David had been the first to do so in centuries and the tests were often completely unfair.

"He needs a little luck," Flutter said as she looked around her to make sure that a cloud wasn't about to hit her with lightning. None of the fair folk would willing attack the daughter of Lurline on her own island but the nice clouds Milo talked to seemed to have a way of carelessly tossing things directly on Flutter whenever she wasn't looking.

"What he needs is one of my machines! Christine do you have any of your Promethean clay?" Sparksia said as her little sister nodded and handed her some of the magical dough that could be transformed into anything just by molding it. With just a little bit of molding from the Technical Princess, she shaped the clay into a mechanized crystal staff with numerous blinking lights and whirls. "With this, there won't be any question of his ability to see through Michael's illusions."

Taking aim at Milo with the magical ray-gun, Spaksia watched Flutter tap her own wand onto the device.

"Here let me add something to it!" Flutter said cheerily. The moment her wand touched the device it immediately started to shudder, shake, and of course shoot sparks.

"No Flutter!" Christine and Sparksia shouted in horror.

Flutter's enchantments were as unlucky as she.

"I choose none of them Lord Michael because none of them are indeed my Ozma," Milo said confidently after checking each one to make sure his answer was correct. Then the energy blast that struck Milo was a terrible black that caused him to shudder and shake in a jig. In an instant all the false Ozmas were transformed from harmless illusions into things considerably more terrifying. Craven Blood Snorters, Kalidahs, the until-that-moment-extinct Gargoyles, Doom Serpents, and at least one Death Screecher.

Milo seeing the sudden appearance of the giant army of evil and being inclined not to be safer than sorry around illusions, which these no longer were had no chance to run or escape before any of them destroyed him. Instead he said "Oh well, I've had a good run."

He adjusted his tie and prepared to die, hoping he'd get some interesting words off first that might be memorable. Aside from 'Please don't eat me' which he didn't expect to work anyhow.

Evile Lackey found the results of Flutter's jinx enormously amusing and plopped himself down to watch the end of our poor Hero. It was then his telescopic eye spotted Milo's herefor unopened Green umbrella starting to glow and sputter. As the monstrous horde bore down on the easiest looking prey in the area, our would be husband of Ozma, the umbrella released a huge cloud of green mist from it's tip that covered the entire area. The Green Magic was able to be seen through and breathed by any resident of the Emerald City but for the Wicked Creatures it was a choking fog.

"Thank you very much." Milo said to the previously useless device and took off in a brisk run. Jumping over Doom Serpent tails, vaulting off Kalidah beeks, and sliding under gargoyle wings as he tried to avoid the blind slashing and snapping of the evil beasts all about. If you believe this to be un-heroic behavior in running away from such a monstrous group, then try to understand Milo fully intended to come back to deal with the creatures before they hurt

The Engagement of Ozma
Book Two in the Umbrella Man of Oz series

anyone. He'd just find doing so very difficult from the bottom of a Blood Snorter's stomach.

Sparksia who had smashed her machine down in anger looked upon Milo's escape with joy as her sister's clapped and cheered the mortal's narrow escape.

"See! I told you he needed luck." Flutter said, quite happy to see the situation as quite lucky given the much more larger amount of bad luck that might have befallen Milo.

"Hmmmph. It would have worked if you hadn't jinxed." Sparksia said with a frown to her sister, and tossed back her hair.

"And it would have never been necessary I think in the first place. I hope our sister doesn't mind nearly getting her true love eaten," Christine said. She was only five thousand years old and very worried about these sort of things. Sadly, Ozma when she found out later was noticeably cross with her.

Evile's reaction was a bit unexpected. While you might expect an evil warlock half-erb to scream, pull his hair out, dance in anger, and spit at a good person's escape from evil (and of course he did all these things) he when he stopped doing so, shook with fear from a sudden realization.

"By the Dark Queen of the Unseelie. It's not possible." Evile invoked the name of Yurline. Taking out his skele-porter finger bone, made from a King of the Restless Dead as a gift for eliminating a haunting of the living while visiting the Kingdom, Evile transported himself to Michael's laboratory in Castle Eternia. The Wicked Alchemist proceeded to barricade the door and cast every enchantment he could to make sure no one but the Supreme Master himself could get through.

"An Umbrella Magician," Evile muttered as he choked on the thought. It was quite possible the man who was extremely close to the destruction of Oz, Avy-Lyon, and the royal family of the Seelie fey had never been more terrified of anyone in his life than poor Milo.

***

Ozma yawned, bored as the High Queen Lurline paraded forth the suitors of every Fairy-Nation in the Otherworld. Her mother's first test was a remarkably pedestrian one that was better suited for Gliteria or Morgan. The Fairy-Princes were the most beautiful men in the world that offered her riches, security for her kingdom, and elaborate untold lifetimes of fawning devotion. Lurline had summoned them through her power as the Queen of all Seelie fey and left them and her to try and work out some sort of wonderful match to break her already committed relationship.

"Thank you very much Prince Farrule. However Oz already is a very prosperous nation, Oz is already a very peaceful nation, and I think my hand would wrinkle up if you kiss it anymore. No offense intended," Ozma added quickly at the end while the particularly ardent suitors got quickly off his knees and stormed off.

Honestly while Ozma wanted to bring Oz's happiness to as much as the world as possible she had enough trouble keeping it peaceful without adding someone's huge domiciles to it that were certainly likely to need allot of help. That wasn't even getting into the fact that she personally did love Milo and wasn't going to be bribed out of it. Some of the Princes were pompous and arrogant bores but most were actually quite nice to her and it hurt her to have to refuse them out of hand.

Going towards her balcony as the piles of treasure and magical artifacts of yore many of the eligible faeries had dropped as part of their dowries were swept up by the Poogies, Ozma caught in the glint of her crystal ivy a reflection of someone she had not seen in years.

"Tip!" Ozma spun around and embraced the person that was the closest to her heart among boys after Milo and in some ways just as much, if different.

Tippetarius was one of the more unusual pieces of Ozma's past in that when she was transformed into a boy by Mombi a young man in the Kingdom of Lostland was transformed into a girl. For years she had thought Tip had been a sort of alternate identity for her but he had proved to be a real person with his own life once his own enchantment had been broken.

Ozma had made him a Prince of Oz for his heroism and he spent most of his time visiting other kingdoms to have adventures with his mentor Zim.

The Engagement of Ozma
Book Two in the Umbrella Man of Oz series

Tip embraced her back as the young man smiled broadly. He was currently out of his usual peasant clothes and dressed in something a little more regal, which meant he was extremely uncomfortable. "Ozma! Your the Princess Lurline once to find a prince to marry?" he sounded as if he couldn't believe it.

Ozma realized that Tip had been away for the entire time that Milo had been at court. In the Land of Oz it was relatively easy to lose track of oneself for years at a time.

"Yes I'm afraid so. In truth I've already found someone but mother has forbidden it because he's a mortal." Ozma said with a sigh.

It wasn't so much that Lurline objected to her marrying Milo that bothered her. She loved Milo but some people's personalities naturally clashed. It was that she objected to it because he was a mortal and thus they were meant to be apart solely because of race.

"You have..." Tip seemed absolutely stunned by the news.

"Speaking of which, what are you doing here? They don't come more human than you brother." Ozma said, giving her friend a gentle poke in the stomach. Ozma was allowed to feel causal around Tip as if he awakened something in her that wasn't touched by the weight of Oz's existence hanging on her shoulders.

"Hey don't call me that. I guess Lurline's spell got me confused with fairy nobility because of the old Switcharoo spell. So what's this mystery guy like anyway?" Tip asked with a bit of shocked interest.

"Hmmm well he's kind, gentle, good teeth, an encyclopedia of interesting quotes, he listens to everything I say about peace seriously..." Ozma noticed Tip was sort of smirking at her.

"Uh huh, uh huh. Standard lovely couple stuff." the Prince did his best to look bored at Ozma's words. Tip of Oz was a man who was already highly suspicious of this Milo character and determined to see if he was hiding some awful secret like trying to take over Oz.

"He's a great kisser," Ozma added as Tip stuck out his tongue in disgust to Ozma's immense satisfaction. The Ruler of Oz rarely enjoyed grossing people out and in fact made it a rule not to.

However with Prince Tippetarius she had her one exception to her rule.

"I really didn't need to hear that Your Worshipfulness. I look forward to meeting the Lucky Guy," Tip smiled. Tip had never quite felt the same way about Ozma that she felt about him. Still Ozma thought that they would get along great once they finally met.

"I'm hoping Tip that you will be able to meet him along with my friends but my mother seems to have lost part of her 'older than the stars' mind. She's got it into her head that Oz should have its enchantment broken and she's using my love for Milo as a measuring stick whether or not to do it."

Ozma shook her head. She didn't mention to Tip that her father was dead as well. That she hoped could somehow be remedied and he had a right to know about the danger Oz was in.

"Ouch. Talk about pressure for a relationship to succeed!" Tip said with a blink. Humor was a defense of her friend against the number of evils Oz had to contend with and he was quite good at deflating a situation's seriousness to manageable levels.

Ozma couldn't help but chuckle. "I don't believe we will fail Tip but things do happen. If you can Tip, please try and contact Zim the Flying Sorcerer to get in touch with Glinda. If Oz cannot be saved then perhaps there is a chance that its people might be. The lands of Oz and a few in contact with it are the only ones where immortality is a part of its life but at least some animals will remain able to talk and Scarecrows able to walk."

Zim was like Glinda, one of the most powerful sorcerers in all the world. Together if anyone could find a magical solution to this problem it would be those two minds.

"The old man is hard to find sometimes but I think he's probably going to be nearby Glinda anyway. I think he's sweet on her." Tip gave a weak smile before descending into courtly bow. At the end of the bow he grabbed Ozma in a tight squeeze. Zim had hinted to him the power of Oz rested still with Lurline and on the insides he was terrified about losing the only world he'd ever known.

Ozma nodded as she rose and called out "Lurline! I am done hearing the offers of your pawns!" it was an overly harsh word pawn but gosh darnit if Ozma wasn't feeling as up to her usual kind and

The Engagement of Ozma
Book Two in the Umbrella Man of Oz series

compassionate self when dealing with attempts to steal her away from her love.

Back in Oz it was a fairly common event and had replaced wooing as the most outlawed act against the Princess-Ruler of Oz.

Tip smiled weakly as he and the other suitors vanished. Lurline herself then stepped in with a disapproving gaze "I assume that none of the Princes met with your approval to be your wedded husband?"

"Or Grand Dukes, or Counts, or even Fairy commoners whom meet with your approval over one good hearted man Mother. If you are quite ready to move into the next test to prove mortals and faeries can love one another let alone live together, I'd very much like to get it over with," Ozma said in a cool but respectful tone to the High Queen of Fairy-dom.

Ironically her pleasantness hurt Lurline more than words might have had she been angered and shouting like all twelve of her other daughters would have been in the situation.

Lurline and Ozma's conversation would have gotten frostier and more courtly as per fairy custom until they were complimenting each other like daggers when the source of their consternation entered into the room.

Milo was looking a little worse for where from his escape. A number of the nastiest had managed to pick him up by scent and tracked him mercilessly. His Saturday best was thus completely shredded and there were numerous splotches of his life fluids about him.

"Milo! What happened?" Ozma said as she blinked in horror, looking to her mother and pulling out one of her poppies to dust on his wounds. Poppies of course in Oz possess healing properties if you prepare them just right before picking, Ozma knows these things.

"Ahhhhhhhh thank you beloved. Your Court Wizard Michael attempted to destroy me," Milo said with a cross stare at Lurline.

There was after all only so much even a gentleman could take from a Lady.

"That's impossible." Lurline shook her head saying. Not only very idea of one of her closest friends in the world (or so she thought) would hurt a guest but that if Michael wished to destroy Milo

Trustworthy Starling, it would just be one of his many powerful spells away.

"It is as possible as this Kalidah bite." Milo said, holding out the rather beak shaped sign of the attack. Milo was a resident of Oz and as long as it was enchanted he had no worry about dying from the attack but it was still quite painful. Ozma's magic managed to heal the wound without a scratch though. "Your Majesty, I know it has been a good many years since you and your daughter have been close but may I request a moment alone with her."

Ozma looked at her mother and nodded.

"Very well. I think I should have a talk with Michael though. Though I do not believe he set out to deliberately harm you despite the evidence, it is obvious that you as a guest in my home have been done a grievous wronged. No matter what the disagreements we may have about the fate of my daughter's hand or her land I want you to know I mean no personal ill will."

Ozma resisted the urge to suggest that she was going to do a great deal of ill will to her by killing the people of Oz but she was still a Lady and Lurline was still her mother.

With a swish of her flowing gown and flap of her wings, the High Queen of the Seelie Fey left and the doors were shut behind her.

Ozma looked up to her love with a sigh as she removed his half broken emerald glasses and gave him a kiss between the eyes. "You certainly do know how to get into these situations my love."

"This coming from the girl who was once trapped in a peach pit beloved," Milo joked as he wrapped his arms around her.

"We'll either eventually run out of villains out to destroy happiness I'm sure," Ozma said hugging him close.

"Hush My Lady. Let us not think of that," Milo replied. He ran his fingers through her dark hair. Before the romance gets too thick for a children's book that everyone goes yuck, let's head back to see what has been happening with the residents of the Emerald City.

***

The Secret Weapon of the Wizard of Oz to the encroaching invasion of the Illumi-nati was the Fabulous Fan of Oz. Now of this I

The Engagement of Ozma
Book Two in the Umbrella Man of Oz series

of course refer to the fact it was a series of rotating blades designed to produce cool streams of air and not any number of my wonderful readers. The huge device stood thirty feet tall and the Wizard had it directly aimed at the army of irritated iridescents.

"Wiz, get those blades a spinnin so we can get onto the winnin!" Scraps called. The Patchwork Girl was wearing a brass metal helmet from World War One that had somehow found it's way into Oz and was quite enthusiastic about defeating the candle army. Scraps absolutely loathed them for hurting her beloved Scarecrow and she was sure that the fan would blow them all away.

Watching all along the walls of the Purple Brick road that the Illumi-nation rebellion was moving down was some of the most important people in Oz. While suspicious all the Good Witches and Wizards of Oz but for the Wizard himself were on vacation or preoccupied with the portents that something terrible was going to happen to Oz from the Island of Avy-Lyon. The Scarecrow, the Royal Family of Oz, Jack Pumpkinhead, H.M.

Wogglebug T.E., The Cowardly Lion, and Kambumpo the Elephant (who had been about to smoosh E. Bused the Jester for poking fun at the measures necessary to prevent tusk-decay when the invasion) had arrived to defend the Emerald City from this great threat.

"Worry not Scraps! I've got everything under control! Lights out for the Illumi-nati!" The Wizard called as he gestured down to Tik-Tok to push the fan's base switch. The copper man was the only citizen of the Emerald City that could be trusted not to fly away in the path of the wind-machine.

"As-you-wish-your-Wizard-ness." Tik-Tock said even as the huge blades began to rotate and blow an incredible cyclone of wind through the air. The device shuddered and shook with all the air suddenly being sucked towards the Illumin-nati and had the Wizard not compensated for the laws of physics with his magic the Fabulous Fan would have turned quite a few residents of Oz's capital into chopped meats of various types.

"You have done well Wizard. I'm sure the position of Mayor shall be yours," Regent Jellia said proudly even as Trot, Betsy, and Button looked on enviously behind the present ruler of Oz.

Charles Phipps

The Illumi-nati leader in a small pyramid shaped candle holder General Wyckburn being a candle in the wind was the first destined to go out in battle. The candlesticks, chandeliers, candelabras, lamps, and torches were soon piled in the absolutely largest pile of candles that Oz had seen since Ozma's last birthday party before they decided to simply use numbered candles to wish her well in the little princess's millennium long life.

"Well all in a day's work for the next Mayor of the Emerald city," The Wizard chuckled and turned to Toto the Dog who was standing next to him. The dog from Kansas then shook his head and pointed his left forepaw toward the pile of candles with a bark of despair.

"What you little..." The Wizard who was growing impatient stared in shock as suddenly the entire group of candles became a huge bonfire fanned by the magical machine. Moments later Tik-Tok was knocked to one side by the device going sailing into the air and exploding, a victim of lowest-bidder syndrome. Specifically the Wizard asking everyone who hadn't voted for him to do the work in hopes they would be glad of his eliminating unemployment.

Never mind, that Oz was a society with no need for employment that is a story for another day.

Jellia took one look at the giant creature of pure fire that was inching it's way slowly to consume the entire Emerald City in it's burning embrace and made her first Queenly decision. "In lieu of new circumstances, I have decided to abdicate my position as regent for the Princess Ozma in favor of he who is next in line for the throne."

"You coward!" Trot shouted shocked at Jellia.

"Do you want the job?" Betsy asked, having a bit more sense than her closest friend.

"Well...no," Trot admitted.

The Wizard having been rather thoroughly embarrassed by this fiasco looked toward the Wogglebug with a bit of a frown. "Very well, who exactly IS the heir to the throne if the Princesses are all out of the running?"

The Wogglebug smiled as he removed his large book of Oz genealogy which he'd been saving for just such an occasion as this.

The Engagement of Ozma
Book Two in the Umbrella Man of Oz series

Flipping through the pages towards the Ozma section, he didn't even bother to look down as he recited from memory the answer.

"Ah yes of course. As I once was telling my niece and nephew Raphael and Cinderella that in the event of the disappearance or permanent transformation of Princess Ozma, Princess Dorothy, and the abduction or otherwise indisposes of the Princes and Princesses under Ozma add etc. Ah yes by natural law of birthright despite by nature not being created by..." The Wogglebug was interrupted from his soliquoy by every single person around him staring daggers.

"Oh alright. The heir to the throne is Jack Pumpkinhead! Philistines!" The Wogglebug frowned and trotted off to go make some more learning pills.

"Me?!" Jack said in shock as the animate man stared all about himself to see if there was another Jack Pumpkinhead. You see Princess Ozma, when she was Tip, had created Jack using the Powder of Life which she'd stolen from Mombi. As such Jack was the first child of Princess Ozma and right now the lawful ruler of Oz.

"HIM?" A rather large chorus of famous Ozites asked. Because of how things resolved themselves, they've asked me not to include their names. Out of respect to Trot, Betsy, Jellia, and Button I've decided not to mention their names.

Toto ran up to Jack Pumpkinhead and barked up to him, expressing his gratitude in dog-ease.

"Well we better hold a very swift coronation because it's looking like a hot time in the old town tonight at present." The Wizard said shaking his head in shame, as a non-Humbug he wasn't used to failures like this anymore. Well not well not often, well not usually, well not since he got his Munchkin assistant, well not always, okay he was very used to these sorts of failures but they still grated.

"I dub thee Pumpkinhead Oz the First!" E. Bused said as he placed Ozma's third best crown on the especially fine pumpkin jack had carved just this morning. How E. Bused came into possession of Ozma's third best crown is a funny story but more or less can be summed up he's a thief.

"Wow! I've never been a king before. I wonder what I should do first. Make a speech? talk about what I intend to do for my term?" Jack fumbled as he really had never prepared for being the

King of Oz. He'd been mostly content to farm pumpkins so he didn't die of spoilage permanently.

"If you have any bright ideas, it might be nice to put out this fire," Betsy said causally, pointing her thumb at the onrushing inferno.

"I usually have my brightest ideas on Halloween when I'm Jack-O-Lantern Pumpkinhead. However I'll do my best." Jack said as he tapped the side of his head, hoping to stimulate some of the seeds into doing their stuff.

"Hurry Jack!" Button said, the little boy going beyond his usual silence for fear of becoming brighter than even he wanted to be.

"Well I seem to recall Oz has a giant floating island of rain makers over it. I lost seven heads in the flood they caused. Since Mom and my Step-dad to be defeated them..." Jack followed the thought well.

"With the aid of a fantastic wonder maker par excellence... and me." E. Bused said as he pulled out a Silver Island fan to cool himself as the air grew hotter. In his left foot he took out a seltzer bottle and sprayed himself too.

"We should probably contact their new King Raspy and ask him to put out the fire. That's my idea." Jack said as he looked at everyone.

Button Bright, Jellia, The Wizard, Trot, and Betsy just stared at Jack.

"That's brilliant," Toto barked.

"Why thank you," Jack gushed, happy his new head could be of service.

Of course there was the question of whether or not his head's thought came in time to save the wonderful city of Oz but given this is an Oz book I'd spot you the odds. Just don't quote me on them given I still owe money to the Bookies in Librasia and the Shark in Toothtown.

***

The Engagement of Ozma
Book Two in the Umbrella Man of Oz series

Chapter 9

The cage that Sita was imprisoned in was a huge, dark, and musty thing that was at the heart of a huge, dark, and muster cavern. The very fact that the Hungry Tiger, King Sean, and the Wogglepillars were imprisoned in a huge glass jar as well made them feel especially claustrophobic. Still each of them had no intention of remaining one of the mad scientist's pets and were currently working on their plans of escape. Since King Sean's plot to will the universe to fix the situation and the Wogglepillar's debate on whether or not a small thermo-nuclear device would be constructed from the dusts present in the jar came to nothing, let us focus instead on the Hungry Tiger.

The Hungry Tiger licked his lips as he sat down on his hindquarters to think out just what he wanted to do. He had found the Wicked Wizard who had long ago kidnapped him from his Jungle home and raised him to be a cruel, vicious, baby-eating monster. Sita was furthermore just a few feet away, sleeping her untouched meal away. The bad thing was that he wasn't even large enough to measure up to the size of one of her whiskers when he found her and if she couldn't get out as a full sized Tiger then what chance did a tiny toy-sized Tiger have in helping her do so?

"So, I take it you know this unpleasant fellow?" King Sean said as Ralph and Cindy began discussing the principles of Algebraic equations in day to day koans for a better tomorrow.

"When I was a cub he kidnapped me from the Tiger kingdoms court in the Gilikens and trained me for his circus. All of his magically created monsters were too ugly for his Magical Circus of Horrors and I was a crowd pleaser for performances with Sita. For years he tried to get me to eat the babies he tossed on stage." the Hungry Tiger said with a bit of a yawn.

"That must have been a real crowd pleaser." Ralph said as he gave an unpleasant look.

"No. Not really. It was a Circus of Horrors but mostly people came for the Circus and we usually ended up run out of town. Finally a young trapeze artist with long red hair joined the Circus and slowly turned all the creatures back into their original shapes. She was actually Glinda the Good Witch of the South you see and Evile didn't have any of the magic needed to fight her once he was stolen of his evil creatures. Sita and I returned to the Tiger Kingdom in the Gillikens and were about to be wed as the rulers of the White and Stripety tigers." the Hungry Tiger's stomach growled. He considered chewing on the bone again but he figured that wouldn't taste very good, there hadn't been any meat on him in years.

"So what happened to Evile?" Cindy sighed with a frown.

"Well despite the Circus being sent over the Deadly Desert one of his machines but Evile found his way back. He kidnapped Sita and sent his assistant to try and get me but I ate him," Rama replied as he wagged his tail a bit.

"That's awful!" Cindy said horrified.

"Yes, ogres taste terrible," The Tiger answered, stretching his legs a bit.

The Hungry Tiger began pressing his paws against the side of the glass jar they were stuck in. "So I left my kingdom to look for her but she obviously left Oz with him and I never did find them until now."

"So your royalty now? I may have to start treating you better!" King Sean exclaimed.

The Skull was of the mind that anyone royal had to be very important and already plotting what sort of power he might have if he could convince the Tiger Kingdom to be their king. He'd discovered he rather liked being royalty and while ruling the dead was no fun, he'd of course have men recognize his greatness among the living.

"Yes but being a Prince is no fun. When I left the Kingdom of the Tigers Sita was the only other Tiger with a conscience. It was always 'Would you like to eat this sire' or 'let's go attack the Kingdom of the Gumps' and that. I'd much rather hang around the Emerald Palace or the Lion's forest where wanting fat babies isn't going to get me any." The Hungry Tiger said as he slammed his weight against the side of their jar and smashed it against the ground of the cage. Babies weren't the only thing the Hungry Tiger craved but he didn't exactly think eating a nice Gump or Farmer would grate his conscience less.

"Ah the wonders of the philosopher-king. I see Plato was right," Ralph said with a smile, observing the Hungry Tiger's wisdom which had freed them.

"But Ralph, the Hungry Tiger by giving up his throne proves Plato was wrong." Cindy said with a sigh.

Plato for those who haven't had the benefit of learning pills yet was a nice old Greek Man who would have been very much at home at Oz. Aside from believing everyone should be nice to each other, he also believed the best ruler-ship was that of really nice Kings or Queens like Ozma.

"Oh don't start that again…" but the Wogglepillars words were interrupted by the sudden awakening of the Tigress Sita.

The huge white Tigress looked at the group of them amidst the broken glass and placed her paw over her face, shaking it sadly. "Oh what have you got yourself into now!"

Sita the White Tiger rubbed her forepaw on the back of Rama to see if he was actually there.

She'd envisioned their reuniting in a variety of ways but never had she imagined that she'd be petting her kitten sized love to keep him from crying.

"MMmmmmmm that's the spot. Watch the claws!" Rama called up in his cooing small voice.

"Greetings oh mighty Rajahess of the Tigerlands. I am King Sean of the…oh stuff it I'm a freaking marble right now. We were shrunk by the warlock outside and we want to know if you know if you have anything that can make us grow up again. Hurry before I get someone to grab your whiskers!" King Sean used his best diplomacy on the Tigress.

Sita gazed down upon the little bone being and raised a claw "Rama would you be terribly offended if I smashed this impudent upstart?"

Sita wasn't actually serious about killing poor King Sean, again, but it was the absolute worse thing you could do to a Tigress to threaten her whiskers.

"I wouldn't be offended my love but my conscience would bother me afterwards…I think." Rama said as he wagged his tail a bit more happily. Tigers were rather dangerous creatures you know, it comes from being wild.

"If we had our Uncle's projector we could fix you up toot sweet," Ralph said sadly. The Wogglebug Professor after all owed his gigantic size to the magical lantern that had projected him to his new height. Unfortunately, said device was on permanent display at the Athletics college Wogglebug Museum 'Chronicling a hundred years of Wogglebug intellegesia'.

"I fear that Evile Lackey no longer does much of his wizardry in the Cove my dear Rama. With the laboratories of the Wizard Michael above the wet cavern we dwell in there is little reason he returns here at all but to do the magics that he knows would give him away as a servant of Yurline. You would need a true alchemist to understand all the various dusts and powders that Evile has collected in his works to working dark magic," Sita sighed.

The Tiger Princess had tried to learn something of Evile's magic by observing him but despite everything we might say about Evile Lackey (and there is a great deal) he was a man who did not deal with simple magics.

"That's alright," Ralph intoned with a weak smile. She was a beautiful Tigress and didn't want such a lovely thing to be sad.

"We know all about the fundamental sciences of alchemy thanks to our wondrous uncle's pills!" Cindy replied, remembering how difficult it had been to chew down those learning pills at their size. Still an education had to be properly endured if one wanted to grow up in the world.

"Then you may yet be able to save us all!" Sita smiled as she looked towards Evile Lackey's work-station. It was an old cracked wooden table with huge drawers, doors, and scientific paraphernalia. If anywhere in Evile's laboratory there was a cure to be found for his shrinking spell on them it would located on that bench. It was located across the room, at least twelve feet away.

"That will be quite a wallllkkkkkkkkkkkkkkk!" King Sean started to say before Sita scooped them up with her tail and flung them with all of her might. I am happy to say that instead of the entire group being splattered against one of Evile's machines they made a not-so-perfect but still serviceable 1.0 landing against Evile's copy of "Magical Transference for Dummies".

"Oooooo my I feel more dizzy that when I attempted the world record for cocoon spinning," Ralph muttered as he felt his head.

"Which I probably why I am still champion holder of it," Cindy reminded her brother ever so gently of her triumph. Of course neither of their cocoons had survived their attempt to enter them to become full Wogglebugs but that is another story.

"Glegg's Fire Vomit formula, Mrs. Yoop's potion for turning boys into Frogs, Smith and Tinker's Troubleshooting Guide to Lurline Engines. I don't think any of these will help us return to our natural size," The Hungry Tiger read the various labels on the bottles and books about him.

"That's okay! According to the magical periodic table the mixing of an anti-magical dust should have all the necessary materials here," Cindy said as she began measured four table-spoons of newt with a half a cup of brown sugar.

"Hmmmmm this is interesting," Ralph said as he looked over some of the documents Evile had been working on.

"What's that?" Cindy said as she tried a mixture of her formula on the Hungry Tiger. Obviously she'd put too much sodium-di-xxxitcan into the mix because instead of growing upwards he was suddenly invisible but for his skeleton.

"Ha! Your all skin and bones!" Sean shouted at the Tiger, laughing before his jaw fell off.

"It's a set of plans for a machine making use of advanced Grand Unified Magical or GUM theory. The essential idea of being able to distill any magical energy into another magical form for use by another wizard. It was a work pioneered on the Magic of Everything paper by Locasta before she stopped teaching it. The potential for abuse by evil wizards was phenomenal. A wizard with proper training could steal a Fairy's immortality, all the knowledge a person has ever accumulated, or stockpile magical energy for huge spells he'd never be able to do normally." Ralph said as he unfortunately became so engrossed in the work of Doctor Lackey that he missed the large crack at the edge of the paper and fell right on through. Being so small Ralph had to move in order to read documents, you see.

"Ralph!" Cindy cried before tossing her latest mixture on Sean and the Hungry Tiger. Hopping over to her brother, the Wogglepillar girl narrowly missed being caught by her companion's sudden restoration.

The sudden transformation of the Hungry Tiger and King Sean into full sized beings again resulted in a rather calamitous crash in the middle of Evile's things. It is only a stroke of luck from the Supreme Master herself that nothing nasty was mixed that would have blown the cavern sky-high or switched the spirits of the Hungry Tiger and Sean. They had enough problems as it was without those added complications.

"Ah I'm my old self again! Was there ever a more beautiful shining being than my bald osteoporosis free self?" Sean said once he reattached his jaw. The Skull was admiring his reflection in a cabinet door's polished surface.

"Yes," the Tiger said walking over to Evile's key rack near the front entrance of his cavern and taking the one key marked with a Tiger shaped end.

"I have waited many years for this day Rama. You have no idea how long in fact," Sita said. The lock on her cage's side fell to the ground with the Hungry Tiger's turn of it's metal gears and the couple was at last reunited. The Tiger kissing that resulted rather looks like rubbing one's face against one another's but since the Hungry Tiger is too nice to comment on what Milo and Ozma looks like to him, we won't comment on how it looks to us humans.

"Hmmmm I wonder what's in here." King Sean said examining the cabinets that Ralph had fallen into. The former monarch of the Restless Dead was hoping that there might be some powerful magic that he might steal to conquer a fairy nation or two. The Skull wasn't an entirely bad individual, just mostly bad and he'd never betray his new friends by conquering Oz. He'd just gladly bring any other into his grip (if he had a hand).

"Hopefully Ralph!" Cindy shouted down the crack.

"I'm here and someone is here with me!" Ralph shouted back.

King Sean gripped the door to the cabinet with his teeth and pried it open, dumping the Woggleleptra and a blonde haired sorcerer in a pile on the ground. The man was identical to the figure Evile Lackey had assumed to kidnap them all and it didn't take a rocket scientist (which none of the parties present were-unless you count Ralph's aeronautics degree for paper based aircraft) to guess it was the true Supreme Sorcerer of Avy-Lyon.

"Mpppppphhhh!" The figure said through one of Evile Lackey's socks, which had been rather grossly stuffed in his mouth when he was chained up.

"ACK! THE WIZARD IS CASTING A SPELL! KILL IT! KILL IT! KILL IT!" Sean shouted, jumping onto the back of the Hungry in fear. You might question why he was so paranoid being dead and all but hindsight is always 20-20.

"No, he's trying to say something," Sita spoke as she removed the sock from his mouth and tossed it as far away from her as she could.

"Egad that Warlock has some smelly feet! Distasteful too! My thanks to you yon Heroes..." Michael said as he spat out the aftertaste of Witch's foot. Michael had to admit that when he hoped to be rescued it would be by a beautiful knightess or princess instead of a assortment of animals with their undead companion but beggars can't be choosers.

"Well that's very nice. A pleasure to meet you. Goodbye," King Sean snarked. Sean began beating himself against the Hungry Tiger's ears to make him go forward.

"Please stop that," the Tiger said causally as he looked at the prisoner. "Are you the Wizard Michael?"

"Indeed I am the Great Sorcerer Michael! He who smashed the asteroid that would have destroyed the Earth in 1000 A.D.! He who cast the spells that turned the sinking residents of Atlantis into mer-folk! He who is without a doubt the most powerful magic-user in all of the Sea of Immortality. I know because I did a count," Michael boasted with a smile even as he struggled in his iron chains. Unfortunately, given that Michael was a half fairy he wasn't possessed of the strength to break through the iron chains, of course a full mortal wouldn't have done much better either I suppose.

"If you are so powerful friend Michael then how have were you captured by a second rate magician like Evile Lackey?" Sita asked a rather pointful question as she unlocked the locks on him.

The Supreme Sorcerer of Avy-Lyon looked embarrassed by the question. "Well it's a bit humiliating but I was taking my daily walk on the beaches when I encountered a half drowned looking man washed up on the shore. Little was I to know that the man was actually one of the evil magic-users defeated by my colleague in Oz Glinda who was one of my finest students. Showing appalling ingratitude...errr he hit me over the head with a rock when I wasn't looking and dragged me to one of the nearby caves." Michael added the last bit in as an after thought.

"And we have reason to believe that he has taken over your position in the Courts of Avy-Lyon." Sita said, remembering the many times Evile came into his laboratory still wearing the illusion of being the Sorcerer Michael.

"Good, then with your magic we can swat Evile like a bug. It'll be easier than taking a baby from its candy!" The Hungry Tiger said with a lick of his lips. Of course this was spoken like a true man who'd never tried prying a lollipop from a determined youngster's grip.

The Sorcerer Michael looked even more embarrassed. Standing up tall the Wizard looked regal but slumped his shoulders as he rubbed his hands together nervously "Unfortunately...no."

"And why exactly is that?" Cindy asked as the Hungry Tiger lowered his head and the Wogglepillars climbed onboard his back and onto the top of King Sean.

"Evile kept me drugged on my own potions for some time. During that time he chanced upon some as yet undeveloped ideas I had made into the field of GUM spells which he unfortunately put to work. One of these machines in this cavern complex contains all of my accumulated magical knowledge which Evile has been using for his own personal gain. Right now I can't even make a leopard change its spots."

Both Sita and the Hungry Tiger looked at their stripes to see if they were alright.

The Engagement of Ozma
Book Two in the Umbrella Man of Oz series

"In other words you're right now completely useless," King Sean rattled his bonebox. The Skull was right now wondering if it wouldn't be better to see if the bad guys side was perhaps a better side to be on. He then recalled that he'd read the Oz books growing up and Princess Ozma had an appalling tendency to bring victory over impossible odds. The King thus decided to stay on the side of good for this occasion and this occasion alone.

The Hungry Tiger's tummy rumbled as he realized that he hadn't had linner yet and dinner was fast approaching. "All this thinking is making me hungry. Can't we just destroy the Warlock and go eat?"

Sita rubbed her love's backside. "Don't worry we'll get you some nice things from the meat trees when we get back...and no fat babies. Not only do you have a conscience but I'm on good authority that they'd make you fat."

The Hungry Tiger winced, suspecting that from this day forward he was going to be even more watched in his diet. Having a conscience was bad enough but a wife? Oh poor Tiger!

"Useless or not my friend I intend to get all my wizardry back from that vile Old Goat and furthermore I fear that unless he is stopped soon then the Great Fairy Queen Lurline herself will not be able to stop what he is likely to possess in mystical prowess!" Michael warned. It was then that he boldly and forcibly marched out the only exit the cavern had. Moments later the Arch-Wizard returned with a depressed look on his face and shook his head.

"What's the matter?" Cindy asked with a wiggle of her antennae.

"Apparently Evile's cavern complex is a little larger than I expected." Michael muttered. Unfortunately the Arch-Wizard was a master of understatement for the sea-side caverns of Avy-Lyon were the most labyrinthine and deep holes in all of Fairy-dom.

"Well we better get started then. I didn't leave one land of Eternal Darkness just to be stuck in another," King Sean murmured as he tried to yah the Hungry Tiger.

"Would it be wrong to eat him? Maybe with a soup?" the Hungry Tiger asked the White Tigress.

"We'll see my love." Sita reassured him as the group began the long trek through the maze defending Evile's privacy. Even Michael unaware of just how much danger that Evile actually was about to put the entire world in.

***

The Forrest of Bygone was famous among faeries as a place where Lurline and her band could spend much of their time dancing when the affairs of court got them down. It was a strange place though for Dorothy who'd been to much queerer places in her life but very few which felt quite so ancient and powerful.

Dusk had explained to her that time flowed differently in the Forrest of Bygone so that mortals who wandered into it might spend three hundred years there and return before they left or spend a day there and come back twenty years later. Dawn had reassured Dorothy though that she knew the paths that would keep them in real-time. Dorothy was beginning to doubt Dawn's words though when she ran into herself for the third time in a row.

"That was funny. I could have sworn that I had the path right that time." Dawn muttered as they waved goodbye to themselves.

"I just hope that when I return there's an Oz left to go back to," Dorothy huffed.

Though the girl from Kansas admitted that since Milo and Ozma seemed to determined to follow that silly rule it wouldn't be so bad to return after nine hundred years so they could be married. Dorothy Gale found it extremely frustrating living with people who were determined to live by the book. If the young woman had her way she would have marched the two down the altar the very next day and to the Nome Kingdom with Lurline or Fairy law.

"I wouldn't worry yourselves too much with Oz right now. Concentrating on finding the Cocky-Trace will be enough for now I think," Dusk said as she sneezed into her handkerchief. The night fairy was unfortunately allergic to a great deal of what bloomed in places bright and well lit.

"I think we're at the center of the Forrest of Bygone Princess Dorothy. Do you think you could tell us what your plan is now and why we had to stop off at the kitchen before it?" Dawn said as the girl buzzed around the forest, soaking up the sunrays. It was somewhat of an equalizer with her sister that she caught cold very quickly in the night air.

Dorothy hefted the bag of corn over her shoulder as she slumped it against the side of the nearest tall tree. It was a particularly large oak that had been standing there a million years or since last Thursday depending on which direction you were staring at it from. "Well you said that the Cocky-Trace was like a rooster and I spent a long time on the farm. So I figure if we spread corn around, he's likely to come and eat it. Then we can catch him."

Both Dawn and Dusk looked at Dorothy like she was crazy but eventually just started grabbing handfuls of corn kernels and spread them around. After all in a fairyland you never know what sort of thing might work.

"Oh I almost forgot. Please put on these." Dusk said as the Night Fairy pulled out three pairs of sunglasses that she had enchanted just the night before.

"Ooooo I'm a Hollywood star," Dawn said as she covered her eyes with the nearly opaque spectacles.

"What are these for?" Dorothy asked blinking as she found herself nearly blind wearing them.

"They are specially designed so that we can see the Cocky-Trace without being turned to stone. I doubt it would help our Mother's mood if she were forced to add two of her daughters to her husband's statue upstairs," Dusk made a joke that was not particularly funny to anyone involved. Dorothy had seen enough people transformed to last her a dozen lifetimes.

"Here chickey-chickey chicks!" Dawn muttered as she began tossing the corn about her.

Some of which managed to land in Dorothy's hair and down her ress. Having nothing else to do and willing to put up with the discomfort of Dawn's causal vegetable tossing, Dorothy began to repeat the Fairy Princess's mantra "I will not get mad about little things."

It was a philosophy that was sorely tested as Dusk threw her corn in imitation of her sister, causing more to get caught in her dress.

"You know if your looking for me, all you had to do was hallar!" the words echoed over Dorothy's shoulders as she turned to see a glowing figure of a rooster with leather like wings under his arms and scales running around him.

The Cocky-Trace was so bright that Dorothy nearly went blind looking at him even with her magical sunglasses on.

"The Cocky Trace!" Dusk said as she got a sudden urge to let out a giddy scream.

"He's so dreamy." Dawn couldn't help but comment, looking on his elegant plumage.

"Thank you. Thank you very much. Feel free to admire the way I wiggle these thighs. The Colonel himself said that it was roosters like me that made his business. What can I do to help you Little Missies?" The Cocky-Trace said before starting to peck up the corn on the ground. It was obvious whatever difference between chickens and cocky-traces were they weren't that divided over food.

"Well we need some of your tears to cure the King of Avy-Lyon from being turned to stone looking at you." Dorothy hadn't been expecting such a lively fellow but she had to remind herself that he did turn someone into an object without staying round to fix it.

"Why sure! I can cry up a storm. Just let me get my ukulele and start telling you about the Heartbreak Henhouse." The Cocky-Trace began rummaging in the knot of a tree for his instrument which he began to strum. Dorothy, Dusk, and Dawn had to cover their ears at the sound the Cocky-Trace made which unfortunately was not nearly as musically inclined as he fancied it was.

"Just think of saving Oz. Just think of saving Oz. Just think of saving Oz," Dorothy repeated over and over as he sang. Suffice to say, Dot began to long for the days of Milo's awful singing.

"A since my chickey left me...I found a new place to dwell...wait a second," The Cocky Trace stopped his strumming and he looked at the three princesses. "Did you say that the King of Avy-Lyon was the one you were trying to turn back into flesh and blood?"

"Yes." Dorothy asked. She was hoping that the Cocky-Trace didn't have anything against King David because then she they'd have to grab him and force him to cry. Dorothy didn't really want to do that since he seemed like such a nice fellow. Plus, she wasn't the type of girl to do those sort of things normally.

"Well I'm afraid that's just impossible. I keep track of every one of my rock solid fans and I've got to say that never in my forty one million years of life did I once turn to stone a King of Avy-lon. I once considered turning the King of Graceland into stone for stealing my bit but never did I turn a King of Avy-Lyon or any other enchanted isle into a permanent addition into my hard rock café," The Cocky-Trace took out a small tea-pot from his knot in the oak and poured himself a cup of molasses laced coffee.

"Hmmm might have another Cocky-Trace done it?" Dorothy asked as Dawn and Dusk looked at each other puzzled.

"They might have but for the fact that I am absolutely positively one of a kind in the universe. There's far too many nice looking henny-pennies for me to settle down with some wizard to reproduce," The Cocky-Trace replied. He gave his ukulele one final strum before putting it up.

The Three Princesses didn't know what to make of this revelation.

"Maybe King David was turned into stone by a wizard." Dusk suggested as she tried to think of who might have hidden in the Castle Eternia and if there was any way of finding them.

"Or maybe he was never stone to begin with!" Dawn had a sudden flash of revelation.

"What do you mean?" Dorothy asked, wondering what the blonde princess could possibly mean by that.

"Well what if the reason all the magical spells that we've used on the statue to turn it back into King David have failed because he's always been a stone statue. It's just a piece of rock that has been carved to look like him!" Dawn said as her mind absolutely raced with the possibilities that were occurring.

"A few minor anti-magical coats to the thing to guard against stone to flesh spells and it gives a very good impression of a impossible to break mystical enchantment. Just like Michael always said 'Never use a sophisticated charm when a simple one will suffice'," Dusk said as the girl gave a brief bow in thanks to the

Cocky-Trace. "But, wait this doesn't make any sense. The divination spells cast by the Court wizard should have revealed this."

The answer to that question was so obvious it embarrassed both Fairy Princesses and disturbed greatly Dorothy.

Casting another teleportation spell to bring them to the Tower of the Forgotten, the Cocky Trace looked upon the group with a smile. Giving his goodbye with a wave "Ya'll come back now! Ya hear!"

***

Evile Tartuffe Lackey had dropped his disguise of being the Arch-Wizard Michael and was pacing around in a furious circle in the luxurious apartments of said magician. Evile Lackey had never enjoyed the fine art and good taste that came with being the Supreme Sorcerer of New Avy-Lyon because he considered it a weakness to love pretty things or enjoy good food.

It was one of the reasons for his amazingly foul disposition all the time though certainly not the only reason for it.

"I am ruined! I am ruined!" Evile shouted before grabbing a Silver Islander vase from the top of a pedestal and casting it with all of his might against the wall. The beautiful thing smashed into a thousand pieces.

Evile was afraid of very few things in his life and one of those few were the Umbrella Magicians of Oz. That he thought Milo to be one is patently absurd given the young minister to be's skill with magic. It is true the young man had managed to learn a few tricks while in Fairyland and even secure a magician's license, the lowest one available and equivalent to a grade school education, but magic wise he was a match to Evile's flamethrower.

"But wait, surely my memories hold some sort of key. My mother dealt with all the old magicians at some point. Yes history will yield the answer. I am sure." Evile muttered to himself. To a scientist like Doctor Lackey, the collected sum of history was solely mankind's mistakes that someone could look over to see how to avoid the stupidity of their past selves.

The Engagement of Ozma
Book Two in the Umbrella Man of Oz series

The only problem was that Evile couldn't stand history and wouldn't be caught dead learning from the past. His solution was a unique one and given the fact the warlock is quite mad, please forgive that his solution makes very little sense.

"Double, Double Boil and Trouble. Split me in to Mitosis bubble!" Evile said as he read the magic words on his bottle of cloning pills and popped one of the foul tasting red beans into his mouth.

A second later an ugly copy of his head started to shift from his back and a few more seconds later a fully formed duplicate of Evile Lackey. The clone was even complete with his ugly taste in suits and a wrongly timed pocket watch to his side.

"My what an evil looking figure you are," Evile-1, the original, said to his double.

"It's pronounced E-VILE you incompetent cretin. Obviously I must have gained a rogue intelligence gene in the cloning process," Evile-2 said with a huff of his chest.

Evile already didn't like himself. "Very well I want you to recite my history as you know it in order to help me discover a means to defeating the Umbrella wizard who now menaces my plans."

"And what if I don't?" Evile-2 sniffed haughtily as he looked around the pig-sty of Michael's room. It was perfect and artistic but Evile-2's standards were impossibly high, as befitting a wicked wizard.

"Then I'll burn you." Evile-1 said as he ignited his magic lighter and a stream of fire shot out three feet in height and took the form of a dragon. When the Wicked Queen Yurline created the Erbs at the dawn of history and at occasionally gloomy points in mankind's past she always gave them a weakness that would allow them to be destroyed.

Wicked Witches would always be afraid of water, Daemons would always be afraid of knowledge, Slavercruds would forever shrivel under salt, Nobalds would turn to stone when touched by sunlight, and warlocks would go up like dry paper when exposed to flame.

Evile kept his magic lighter from the time a well meaning wizard had wanted to put an end to his wickedness but ended up a toadstool for his troubles.

"You make a very good point brother," Evile-2 said. "Let us start at the beginning then. You were originally born in the Dark Kingdom of Boogeyland between the land of Ev and the Lands of Dreams. The kingdom was ruled at that point by four powerful witches who had divided the country between them called Basty, Gingy, Mombi, and Taarn. You were the child of the strongest of the witches Basty but being half fey matured very slowly compared to the other evil creatures which grew up into monsters quickly before dying."

"Ah yes, royalty from the beginning." Evile-1 mused.

"Boogeyland has no real royal family of course because the population is too chaotic and violent to ever have a long lasting government. Furthermore, none of the witches were content with their land because it was blackened, horrible, and ridden with creatures even they feared to tamper with. They probably would have eventually destroyed each other or perished as their spells of long-life failed if not for a fairy of Lurline's band accidentally losing her way and crash landing in the country of the Erbs," Evile-2 said as he pulled out a chalkboard and began making illustrations so his double didn't lose track of what was happening due to boredom.

Evile was a clever man but he had been a terrible student his entire life.

"Ah yes. Hehehehe I remember all I had to do to get her to talk was threaten to cut off all of her hair and break her pretty nails with my teeth to get her to tell my mum, aunts, and cousin everything," Evile-1 reminisced fondly as he clenched his shark like incisors together.

"Yes and they discovered there across the desert which bordered the Kingdom that the Fairy Queen Lurline was enchanting a land that everyone would eventually be immortal in. Furthermore, that it would be the most magical country in all of Fairy-dom when the enchantment was complete. Turning the fairy girl into an object, the Four Witches gathered up their most innocuous henchmen and magical tools to set off to the land of Oz. Boogeyland of course collapsed back into anarchy for a time but the Witches were unconcerned with that." Evile-2 drew on his chalkboard an image of four lines heading into the Land of Oz.

"If the masses lack bread, let them eat children as my mother always used to say," Evile-1 said of the Erbs in Boogeyland's distress.

"Pretending to be refugees from a horrible country which was true enough to get by Pastoria's wizards the Witches appealed to the Kind heart of the Monarch of Oz to help them set up new lives even as they plotted to find a way to take over the kingdom. Manipulated shamelessly, Pastoria gave each of the four witches a position as a housekeeper to one of the royal families in his homeland. Perhaps Pasty was more canny than he appeared or at least one of his advisors was because Basty and you were sent to live in Winkieland. The homeland of the fabulous Umbrella Wizards who were the greatest Witch-fighters in all of Fairy-land. Other wicked folk had tried to take Oz in the past but the Umbrella Wizards had defeated them all," Evile-2 said as he drew an image of an umbrella pointed to the sky and dozens of melting witches in the rain.

Evile-1 winced and bit his thumb. He'd been captured by one of the Umbrella Wizards while trying to feed one of the Winkie Royal Family to his pet Blood-Snorter.

Thankfully Evile had been using his father's ability to transform at the time or he certainly would have been revealed as the son of a Witch and his mother would have done terrible things to him. Still Evile had spent the next three months in an iron cage as the Umbrella Wizard tried to teach him good manners, honor, and decency. It had been the worst experience of the Warlock's life by far. "But mother did eventually defeat those wizards! She and the rest of the Compass Witches eventually wiped out the royal families of Oz and did away with Pastoria."

Evile-2 nodded "Indeed so. Maybe Old Basty cast a glamour on one of the lonely old goats or maybe they were too confident in their ability to smoke out a witch among them but she eventually stole their magic and with the Magic Cap sent the Flying Monkeys to wipe them out with Winkieland's Nobility. They succeeded because the Umbrella wizards were too good to harm an innocent with their magic, even in self defense."

"Haha, suckers!" Evile-1 smiled then frowned at his next memory. After his mother had freed him, she'd forced him to clean all the palaces by himself. It was less than a year later he was thrown down the side of the castle cliffs by his leg for trying to douse her with a bucket of water. His mother was a neat-freak and wanted a clean castle even when it might mean her bane. It was a pity because Aunt Mombi had promised him a shiny scaled green dragon hatchling if he liquidated her and he'd never gotten it.

"Of course they're all dead and you're the only one of their minions left alive. Plus Princess Ozma is restored to the throne and likely to rule forever more," Evile-2 mentioned causally as a taunt to his progenitor.

Evile-1 muttered. "Never mention that again. So do I have any chance whatsoever against the Umbrella wizard?"

"Truthfully? No not a single chance in the world. If you still had your ability to create magical monsters or the universal magical solvent you might have had a chance but Glinda took those powers away when she broke your wand," Evile-2 took special pleasure in informing Evile-1 of his impending doom.

Evile-1 grumbled a bit about that memory. Glinda looked so cute in that acrobat's outfit and she had such a cheery disposition, Evile should have suspected something was wrong with her. "Well thank you very much. Goodbye," Evile-1 said causally before pulling out his lighter and blowing the flames on his duplicate.

Evile-2 had no chance to react before the fire consumed him and left in a split second nothing more than ashes that made him look like a warlock shaped burned cigarette. The pieces crumbled to the ground next to the original Evile as the mad scientist pondered what to do next in his increasingly bleak situation.

"I will have to accelerate my plans considerably," Evile finally decided. He'd hoped to have a longer time to destroy Ozma's love for the mortal man and have the satisfaction of Lurline herself destroying Oz for him but Doctor Lackey knew that the final results would be just the same when the vile magic he'd spent years preparing reached fruition.

"But first to dispose of the Umbrella magician!" Evile intoned as he cast open the shutters to the bright light of Avy-Lyon. Evile had

The Engagement of Ozma
Book Two in the Umbrella Man of Oz series

just about run out of tricks but he still had his mother's power over animals, one of the reasons that her castle was in always need of cleaning.

Kawing into the air like a great bird he sent out a call to the Great Eagles of the Sea of Immortality in the Rocs. One of the huge forty foot long birds was unable to but answer the power of the magician as Evile gave him a simple order.

"Destroy Milo Starling!"

***

Chapter 10

The Garden of Not-So-Earthly Delights was the brightest spot in Avy-Lyon and the most tranquil.

Long ago Queen Lurline had grown to miss the many enchanted lands that she had filled with wonders and her Band had gathered select plants and animals from all over those countries of Fairy-dom to construct this garden as a some odd billion year birthday present.

It was here that Princess Ozma and her fiance were retiring to for a bit of relaxation after the usual troubles of the day in being tempted by handsome princes and nearly being eaten by unpleasant wildlife.

"So do you think your mother is going to keep making you take these tests? I was rather hoping that with the latest calamity she might have seen the light of day," Milo said as he tapped his umbrella to the side of the cobblestone walkway they walked. It truly was a paradise to his eyes.

Milo was not as intelligent as Ozma being she had a thousand years of experience on him and was also naturally more clever but he was hardly stupid and nearly as wise as the beloved ruler already. Thus they made good sounding boards for each other for resolving problems and of course could enjoy the time together solely for the company.

"I would like her to just give it up but I'm sure she'll insist on more tests for the both of us. I'm not even sure she'll honor her promise to spare Oz if we pass them all in fact," Ozma had to admit as she picked up a cute little birdy on one of her fingers and gave it a pet across the back.

There was something about Ozma that was attractive to the wildlife and it was occasionally troublesome, especially when a squirrel might fly out of her hair while being hugged.

"I thought Fairies were forbidden to break oaths." Milo said in a rathre curious notion as he tried to ignore the daytime flying Owl that took root on his head. It had started burying its claws into his noggin.

"Yes but so is destroying an entire fairy-land. I'm not sure what she will do at this point if you want to know the honest to Heaven's truth Milo," Ozma had a unique aspect as far, at least as far as Milo was concerned, in that she had been raised three times in her life.

Once as the Fairy-Princess of Avy-Lyon under King David and Lurline, next as the Princess of Oz under Pastoria the Second and his wife, and finally as the enchanted boy Tip by Mombi. Even Mombi she had felt some affection for despite the terrible accident that had claimed the old witch's life and Lurline's betrayal cut at the very core of who she was.

"We can make our plans but the final outcome is in the Supreme Master's hands my lady Ozma." Milo quoted the Fairy Edition of the Good book.

"You're just a bundle of reassurance there my love." Ozma said as she gave a brief wave to the Day-time Owl and sent him flying.

"I do my best." Milo joked. The young Kentuckian then sat down on a solid platnium bench in the middle of a blue forrsted section of the garden that reminded him of his home state of Kentucky.

"Ozma, do you be...do you think...what would happen if we agreed not to see each other again?" the words started to choke him in his throat he maintained enough calm to finally force them out. The look on Ozma's face when they were said was enough to make him want to become violently ill.

Ozma looked at Milo stunned at his words, not sure she'd heard her lover correctly. Was this some sort of way of telling her that their relationship wasn't worth all the trouble that it was causing? Did he not care for her anymore and her mother's tests had broken his spirit? Did he just not want her anymore? "Milo you'd be willing to do that?"

"My L...Ozma I have loved you since the moment I first saw you. No matter what I consider you the woman who is my wife in spirit if not in fact yet. I know though that Oz is a place that is a part of you and it's a part of me now as well. If I had to leave this world to save it...I.I would but I would never abandon it in spirit or be any less a part of it." Milo bit his fist as he tried to hold back tears at the thought, he didn't want to think like this but it was something that had to be addressed.

Ozma looked at the man and then grabbed him in a tight embrace, rubbing her face against his in a tiger-kiss. "Oh Milo, you really are too noble for your own good."

"Pot, kettle, black my love." Milo smiled and gave her another kiss on the lips.

Ozma smiled to herself as she kissed back. The ruler of Oz thought of herself as a mischief prone woman with a bit of a temper, brash personality, and a bit of a stubborn streak yet there were those in Oz who thought she could do no wrong. Milo had a dark side Ozma knew, or at least a side that was twenty percent less white than the rest of him but sometimes she just wanted to shake her love until he talked some sense sometimes. "Under no circumstances Milo would we offer that thing. This is an order from your liege as a citizen of Oz."

Milo gave a weak nod before saying "As Your Ladyship wishes."

"Milo, may I ask what your family is like?" Ozma looked at Milo as she sat down beside him and took his hand into hers.

"Direct descent from Scotch settlers to the wonderful flowing land of abundance in America they were noted for their propensity towards being fairly religious folk with an odd tendency to produce the odd snake-oil salesman or lawyer every few years. The name Starling roughly mean..." Milo was interrupted by Ozma putting two of her fingers on his lips.

"I meant individually." Ozma said with a chuckle.

"Oh well that's much easier." Milo said before wincing. "Well my father is a man I deeply respect and has made his business to be an absolute pillar of the community in the region where I grow up. He's enthusiastic about making deals, hard-working, deeply honorable about his business practices...such as they are, and he quickly gave his blessing to our union," Milo neglected of course to mention that it had only taken the knowledge that his son would be marrying a woman of means to make him quite happy for his son.

"What about your mother?" Ozma asked as she thought about the wedding they would have in a few centuries. Ozma was certain to make it the most spectacular affair in all of Oz's history and they'd had quite a few in its time. She didn't give any further thought to the danger it was in from her mother because failure to save Oz or to marry Milo was simply not an option anymore.

"I learned most of my quotables from her. A good Presbyterian woman she a former teacher and one of the strictest women around with her learnings. The Good Book I carry around was my first real gift from her. She is a compassionate, decent, and a wonderful cook," Milo didn't particularly want to go over his conversation with her regarding the Lady Ozma which had been reassuring her he wasn't marrying into a family of devil worshippers.

"And your sister?" Ozma remembered that Milo had mentioned he had one but of all the people he spoke of, he mentioned her the least.

"She has very good teeth." Milo pointed out as he looked guilty under Ozma's gaze. The less said about Fancy Starling the better was the common attitude in the Starling Family and Milo was occasionally ashamed of his own part in it. Occasionally.

"Milo..." Ozma gave a rather unpleasant glare. It brought home how important family was to her ironically when she felt most alienated from them. Her sisters teasing and the years she had spent away from them seemed a distant memory compared to the feelings they had when they were around each other. Sure they had set her hair on fire, brought her high up in the air and dropped her before she'd learned flying magic, and occasionally turned her into things but they were family.

"I know, I know burning bridges must be simply rebuilt." Milo tried out one of his own sayings that he was still having trouble with. Your lucky he didn't share of his other less socially graceful ones like 'Never talk to lightning faeries next to a puddle' or 'Two in the hand is worth three in the bush if you divide for taxes.'

"If that means you should make amends with your sister I very much suggest you do so. I intend to see all of your family at our wedding including your sister," Ozma corrected as she maneuvered past her lover's occasionally impenetrable wall of allegory. There's had occasionally been bumpy parts in their courtship such as when Milo had proposed with his grandmother's ring but E. Bused had eaten it, at which point Milo hadn't blamed her for not wanting it as much.

"Well I don't know how that will be possible but you have my word as a gentleman," Milo said as he moved his Oz national colored scarf across one shoulder to compensate for the chilly atmosphere as a draft flew in from the ice garden just a few feet away from the loving couple.

Ice poppies, Ice roses, Sculpted Ice Hedge animals, and more made it one of the more interesting places in the garden. Milo's reluctance on invitations was something he knew Ozma knew about but chose to ignore in that in less than a ninth of the time it would take to have their wedding all of his family and friends from the Outside World would grow old and die.

Milo still gave his parents a call every weekend on the special two-end line the Wizard had set up for the Magic Picture and occasionally dropped a line on old friends like Thomas from the Scouts but even then he'd eventually have to part as they chose to live out their lives, weary, and finally lay to rest. It was a sobering thought comforted only by the knowledge they'd be immortal afterwards.

"I suppose I can ask for no more since my mother has given her word as a Fairy Queen." Ozma smiled and then cast a brief incantation that turned their summer wear to winter garments. The ruler of Oz had never truly understood why Milo wore his scarf even in spring but now they matched and headed off directly into the Winter garden. Lurline's garden was beloved partially because it was eternally divided into four districts for the four seasons so a person in the mood for Fall could jump in fallen leaves or with Summer bathe in a warm gentle pond. "Milo do you ever miss the outside world?"

It was a question that Milo was hard-pressed to answer. Ozma was part mortal and part fairy so Avy-Lyon had never been her home while Oz truly was yet she'd never lived in the realm of humanity and God willing Milo hoped she never would, yet he couldn't deny his

The Engagement of Ozma
Book Two in the Umbrella Man of Oz series

occasional longings. "I don't miss the world so much as I occasionally miss the people in it my Lady.

Still on occasion I miss the cardinal's song, the hooves of the Derby, and the smell after a fresh rainstorm. If I had to compare my old life to the world of Fairie though I would have to say that it was like watching a movie on a screen while Oz was being in the real world. Rather like that scene in the Wizard of..."

Ozma gave Milo a look that immediately shut him up from his comparing his favorite philosopher to the MGM film. It wasn't that Ozma disliked the movie, far from it, it's just that she wished they could do something as popular after the beginning of the Dorothean calender for general consumption. It had been shocking to Ozma that aside from seeing the movie once during his childhood Milo had never been exposed to the wonderful Historian works. "That's beautiful Milo. I'm often worried about how your adjusting to life in Oz."

"Well if I have trouble Ozma I must say that it's probably not going to be from missing the old world. It reminds me of what your father King Pastoria said to me when I asked him for his blessing on the marriage," Milo said as he remembered going to meet the most noble King in his home in the Emerald City, a true man of the people.

"What did he say?" Ozma asked as she walked over to some of the snow on the ground and began to make a nice snowball while pretending to sniff one of the ice flowers.

"He said that he was happy that his daughter had managed to find someone and then he privately took me to one corner of his shop. I believe his exact words there were 'should you ever hurt her, I will hire a wizard to turn you into grass to feed to the Woozy.'" Milo said causally as he chuckled at the image even as he was sure the man was quite serious.

"I can't believe it! My adoptive father wasn't even the type to persecute Wicked Witches!" Ozma stared, unable to believe her father would do such a thing. It was in that pause that she was hit in the face with a snowball by Milo. Blinking the flakes off her eyebrows Ozma replied in kind with the ball she had been intending to throw as a small war was touched off. It finally ended when Ozma cheated with her wand and dumped an small hill of white ice crystals on the top of her fiance and he waved his hands up in surrender.

"Never mess with this witch," Ozma said as she blew on the end of her wand as it steamed.

A small penguin then slowly waddled it's way up toward's Ozma before bowing and saying "Hello my dearest sister!"

Ozma looked down at the penguin's green eyes and chuckled "Hello Kirri, nice to see you. I see your still practicing your shape-shifting." It had had occurred to the Queen of Oz that she contact her sisters and make an appeal to have her mother removed from the position as the Queen of Fairy-dom by a Burzee conclave but Ozma didn't believe that would work.

Ancient Fairy Mothers like Zurline and Lulea may enjoy the presence of mortals and care for the innocent but many thought Oz was a threat to the security of Fairy-land. They thought mortals shouldn't be made to live forever (hence the name Fairyland as opposed to Immortal Mortal land) or least all mortals shouldn't be immortal by virtue of just living in a land. Santa Clause had done many incredible deeds before being presented with eternal life after all.

"Practicing? I will tell you sister that I have long since mastered it! Mother says it is time for another one of your tests," Kirri said with a frown as she transformed back into the young sprite dressed in leaves she normally was. Kirri was a true nature spirit and thus could endure sweltering sun, blizzards, and even bathe in hot lava without being the slightest bit uncomfortable. Yet she couldn't sleep in a prepared bed of Castle Eternia if her life depended on it. She needed the wild open outdoors to go to sleep.

Ozma sighed audibly with a long face. "I understand."

The Queen of Oz took her sister's hand as she looked back at her fiance for one last time and said "I'll be back soon. Why don't you go check up on Dorothy and the Hungry Tiger? I'm getting rather worried about them both. It's been some time since I've seen either of them and there's something…" Princess Ozma didn't want to say that there was something wrong in the very air itself. She had a almost mystical sense that evil was afoot.

The Engagement of Ozma
Book Two in the Umbrella Man of Oz series

"I will," Milo said as he gave a salute to his love and began to walk off to the sunset that was burning many colors into the skyline. Milo unfortunately didn't have much time with his thoughts because at the moment he stepped out of Ozma's sight and hearing range he was carried off by the claws of the huge Roc.

"AHhhhhhhhhhhhhhhhhhhhhhhhhhhhhhhhhhhhhhhhhh!" Milo expressed his sentiments to the beast about his abduction.

"Oh terribly sorry there mate. My name is Rocky and I'm a Roc. I hate to tell you this but a warlock has geased me to kill you in some unspeakably horrible way. I can't do anything but obey because he used Animal magic on me like the Old West Witch of Boogeyland used to use. I hope you don't bear me a grudge because of it." Rocky the huge flying bird said. Rocs weren't really unpleasant people and were in fact the noble friends of Jinn with their only enemies the Giant Clams that they hunted out of the ocean.

"Well if your being forced to do it I suppose I can't really blame you for it. Still I reserve the right not to be happy about it," Milo said rather off-handedly as he watched the Isle of Avy-Lyon pass him by. They were now over the Sea of Immortality which was the absolute most dangerous sea in all of Fairy-land or so the legends spoke. Olympus, Edenia, Ozcadia, and the other isles of mythology were all about him too like tombs waiting for an occupant.

"I'll tell you what! How about I let you choose how I destroy you? I suppose it's a small comfort but it's the best I can give you." Rocky said to the man he was holding in his talons. Rocky already liked him and would feel pretty guilty for killing him but these sort of things couldn't be avoided when dealing with black magicians.

"Well what exactly are my options?" Milo of course had no intention of dying under these circumstances but he had very little idea of how to turn this situation to his advantage.

"Well I could eat you." Rocky preferred this option himself.

"Let's call that plan B." Milo argued gently.

"Well I could cut you up with my talons," Rocky offered another option. Personally, Rocky hoped that the man would choose his first suggestion. He had been hunting clams when summoned by Evile and hadn't had lunch yet.

"Let's call that Plan C." Milo said, hoping the Roc alphabet worked much like his own.

"Well I could drop you in the Sea of Immortality," Rocky suggested for his third option. He hoped the mortal would choose soon and wasn't merely trying to stall for time, Rocs are very impatient creatures after all.

"Hmmmmm," Milo didn't think that sounded so bad and was about to say he chose that when Rocky went on with his description of what would happen.

"Of course then the Whale-Sharks are likely to get you or the Giant Salt-Water Pirranah or the Million Tentacle Octopus. You might even get swallowed by a Giant Clam which means I could end up eating you anyway!" Rocky said to Milo, hoping to nudge him into the direction of choosing to be food.

Princess Oceania had a palace at the bottom of the Sea of Immortality and unfortunately had gathered around it a number of unpleasant creatures. Sadly she believed it was wrong to change a creatures habits and thus, unlike Ozma, none of her monsters ever reformed thanks to her influences.

"Do I have any other choices?" Milo asked weakly, it was shaping up that being eaten may actually be his best chance for survival. "Well I could dash you against the rocks of one of these islands but that's going to hurt more than my nice sharp talons or my beak." Rocky said as he suspected the mortal was still going to choose it.

Milo winced, as a citizen of Oz he would survive anything aside from total destruction. Dismemberment though would hardly help his situation and being devoured probably would result in his final death. He'd survive the fall easiest with the least amount of damage, the young man was sure but it would still be very painful and he might be unable to move thereafter to try and get back to his beloved. Still it didn't seem like there was very much of a choice "Very well I choose to be dashed against the rocks."

"Well suit yourself." Rocky said as he made a dive for the reefs of Edenia. Edenia was the most beautiful island in all the Islands of Immortality, even moreso than Avy-Lyon. However, the Island was completely free of inhabitants by Fairy-tradition save for those who were exiled to it for crimes against the Escheat of the Courts and the Talking Animals who had lived there since it arose from the Sea. It was said that on the island were magical fruits that could grant a mortality immortality or take it away and a gigantic serpent that was said to longer than any other on Earth.

Milo gave a brief prayer to the Supreme Master as he adjusted his hat and was flung forty feet to the rocks below where he hit with a *CRACK* and bounced rather unceremoniously onto the beach shore. Being from Oz didn't make him invulnerable and he had a crushed…well a crushed everything and would have spent perhaps months on the beach recovering had not his umbrella unfolded beside him and from it's confines dropped a bottle of "Herby's pattented Healing Juice-Guarenteed to fix bones, cure any disease, and even regrow organs". Herby's juice also had some unpleasant fine print about not being able to work on the common cold and a tendency to give a green skin but even the best medicine has side effects. The Umbrella bounced up beside Milo as it popped upon the top of the bottle and stuck it into his mouth before laying down beside him.

"Ack!" Milo said as he rose up beside his umbrella and blinked a few minutes later. The preacher-to-be had been unconscious when his umbrella had poured him the magical juice and wondered where the now empty brown bottle had come from and why his skin was now suddenly green.

Looking up into the sky to make sure that Rocky had come back to his clam hunting, Milo rose unsteadily up on his legs and gazed across the Sea of Immortality. Across from the lagoon before him there were huge fins of Whale-Sharks encircling the island and a mass of jungle that was directly behind him. Clutching hold of the handle of his umbrella he picked it up and gazed about for some sign of Avy-Lyon. The Sea of Immortality is a strange place though and while the island was not so far away from it a few minutes ago it was now nowhere in sight.

"Oh bother. This is a pickle," Milo said plopping himself back down on the ground. The young man had been a Boy Scout for a while but while he'd gotten quite a few nice merit-badges and done plenty of civic-service he'd never been a very good camper. He'd furthermore eventually resigned because of his favorite President

Charles Phipps

Jimmy Carter and their attempt to get him to hunt a poor animal called a Snipe during one of those trips. Milo was certain while he wouldn't starve (being from Oz he couldn't) that he wouldn't be able to do much to help his situation.

Still he had to try, for Ozma's sake.

***

The Engagement of Ozma
Book Two in the Umbrella Man of Oz series

Chapter 11

Dorothy Gale was worried sick for her friends right now and it was hard for the two flying Princesses at her side to keep up with her, which shows how fast she was moving.

She ran through the magical castle checking every crevice, nook, and cranny for some sign of them. There was no sign of the Hungry Tiger, Milo, or Ozma at all and the young woman was certain something dreadful had happened to all of them.

"Slow down Miss Gale! We have to think about this logically!" Dusk said with a breathless sigh, as she looked herself for some trace of her mother.

They had no idea that the Supreme Sorcerer of Avy-Lyon had been replaced but the thought of someone having the magic of him or the power to defeat him was enough to make the frumpy fae very afraid indeed of every shadow in her once secure home.

"We've got to find them! They might have been turned into cheese or wogglepillars! Swallowed alive by gigantic fish or eaten by universal solvent!" Dawn said as she frantically buzzed through the air and looked over her shoulders at least three times every second.

Dorothy stopped a moment to lean up against a huge statue of Atlas the Titan who inspired many great deeds, art, and a very important book of maps.

"You're right we just can't willy nilly about hoping we'll catch some sight of them. Especially since…" Dorothy didn't finish her sentence as she looked up towards Dawn and Dusk. The twins didn't have any answers to Dorothy's query but they were soon to have an answer to their question. Floating down the main hallways of Grand Castle of Lurline was the High Captain of the Guard Zolos.

The incomparable warrior who had defeated armies with his bare hands, tossed Manticores into oceans, and never missed once with his spear. Of course, High Captain Zolos was a poogie and only a foot in height with a very large amount of baby-fat but that just goes to show you never judge a fairy by his fodder. The High Captain was currently leading a security detail that he was hoped to train to protect the royal family. Poogies only live until they are sixteen when they 'pop' much like balloons. Thus working for immortal fairy queens like Lurline is a lifetime occupation.

"And over here is what we like to call a Princess who was also a mortal. Take careful note because you probably won't see another one in this lifetime. The human princess is sadly a dying out species due their recent focus on the world destroying idea of..." High Captain Zolas said as he poked Dorothy a bit with a spear as the heroine of Oz took him in her hands.

"Do you know where Ozma is?" Dorothy asked, resising the urge to shake the Poogie. Shaking children is something that you just don't do you know.

"Ah yes, the High Queen and her band have gathered around the Rebel Princess for an elaborate series of tests to prove that the Great and Glorious one is correct in her perfect wisdom while all others such as her young deluded daughter are not..." Captain Zolas looked at Princess Dorothy who narrowed her eyes at him and gave him such a look that he decided to think better of his words.

"Oh really?" Dorothy said unpleasantly.

"They are at the Stone Circle I think." Captain Zolas blinked. The Stone Circle was a large number of arranged rocks that was much like Stonehenge and where many fey in the courts held their rituals to celebrate the passing of the days.

Dorothy nodded and looked to Dusk "We've got to get there fast! Why don't you take us there with your magic?"

Dusk winced and pulled out the bag that she carried her dust of transportation in. The sparkling dust that was left over from all the magical movements had completely depleted her supply. A few shift shakes were enough to convince Dorothy that they weren't going to get there in an instant.

"Why don't we take some of mother's steeds to the Stone Circle?" Dawn suggested as she spun around Dorothy and eventually landed on the top of the globe Atlas held aloft.

"Magical steeds?" Dorothy said, not sure how she was going to like this. At a hundred years old Dorothy was a very good rider but quite a few of the animals you encountered in Fairy-land were temperamental and she didn't know how much time they could waste trying to calm them down. Finally she decided it would definitely be

The Engagement of Ozma
Book Two in the Umbrella Man of Oz series

less time than it would take to cross the sum of Avy-Lyon on their own.

"Yes absolutely. This way," Dusk gestured as Dorothy made a jog behind the dark fairy princess. Captain Zolas merely watched the three with a detached interest and decided to go back teaching his trainees, focusing next on the dangers of allowing Animal Royalty into a castle without checking to see if they are carnivorous or not. Down, down, down the three went across twenty halls and down a dozen flights of steps. When Dorothy reached the bottom she was quite exhausted.

"You'd think...*huff*...you could stick them anywhere in the Castle...*puff* if they can fly and *huff* not just the basement." Dot said, wiping some of the sweat from her forehead.

"True but then people in the basement would have a much longer ways to travel anyway." Dusk pointed out as Dawn collapsed in a pile of straw next to some riding tackle.

The stables of Castle Eternia were a huge affair with a beautiful menagerie of strange and wild creatures that had been gathered for the Airby of Kirri and Flutter (Airbys are like Derbys only in the sky). The beasts were quite fond of both when the later wasn't causing them to throw their riders and trip (a hard thing to do in the air) by her mere presence. To Dorothy there was such a bewildering array of critters that she had no idea what she might possibly choose to mount.

"Just choose one Miss Dot. We'll follow along the old fashioned way," Dawn said as she took a moment to catch her breath.

"Hmmm do you have a pigasus?" Dorothy asked looking over a particularly ugly creature with bat wings.

"A what?" Dusk asked blinking at the odd word.

"Yeah, a pig which flies. The only downside is odd things happen whenever he does." Dorothy made the odd comment. Still as a farm girl she had plenty of experiences with pigs and had ridden on the back of the only flying one she knew of many times.

"I don't believe so." Dusk answered with a frown.

"But we should get one!" Dawn readily answered.

"How about an Iffin?" Dorothy suggested next because she really didn't want to ride anything dangerous.

Charles Phipps

"An iffin?" Dusk looked perplexed at the young woman from Kansas.

"It's a Griffon which has lost it's Grrr," Dawn merrily explained.

Dorothy nodded but Dusk shook her head on the Griffon idea. They had plenty of Griffons but unfortunately they were all very grry and that was something Dot just couldn't stomach.

"Well why don't you just choose one that you like? They're all very nice once you get to know them and loyal to mother." Dawn suggested.

Dorothy looked through the magical steeds and eventually her eyes settled on a giant bald eagle. Because Dorothy was a patriotic American before her immigration to Oz and still remembered fondly her homeland, she thought he was the best choice of the lot of wondrous fairy-born animals.

"Hello. I was curious would you let me ride on your back and take me to the Stone Circle of Lurline?" Dot said as she stroked the side of the Eagle's head and asked politely.

"I am afraid I cannot take anyone in the presence of her Majesty without express permission from one of the riding masters," the Bald Eagle said proudly as he stretched out his wings in a pose very similar to the United States Seal.

"But we are princesses of Avy-lyon!" Dawn said outraged as Dusk only looked slightly less so.

"I'm sorry but I have no way of verifying that." the Bald Eagle strutted over to the magical feeding trough of the stables. Ordering a trough of fine tofu pigeons the Bald Eagle was followed politely by Dorothy who just continued to smile.

"Isn't there anything we can do to convince you to help us?" Dorothy said batting her eyelashes a bit.

"Well I..." The Bald Eagle ruffled his feathers a bit as he looked and said "I might be willing to negotiate if you could provide me with something."

Dorothy got closer to the Bald Eagle's head with her coy smile "What?"

The Bald Eagle looked embarrassed and looked a bit about to see that he was alone with the three. "I'd like a toupe."

The Engagement of Ozma
Book Two in the Umbrella Man of Oz series

Dot blinked at the words of the Bald Eagle "You want a what?"

"A feather-piece to be precise. I am sick truly of being mocked by the rest of the bird community for not having a gloriously elegant plumage to signify my greatness. If you can provide this with your magic I would be happy to risk the wrath of the great and glorious Lurline," The Bald Eagle said before finishing his meal in three swallows.

"Well I suppose we can take care of that but I think you look distinguished without any...err elegant plumage." Dorothy said as she rubbed his head a bit.

"You're just saying that. Climb aboard and we shall be off to the Stone Circle immediately." the Bald Eagle said as Dorothy eagerly did so.

It only took a moment for the Eagle to take to the air and the Princess of Oz had to hold on for dear life due to the great winged creature's speed. Dawn and Dusk followed swiftly behind the young woman as they tried to match the pace of the graceful King of the Birds. She only hoped that she would be in time to warn Ozma and her friends about the evil afoot.

***

Ozma walked down the twisted mesmerizing halls of the Labyrinth her mother had constructed out of the Queen of Oz's own insecurities and fears.

It appeared as an endless hall of mirrors with countless twists and turns. The only light in the hall was the Princess's own wand that she kept illuminated in front of her with a simple magical spell that did little to cast away the overwhelming feeling of dread all about. Each passage lead to dead ends that provoked the worst possible outcomes of Oz's enchantment, and more bitingly the possibilities of betrayal in her love of Milo.

"I have lived centuries and seen hundreds of beautiful maidens more lovely than you Princess Ozma. I cared for you at first but I think it is time that I spread my wings as a mortal man further. How was I to ever know there was so much to do in this universe and what was paradise to a young man would so quickly stale to an ancient?" the false image of her lover words echoed with a bitter cynicism that betrayed none of her fiance's idealism.

This Milo Starling had been there, done that, and all that was left was a endless ennui that would eventually be satisfied only with his own self-destruction.

"Love is not a single thing that can be beautiful at first then grow stale but a vibrant living thing that must be constantly challenged and reborn," Ozma said to the shade as she placed her hands on the illusion and dissapated it like it was a reflection in a pool of water.

The next image was of Dorothy with her eyes cracked with horror, sorrow, and sadness as she rocked gently back and forth. This Dorothy was a much older one and looked like she could be seventy years of age or older but it was still recognizably Dot.

"What is wrong Dorothy?" Ozma could not help but ask. The Queen of Oz knew this was but an illusion but the sight of her like this was enough to break down any of her resolve to ignore these phantoms of her mind.

"I am a little girl. I am a little girl..." Dorothy repeated the words over and over again. Ozma finally just dissapated the image in disgust. Her mother obviously had no conception of what a human's mind really worked. Further she was trying to convince herself and Ozma of its truth.

"Childhood does not have to be something that is clung to because it is part of a greater cycle. As we pass from child to woman we learn to recover what we have lost." Ozma said to no one in particular. She doubted that Queen Lurline was even listening to her anymore. Dorothy could be a child, a maiden, or even a mother like Ozma hoped to someday be but being immortal wouldn't inhibit that as all in Oz would simply gain a chance to saver each stage much more. The monarch of the Emerald City had even considered modifying the immortality spell so that mortals in Oz could choose to age backwards when they wanted as well.

Ozma found the Labyrinth beginning to straighten as she soon discovered it becoming a straight line. If Ozma recalled how her mother's mind worked, this would be the way to the exit but also the final illusion that would be what Lurline thought most devastating to her psyche. At the end of the Hall Ozma did indeed see a large red sign that said 'Exit' right above a plain wooden door with a gold knob.

Before Ozma could extend her hand to open the door and leave the cursed Maze, she found it opened for her and stepping through was an almost exact representation of herself.

"Hello there me," Ozma-2 said as she stepped in front of her.

Ozma-1 crossed her arms and sighed "Your not me, your an illusion conjured by my mother which is designed to act like me but is limited by how she knows me. Besides your nose is too big."

Ozma-2 felt her nose then looked crossly at her double "No, I think you just need to look in a mirror lately."

Ozma-1 didn't think that her nose was that big at all. "So what exactly are you hear to say about me?"

"Well I'm the biggest doubt and insecurity of them all so you had best prepare yourself," Ozma-2 cautioned.

Ozma-2 was after all based on Ozma-1 and while it was her job to make sure that the Ruler of the Five Districts of Oz had her faith crushed, she wanted to make it as painless as possible.

"Thank you," Ozma-1 said as she blinked. She was not exactly comfortable with her double being so polite.

"Very well I'm going to ask you a single question," Ozma-2 said with a smile as she cupped her hands together.

"Okay. Please ask," Ozma-1 sighed. She was really hoping this wouldn't last much longer.

"What makes you think you can do all this?" Ozma-2 leaned against the side of the wall and played a bit with the poppy in her hair.

"Pardon?" Ozma-1 asked, not sure what the question was.

"Well we know Milo loves you and would never betray you. We know Dorothy is strong and so is Trot, Betsy, the Wizard, Glinda, Button and the rest. However, why are you exactly worthy of being his husband and their Queen?" Ozma-2 asked as she blinked curiously.

Ozma-1 found the question ridiculous and was about to shove past her duplicate when she stopped and blinked. "I don't know."

Charles Phipps

"I mean you really are a very bad ruler. You know that don't you? You do your hardest but you've been kidnapped so many times and Oz has nearly been destroyed many more times. You've managed to survive by luck them so far but each year more people look at you to be perfect and your not. Eventually someday the people of Oz are going to find something that you aren't able to protect them from and there won't be any way to fix Oz from the destruction some evil person inflicts on it," Ozma-2 just tut-tut-tuted.

Ozma-1 bit her lip and acknowledged the truth that several times in her career as ruler of Oz she had failed to protect her people and it was others who had ended up having to rescue her and her kingdom.

"You're a thousand years old but you've been a child in the Court of Lurline when you could have been a woman learning your own way. Milo loves you as do your subjects but how much is that love worth to an ideal that you can't live up to? What happens when someone turns him into an inanimate object and instead of keeping him around they shatter it to a million pieces just to hurt the 'Invincible queen of Oz'? What happens when someone does that to anyone in your kingdom and you can't stop it because your just a little girl after all?" the words from her double were sympathetic and warm. At heart too Ozma-1 knew that the illusion was right and that no matter what she couldn't protect her loved ones from all the jealousy, hatred, despair, and anger that would be directed at them.

Things directed at them solely because they lived in a land filled with happiness the monarch of Oz couldn't share with the entire world no matter how much she wished she could.

"I cannot protect them it's true from all possible dangers nor can I be the perfect queen that they deserve to be. I have to trust them to be strong on their own and forgive me when I fail. In the end I can only hope that it will turn out all for the best like every other person in the universe." Ozma said as she swallowed her pride and watched the illusion fade.

Tears slowly fell down her face as she thought of all the things that might happen because she couldn't do better than she might have. Where the tears struck little poppies grew from the ground. Stepping through the door she found herself in the Stone Circle outside the

Castle Eternia. It was a huge set of rock arches that had been constructed by the Great Wizard Michael to focus magical energies before they had discovered such wonderful things as Lurline Engines.

It had been here that Ozma and her family had planned the many enchantments that went into making Oz the spectacular fairyland that it was. Her mother was sitting on a ivory and gold throne with her wings fully extended as ten of her sisters were present at her side. All of them had been watching the misery she had been going through the labyrinth and not one face did not seem longer for the experience. All except one, Michael the Court Wizard who had been Ozma's instructor growing up the first time in the courts of Avy-Lyon merely seemed bored by the entire thing. She wondered what could have possibly hardened his heart so much that every ounce of sympathy was drained from the Sorcerer Supreme.

"You have passed yet another of my tests set before you my daughter. You are possessed of great maturity and wisdom, I am proud of you for that," Lurline said with a look of acknowledgement that the tiny princess hoped included how wrong she was.

"That means a great deal to me mother," Ozma said truthfully. She had always felt like she was something of a second rate Sidhe in comparison to her statuesque parent.

Lurline looked to each of her daughters who gazed at her expectantly. The High Queen felt very alone on her throne and weary of all these games that she had been playing with her daughter's feelings.

The Seelie Fairy had many more tests planned for her daughter to convince her that what she was doing was for the best but she didn't know if she had the will to face her daughter's every honest defense of her friends and family. Lurline who had defied all the fairy-elders and rose to become Queen by virtue of her just heart did not feel at heart what she was doing was good or just. If she felt that way though she had to ask herself why she was doing it at all?

"You indeed have shown great cunning in your trials Princess Ozma but the High Queen Lurline has existed since nearly the birth of the world and she is not so easily convinced of your..." the Wizard Michael was caught off by the rise of the High Queen Lurline.

"I have decided to spare your kingdom." Queen Lurline interrupted the false Wizard at her side.

"WHAT!?" Evile Lackey could not contain his outrage even as he barely managed to keep hold of his disguise as the Arch-Wizard. Even the thought of what that nasty two-faced snake had planned wasn't enough to lessen his anger at watching his spell over the Fairy Queen broken by a mother's love and goodness. It gave him an odd feeling akin to diabetes to see decency triumph. A common enough affliction among evil-doers it still hasn't been found a cure for despite numerous attempts by villainous magic practicing pharmacists throughout Fairy-land.

"Goody Gumdrops!" Princess Rebecca the Jester shouted as she fluttered high in the air.

"You have made a very wise decision Mother. I am glad Ozma had the courage to stand up to you like she did. She shames me with her strength of character." Morgan said as she took her mother by the arm and gave her a hug.

"You did it!" Kessily grabbed her sister in the Queen of Oz and gave her a hug that nearly split the Princess in two.

"Ooomph!" Ozma managed to give her most formal reply under the circumstances even as she was soon joined by all of her other sisters in turn but for the eldest who stood to comfort their parent.

The False Michael positively fumed and gritted his teeth. If it wouldn't have leveled the greater area of Avy-Lyon he would have snapped his magical staff over his knee. Lurline looked at her wizard with shock and had not the witch's powder done such a good job she surely would have suspected that her difficulty arriving at this very sensible decision was the product of his wicked magic.

"I had no right ever to break the enchantment over Oz and I cannot imagine what compelled me to think so. It seems like a weary dream that was a good idea at the time but only stubborness and weak will prevented me from seeing the truth of," Lurline explained as she let her golden wings flutter.

She approached her daughters with her head held low.

As Ozma struggled to move between the mass of her sisters she finally managed to exert herself and say "I understand dearly the

The Engagement of Ozma
Book Two in the Umbrella Man of Oz series

pain you've been going through with what you've shared mother with the loss of my father. I forgive you the threats and I can only hope now that I can count on your blessing upon my own marriage. I also swear that we will find a way to…" Ozma was about to speak about finding a cure for her father's enchantment when she saw Dorothy riding on the back of one of her mother's pet Great Eagles. Beside her were Dawn and Dusk who were flying as fast as they could with their wings towards Lurline and her band.

"Ozma! Look out! That Wizard beside you is a Traitor! He's the one who did away with your father!" Dorothy shouted on eagle-back even as she tried to find a safe place to land near the Forrest of Bygone's huge trees.

The Little Queen of Oz didn't have time to react for as soon as the words were spoken Evile Lackey pulled out a small remote with blinking buttons even as a bright red light filled the entire air around Ozma, her sisters, and the High Queen of the Fey.

"Hahahahahahahahohohehehehehehe." Evile could hardly keep from falling over with laughter. He was positively bristling with magical energy and even in broad daylight cast a glow around himself. A glow that was bright scarlet with black lightning shooting about it every few seconds. Evile's hair stood completely on end and he looked much like he had been the victim of an electrocution. Gone was his disguise of being the Arch-Wizard Michael and the shock of seeing the Warlock for the first time caused all of the Fairy-Princesses to gather around their sister protectively as Lurline raised her wand in defense of her children.

"Who are you and what do you want Dark Magician?" Lurline said in a commanding tone that would have frightened the spots off a charging leopard, not an easy thing to do.

"I am Evile Lackey, son of the Wicked Witch of the West and father of Igor Lackey the Grand Weathermaster of Zo. I come to claim rights of Vengzzzzzzzzzzztt…Vengencccczzzzzt…I come to claim rights of Revenge for my Famtzzzzzt errr Kin." Evile said as he sputtered out his words with quite a bit of saliva that the lighting sizzled. It was quite annoying to be a living magical conductor sometimes.

Dorothy set down the nice Eagle that Dusk and Dawn had lent her as she looked fearfully at the terrifying monster that had emerged in their midst. Something in the Kansas Girl's Common sense told her that this wasn't going to be an easy dip in the Fountain of Oblivion to fix.

"Your claim is denied! Revenge is the right of no being in my Kingdom!" Lurline said as she pointed her wand at Evile and looked on in shock as nothing happened. Each of Ozma's sisters tried their own wands on the warlock as well only to find that they too were berift of magical 'juice'.

"Behold my alchemical bio-magical scientiffic genius! Harnessing the power of a Lurline Engine and the common simplicity of Grand Unifying Magic or G.U.M.S I have transferred all of your magical powers to my own malicious personage. I am literally overflowing with mystical energy and with your power have transferred myself to a full ten point one on the Victor's Scale of Magic, one notch higher than Fairy Queens and below nothing but the Supreme Master herself!" Evile Lackey chortled as his laughter grew to such a terrible squeal that it could be heard in the Lands of Titihoochoo, Atlantis, the Silver Islands, and the greater Harrisburg area.

"Ozma!" Dorothy called out to her friend as she looked on in shock at what she had inadvertantly caused. Unaware that Evile had been planning much more evil that would have come to fruition had she not warned them.

"It is now time for the final page in your billion page novel Queen Lurline! Goodbye!" Evile chortled as the Warlock suddenly started to grow in size substantially. Still surrounded by his terrible red and black-aura the devilish figure lifted up his fingers and recited the most terrible spell in all of Fairyland.

The Lament-Everlasting, that was the only spell in the universe that could destroy an immortal fairy utterly. With a hushed whisper of suddenly all sound on Avy-Lyon the terrible ball of 'nothingness' was tossed forward down onto the Band of Lurline.

"Ozma!" Dorothy cried out as tears came to her face before she saw what was remaining after the terrible spell by Evile. Instead

The Engagement of Ozma
Book Two in the Umbrella Man of Oz series

of being-utterly destroyed Ozma and her family remained untouched by the wicked magic.

Raising her wand above her head it glowed brightly and the Magic Belt shined like a miniature sun, the power of the Little Queen of Oz enough to challenge even the darkest of powers.

"You will find me a stronger witch than you think," Ozma said as she began to speak all of her greatest magic to try and turn the tide against the evil wizard. Evile Lackey's GUM spell had not taken away her powers for the Otherworld Princess was both a fairy and a human girl in her blood.

With the magic of both, the protective power of the Nome King's Belt, and the cause of right she could fight the alchemist but whether she could beat him or not something only the Supreme Master could see.

***

Raspy the First King of the Oz Province of Zo was enjoying his dessert after a late dinner which had been paused for dinner which had followed a large lunch preceded by a warm brunch and hearty breakfast. Yes it was good to be King when you had a hearty appetite but unfortunately had learned to indulge far too much in the many delectable treats available to him as the ruler of the flying kingdom and now was too heavy to fly in the air.

Raspy was content though to take food over his love of crashing though and had decided instead to rule from a simply expanded throne.

It was then that Coughy the Prime Minister of Zo zipped through the air and smashed deliberately into the wall behind the Throne. He was a midget among the hissing-wings that was only a foot and a half in size at his longest but his wisdom was greater than all others in the flying island combined. In the small one's hand was a fire-works rocket that had a message tied to it emblazoned with the Royal Seal of Oz.

"Nephew!" Raspy shouted as the umbrella shaped crown bobbed on the High Hissing-Wing's head. The Throne room looked more like a banquet hall that a place of business as a huge table was set on the shimmering stones of the Crystal Palace floor laced with sweet drop cakes, gummy beans, and delectable Evian Delight. Gone was all the soot, war celebrating tapestries, and other creepy decorations of the Wicked Queen Zoam.

"Yes Mighty Master of Crashes!" Coughy said as he let loose into a torrent of violent coughs. Coughy was also the acting Master of Rain-Making machines in Zo and was quite succeptible to flu. Thankfully since no one ever dies in Oz and the hissing-wings enjoy pain a great deal it was something of a blessing, something of.

"What have you brought for me my most noble assssssssssistant?" Raspy said as he prepared another napkin over his already five soiled napkins wrapped around his neck. Raspy was for all of his noble qualities also a messy eater but he was such a kind, compassionate, and blissfully unaware ruler that his subjects gladly overlooked his appalling table manners.

"It is a letter that arrived by the Wizard's rockets from the Land of Oz below Most Obese Yet Happy with Oneself One." Coughy said as he coughed once after his words and handed over the device in his hand. Rapsy took it into his claws and pulled them out a huge pair of emerald spectacles that he had made in the likeness of his dear friend Milo's though much bigger for the head of a hissing-wing is large. "Sssswitch and Blazzzzesssss! Princesssssss Ozma hasssssss been overthrown!" Rapsy said in shock as he read the letter to himself.

"NO!" Coughy said before coughing a hideous fit.

"You're right. Ssssssshe's merely on vacatttttion. Unfortunately, her kingdom isssssss sssssufferring an invasssssion by a group of militant candlessssss and they need our help to put them out. It has been requesssssted by their new King Jack Pumkinhead the Firssst," Raspy said with a smile of his many layers of teeth.

Coughy was not amused. "Sounds like a seedy sort of fellow. Are you sure he's on the up and up?"

"We have a duty to protect the Land of Oz and not a moment to lossssssse." Rapsy said with a nod as he struggled to get out of his throne and finally managed only with the help of three of his hissing-wing guards.

The Engagement of Ozma
Book Two in the Umbrella Man of Oz series

Coughy meanwhile sped up to the tower of the Grand Weather-Machine which contained the great Weather-Machine of Zo which had been rebuilt using the plans of Igor Lackey fixed with the educated guesses of all of Zo's finest minds. When that mess was completely scrapped they appealed to the Wizard of Oz, Glinda, and Zim the Flying Sorcerer who presented them with a lost book of the Umbrella Wizards of Winkieland that allowed them to build the beautiful machine that allowed Zo to create rain or end it wherever it liked.

"Cough Wheez Sputter Choke!" Coughy shouted the moment he landed within the huge building of gears, pulleys, humming generators, and water-wheels. The hundreds of white-dressed rain-makers looked at the Prime Minister of Zo for a moment, trying to figure out exactly what this peculiar demand was.

Phil the head of the Zo Introspective Religious Order of Stoic Layabouts formerly the Prime Minister of Ozzification, formerly head of the First Revolutionary Council of Zo, formerly the Captain of the Black Spectacled Order looked toward Coughy as he said "I believe he just ordered us to cough, wheez, sputter, and choke."

Coughy smacked his head as the tower was filled with the sound of very sick individuals. "No I meant to say that we need to start up the rain machines full blast and drop their water on a very specific spot!"

Phil the Stoic Layabout thought about that for a moment, shrugged and said "I must have missed a vowel translating it from Hissing-Wing." Coughy who knew hissing-wings spoke English just shook his head from that particular bit of excuse. The Introspective Religious Order of Stoic Layabouts had formed when His Majesty had discovered that the former Spectacled Order could do virtually nothing normally without their glasses or earmuffs and were among the stupidest individuals in Zo. To that end he had appointed them in charge of the educational and philosophy. Jobs which had made sense at the time.

"Here you go sir!" one of the smaller weather-makers in a boy named Fiz said rushing up, dirt and soot covered and happy like all boys who are should be.

Charles Phipps

Fiz was a intelligent lad with eastern eyes, a warm heart, and short black hair. He was also the first to be born in Zo after the Great Liberation and had shot up quite swiftly.

In the young boy's hand was Zo's Magic Periscope which had been a gift from the Rainbow King and allowed the viewer to be able to see anything below Zo no matter how distant or covered.

Handing the device to Coughy, the tiny prime-minister of Zo adjusted its knobs and dials until he saw the huge moving bonfire that was moving over the fore-gate to the Emerald City.

"Prepare to fire…err water at 12 degrees by fory-seven!" Coughy shouted and wished he had a little white hat as he did so. The weather-masters adjusted the huge machinery and with a grind the gears turned to transform the white clouds of Zo into a heavy black rain cloud. The rainclouds of Zo filled like water-balloons and where they allowed to fill beyond their size it was possible the entire country of Zo would pop and scatter across Oz. Coughy was much too observant for that and as the clouds filled to the brim the miniature hissing-wing gave a thumbs down signal to Phil.

"I interpret the portents of the Master of Rain-Machines as wishing us to drop the water of Zo upon the Land of Oz below. That is of course unless he is using Ancient Roman thumbs down techniques in which he is saying we should drop someone off Zo." Phil prepared to open a philosophical dialogue regarding the matter with his partner the rain release operator Bob.

Coughy stared at the rain-release operator in horror as a coughing-fit overcame him and the alarms started blaring throughout the Tower about the imminent explosion of Zo. Bob standing next to the giant red- button that would release the rain and save both countries was meanwhile scratching his head over the implications of Phil's statements. At the last moment the young boy Fiz pressed it in with both hands and caused the water torrent to pour down from Zo's clouds.

Coughy finished his choking and looked at the boy "Good show young man! I appoint you Official Button Pusher of Zo."

Fiz gave a salute to his commander as he says "Anytime then!"

The Engagement of Ozma
Book Two in the Umbrella Man of Oz series

King Raspy the First finally arrived as the rain steamed on the Illumi-nati far below and eventually quenched them. The Hissing-Wing King was unable to fly on his own and thus escorted in by the efforts of six of his best guards carrying him as he flapped his wings futily to help in the process. "Excellent job there Coughy! I insist you get a medal for your efforts!"

Coughy nodded to his monarch as he plopped himself on the ground and said "Your Most Round Greatness is wonderful but I am simply do my job sir. This young boy here is the true hero."

"Is this true?" King Raspy said with a curious raised eyebrow and if you know anything about hissing-wings, they have very large eyebrows. Being a loyal citizen of Zo Fiz could only reply "I cannot tell a lie sir. I only pushed a button."

"Ah being a loyal citizzzen of Zo I know your not telling the truth and thusssssss you did much much more." Raspy said, being of the mind that citizens of Zo were not quite as reformed as they thought he thought they were.

"Excellent Reasoning Your Largess," Phil the Philosopher bowed before the wise monarch.

"Uhhh," Fiz wasn't sure how to respond to that and looked to Coughy.

"Just go with it. Wheez!" Coughy said as he spat into his fist and went to fetch himself a steaming hot cup of his namesake.

"In honor of your acomplisssssshment I name you the Prince of Zo and I knight everyone here. I declare furthermore a celebration banquet in honor of our ssssssaving the Motherland." Raspy said as he pulled out his umbrella scepter and tapped the boy on the shoulders.

"Sir, we are already celebrating the centuries comming nuptials of Queen Ozma and the Founder of the Umbrella Order Milo the Conquerer." Coughy reminded the monarch of Zo.

"Oh? How long as we've been cccccellabrating that?" Raspy asked with a blink of his huge eyes.

"Some years now," Coughy said as he gargled the black bean based drink in his mouth and swallowed it.

"Exccccellent! We have an excusssssse for many more banquetsssssss then," Raspy smiled as he lifted his umbrella high in

Charles Phipps

the air "To Oz! Let ussssss hail King Pumpkinhead on hisssssss victory!"

And they did indeed.

***

The Engagement of Ozma
Book Two in the Umbrella Man of Oz series

Chapter 12

Milo Starling had decided to walk through the gardens of Edenia and was already starting to regret the decision as the island was positively massive. The island was much like Oz in that the magic practically soaked the air but unlike Oz there was a much wilder feeling to the place, as if at any time you might encounter something supernatural but never another human being.

Milo wasn't a bigot you must understand and was perfectly comfortable conversing with birds, beasts, or walking lampshades like any good citizen of Oz but it might have been nice to know that some part of the island was made to accomadate his bipedal nature.

"Harps and Halos I can't go on any farther." Milo said as he finally collapsed on a particularly nice patch of blue grass. He had at least found a particularly nice spot in the island to take a moment to rest. It was much like Munchkinland which of course reminded him of his native Kentucky which reminded him of Scotland. The only main exception was the forest around him was filled with trees that were growing objects.

Not just bread or types of food which were common in Oz but furniture trees, book trees, appliance trees, and even a tree which was growing toys for children. Milo had no doubt in his mind that if he continued looking around he'd find a tree for virtually everything in existence.

"Oh look at that." Milo said as he managed after a few moments to get up and go to a particularly inviting tree. The tree's allure wasn't because of its delicious fruits or it's bottles of iced tea which Milo could do with greatly right now but instead of the musical instrument that the young preacher loved. It was the grand instrument of the winds that Milo plucked a ripe one off and cuddled against his chest in a set of bagpipes.

Taking a huge breath Milo began to blow into the device as he squeezed it rhythmatically. Those who knew Milo who like the Good Book said often made joyous noises would have been surprised to discover that the noise that came out of the device sounded suspiciously like music.

Milo had always wanted to learn how to play the bagpipes but the Wogglebug refused to make pills for their playing because of what the young preacher termed 'no appreciation for the High King of all wind-instruments'. Instead the young Kentuckian had travelled far into the Gillikens to the High-Lands and learned it the old fashioned way. The Kentuckian you see viewed Scotland and all it's history as a magical thing much like you and I see Oz and playing the pipes was a way of bringing that all together.

"Pardon me." Milo heard a voice say as he worked on a rather rousing nationalist tune and stopped blowing. The young preacher took a moment to look up and saw an entire flock of red cardinals had gathered around him. All of the cardinals were wearing little red caps on their head except for the largest and most impressive of them which had a large pointed white hat on his head. Furthermore, the leader of the cardinals was carrying a little shepherds crook that fit on the edge of his wing.

"Ah. Top of the morning to you," Milo said as he bowed his head to the leader.

"Forgive us brother but we the College of Cardinals are having a most religious meeting regarding the impending beatification of a worthy protector of this magical land. Your playing, while beautiful, is disturbing the hallowed sanctity of the occasion." The leader of the Cardinals said as he waved his shepherd's crook a bit at Milo.

"Oh dear how embarrassing. Was she martyred recently?" Milo asked with a frown. He'd spent a number of his education years at parochial school and learned to respect the priests and nuns there a great deal. One of the things you just don't interrupt is choosing a person to become a saint, which is the highest honor one can be given when one is dead.

"Oh she's not dead yet which is why it's impending. Vorestia the glorious Unicorn has guarded this island for two-hundred years but unfortunately the Far-Guard Serpent has awoken from his million year sleep thanks to some villain dropping a monarch on his head. Now he is awake and we expect him to eat her any time now. Oh Woe. Woe. Woe." The Ponitif said as the cardinals behind him agreed with him by nodding their heads.

The Engagement of Ozma
Book Two in the Umbrella Man of Oz series

"Woe. Pardon me sir but I am a man from the Land of Oz and in these sort of situations it is my duty to help. Could you point me in the direction of this unpleasant altercation? If I am to die at least let it be in the service of something good." Milo said, having no intention of dying but really wanting to head off the accusations by the locals that going to face an unknown enemy for someone he didn't know might entail.

"Oh you must be the great young hero Tippetarius! Please do not allow us to delay you most noble wizard. She is down by the north side of the beach. No doubt waiting for the creature now." The Pontiff of the Cardinals said as shooed him gently with his wing.

"Uhhh n...Thank you." Milo tried to explain the truth but decided to simply be polite and go on a rescue mission. In truth Milo didn't like to admit it to himself but he was often jealous of Tip. Tip after all was Ozma's closest boy friend and they had shared more than any being could expect to share with another one, even when magic is involved. Milo knew it was wrong to covet another's gifts and life but Tip had done a great deal more than the preacher and he felt something of a need to catch up with him.

Ozma of course would have told Milo he was silly and that she was marrying him not Tip, which would have been more than a little gross to her, but getting back to his queen for just those assurances was part of Milo's goal.

The Far-Guard Serpent you must know is one of the most unpleasant creature's in all of Fairy-Land. The huge mile long creature had been originally a much smaller snake which had a mildly poisonous tongue that could only sting away people who disturbed it. Then one day it went crawling into High Queen Dana's gardens who Lurline's grandmother and thus Ozma's great grandmother and ate some of the fabulous enchanted apples which gave Avy-Lyon it's great magic.

A similar tree existed in Oz and in a number of other fairy-countries and a single bite is enough to grant a person immortality, great magic, and if they are given willingly great wisdom. The Far-Guard serpent ate many and fell asleep after it was done and when he awoke he was huge beyond belief and Queen Dana furious with him.

The Supreme Master in order to be nice to the serpent which was really more greedy than it was maelovolent suggested then that it serve as the Guard for the Island of Edenia where all magic trees and animals originally hailed from. It usually did a very good job of defending Edenia from thieves and overly curious travellers but it occasionally forgot it's mission as well. It was at this time that she gave birth to awful things like the Doom Asps and tried to eat the inhabitants of the island it dwelled underneath.

A few hours earlier it had woken up in one of those moods and had by chance come across the Unicorn Vorestia. Vorestia now you must first understand does not look like a unicorn at all and instead due to a series of unfortunate looks like a pretty young woman whom Milo would be quick to say was the loveliest he knew after Ozma and Dorothy. Being a gentle creature by nature Vorestia tried to reason with the Far-Guard Serpent, who enjoyed being called Maggie, but instead it had merely led to the unfortunate scene Milo came across where Vorestia's two legs were wiggling outside of the gigantic snake's mouth.

"Saints and Seraphim! Spit her out this instant!" Milo shouted as he looked at the huge beast before making a mild apology to any saints and seraphim who might have been listening to the air.

Maggie remembered then what her job was and indeed did drop the unicorn from her mouth on the ground below. Milo was so stunned at being obeyed that he was nearly eaten as the Far-Guard Serpent snapped down to bite the intruder to the island in two. Milo thankfully had learned a number of dance-steps which in this case allowed him to gracefully avoid becoming the creature's dinner.

"Hatred stirs old quarrels, but love overlooks insults…but not cannibalism." Milo altered one of his favorite passages as he swung his umbrella like a baseball bat and swatted Maggie across her huge draconic mouth. The wooer of Ozma then watched the Far-Guard Serpent teeter over and collapse to the ground unconscious. Stopping a moment he then walked over and poked her gently with his foot. The Far-Guard Serpent did not stir would remain unconscious for a hundred years until she awoke with a much better attitude and dedication to her cause.

The Engagement of Ozma
Book Two in the Umbrella Man of Oz series

"Well that was easy." Milo said as he twirled his umbrella. The young man should not have been surprised to discover his umbrella having such an affect on the giant beast however, it was made by his true love Ozma and that makes magic much more powerful. Looking down Milo then saw the Lady Vorestia covered in the black poisonous spittle of the giant snake.

"Drat, Drat, and Double Drat!" the woman plopped herself up even while Milo began to offer his hand. Her eyes still stinging from the black tar of the snake salvia she blinked a bit at Milo.

"Good morning. May I help you?" Milo said, getting slightly uncomfortable at her gaze.

"Are you a beautiful princess?" Vorestia asked as she felt Milo's face.

"No. No. I'm quite sure I'm not," Milo said, looking down at his Saturday best to gage whether or not he looked like a beautiful princess in them. To his relief he couldn't see anything that would help her mistake him as one.

"Darn the luck! I need to find a beautiful princess to marry the handsome king of this island so I can get off it," Vorestia sighed as she finally wiped the last of the poison from her eyes.

"Perhaps you should start at the beginning of this story. I'm sure it would be interesting." Milo suggested. He had nothing else better to do at this point after all.

"Well I am Vorestia the Unicorn," Vorestia said with a slight bow as she introduced herself.

Milo frowned, not wanting to point out in no way did she resemble a horse or even have a horn.

"I know I don't look like one but I'm forbidden to take my natural form because of a mistake I made. The High Queen Lurline banished me here for breaking up the marriage of a woodcutter and his wife. I can't come back to Avy-Lyon or travel to any of the other fairy-lands until I get another couple to reconcile," Vorestia frowned and pouted, the woman falling to the ground and crossing her arms across her legs.

"Well I hardly think your going to be able to do that with no one here. If it's any consolation I do need to be reconciled with a woman off the island however." Milo politely didn't ask how she had broken up the woodcutter and his wife, it was really none of his business.

"Yeah tell me about it. Well the problem isn't finding one person to reconcile because the King has a missing love too. The problem is finding the other half of the love…oh you know what I mean." Vorestia pouted and pulled at the grass on the ground, throwing the pieces of it into the air in fury.

"Well I'm sorry but if I reconcile with her I'll be sure to say you had a part in it," Milo said as he patted her on the shoulder and helped her back up.

"Oh would you?" Vorestia said with a smile as she planted a dozen kisses on Milo's face.

"Yes I would. You say there is another man on this island?" Milo gently pushed away the lovely unicorn woman.

"Yes indeed! Want me to show him to you?" Vorestia says off hand in hopes that she might get a hold on the Milo fellow.

"Certainly," Milo had a slight idea of who the other man might be on this island and if he was correct then escaping this island was something much more important for both Ozma and Oz as a whole.

Walking together through the maze-like forests, jungles, swamps, lakes, mountains, and even a volcano the pair managed to make their way to the other side of the island where a huge tree lay. The tree was unlike any other in Oz because instead of growing on it the small but useful things that grew in Oz there grew on this tree an entire Castle. The Castle was a massive one with a green center, yellow north west tower, red southwest tower, blue southeast tower, and purple northwest tower. Out of the front of the castle was an orange drawbridge which dropped with a heavy thump as a dumpy man with a long golden beard walked out whistling with a heavy gray robe draped about him.

Milo bowed his head before the man and then said "King Ozroar I presume?"

***

The Engagement of Ozma
Book Two in the Umbrella Man of Oz series

Princess Ozma had never been very good at magical dueling. It was something of a sport among witches, wizards, and magically inclined faeries so she had been taught it growing up but to her recollection she'd never won a single spell competition with any of her sisters.

To Ozma dueling was essentially a nasty thing and she simply let her sisters win by setting her hair on fire, turning her into china sets, and paralyzing her for hours on end. Those wonderful memories of her family spurred the fairy-queen to battle harder to protect them from the monstrous beast that was doing everything in his power to destroy those close to her. It's sometimes amazing what Ozma can look back upon as pleasant memories but that's why one cannot help but love the little ruler of Oz.

"You cannot possibly defeat me little girl! Everything you know of magic was taught to you by those who have learned their magic from Lurline! I even remember teaching it to you! I could make you a snowflake in a heat storm or a match burning in an ocean or turn you into today which would only last until tommorow. You should just give up yourself to me. I might keep you around as a maid to clean my castle when I've conquered the universe," Evile Lackey gloated as his red aura flickered on and off around him.

Despite what the confidence of his words he was astounded at how powerful the young fairy woman truly was. With the Nome King's belt, the witchcraft of her human side, the magic of the fairy, and the fact Evile was not yet used to his grand power she managed to hold her own against his terrible spells.

"If you could have done so warlock! Ummph! You would have…uhhh…done so. I furthermore…ooooo…have no problems serving in the honorable cleaning profession but…uhhhh I think you would be better advised to learning how to clean your cell!" Ozma said as she held her wand before her and concentrated on it's bright light. Evile's current spell which would have sent Ozma and her siblings to the darkest cavern of the moon to live with the rats that feasted on the green cheese that grew there was being forced away but the dark wizard kept casting it around them.

"Just once I'd like to go on a trip without something like this happening," Dorothy bit her thumb in agony as she watched Ozma struggle against the Wicked Wizard. Dorothy Gale had faced a vertible army of evil magicians in her lifetime and had managed to survive by the grace of good fortune, good friends, and common sense but as a young woman she had no inkling of just how powerful the vicious erbling was or she never would have tried what she did next. It just goes to show you that ignorance is occasionally bliss even if it usually ends up hurting you in some horrible way.

"Dorothy what are you doing!?" Dusk said shocked while the young woman from Kansas ran up in-between Evile Lackey's feet and grabbed his gigantic shoelaces. Dawn figuring out what she was doing was soon joined reluctantly by her twin as the pair helped Dot tie in seconds a rather hefty knot between the wicked one's shoes.

"What in Yurline's name?" Evile said as he looked down at the pair dodging from his red lighting and escaping under him.

"Good show!" Ozma said with a smile as she conjured a magical ball of snow in her hand and blew a storm of ice in the face of the warlock. With a gasp of surprise the monstrously large wizard lost his footing as his feet betrayed him and he went sailing onto the ground with a thump that could be felt a quarter mile away.

"That was a worthwhile trip! See you next fall Evile!" Rebecca the punster couldn't resist taunting from the sidelines.

"Rebecca don't taunt the warlock, it's very bad manners." Morgan said to her sister as she looked on for a sign of what might happen next.

"Dot! Dot! She's our gal! When Nasty-No-Goodniks tumble she's our pal!" Kessily cheered on and wished she had her magical pom-poms. This was even more exciting than Rugby which was the second most violent sport in Fairy-Land after Broom-Polo.

Lurline rushed forward to her daughter's side as her eleven other daughters looked to one another and tried to formulate some solution to take advantage of the half-erb's distress. Unfortunately, Ozma was already exhausted by her magical ordeal and all of her family was so used to magic that without it they were unable to think of anything before the terrible villain recovered.

"Half-pint wretch! I'll evaporate you good!" Evile squealed in anger and pointed his left hand like a gun at the young princess of Oz,

The Engagement of Ozma
Book Two in the Umbrella Man of Oz series

intending to wring all of the water out of her body like a sponge with a twister spell.

Thankfully Dorothy didn't end up getting dehydrated into something that Astronauts might be able to eat as his spell bounced harmlessly off her.

Dorothy had been long ago given the most powerful permanent charm in Oz by the Good Witch of the North to guard her against the evils that had still abundant in Oz at the time.

"A Kiss of Protection! Well that's easily removed enough..." Evile said as he had a terrible plan in mind. The Phanfasm blood in Doctor Lackey was very strong and if there is any other creature in Fairy-Land which is better than tricks than them, the people who are better certainly won't admit it to their faces. Mostly because the Phanfasms would probably do something unspeakable to them but they are actually very good at trickery, which I probably should have just said from the beginning.

"No!" Ozma said rushing forward as Evile grabbed her in his hands and snapped his shoelaces in two getting up. Holding the little fairy-girl like a doll in his hands he ripped the magical belt from her hands and tossed far away in the middle of the Great Stone Circle.

"Ozma!" Dot cried out even as all of Ozma's sisters ran toward Evile's legs and pounded against his ankles for him to let her go. The Wicked Warlock of Avy-Lon ignored their poundings as he looked with an evil grin at Princess Ozma.

"Who is going to save you now My Dear?" Evile taunted as he poked her in the tummy with a big clawed finger.

Ozma didn't have an answer.

***

The Hungry Tiger was getting even hungrier trying to find his way out of the seemingly endless caverns that were underneath Avy-Lyon island. They had been travelling for hours and not only was his fur wet from the damp salty cavern air but there was no sign that they were getting any closer to the surface to warn Ozma, Dorothy, and Milo about the traitor that was in their midst. Finally unable to go any further without a sandwich, piece of tender meat, or other tigery treat Rama simply plopped down on the ground.

"Oh dear, come on Rama My Boy. We haven't that much further to go…I'm sure of it," Michael the Arch-Wizard said. He was looking around nervously and generally not appearing sure at all.

"My love let me say that once we are return to Tigerland we shall prepare for you the biggest feast Oz has ever seen. They'll be venison, pork, beef, chicken, eggs, and everything you could possibly want save small human children." Sita placed her white paw over the Hungry Tiger's neck and snuggled him close.

"You mean it? Maybe we could shape some of the beef to look like one?" Rama asked as the Tiger licked his lips and regained some of his vigor.

"No Rama, it's best not to tempt yourself with these things," Sita corrected and turned her head to look revolted. She absolutely loved her prince with all of her furry heart but he really had to get over this obsession of his.

"Do not fret my two Tigers! I the great King Sean have already managed to resolve the problem of our being lost!" The little skull man bounced passed the entire group and plopped himself on one of the stalagtites that was jutting out of the ground to speak.

"This I have to hear." Michael the Atlantean Sorcerer said with a sigh. After so many thousands of years of life the greatest of all wizards, who couldn't even make milk turn sour with his magic now, had learned a great deal of patience but the Boise Idaho Car salesman's restless dead skull was starting to try even his considerable reserves.

"In the manner of Theseus and the Minotaur I have marked the trails of our path. Thus we should have no trouble finding our way out. You may thank me with adulation and expensive gifts," King Sean bobbed himself a bit in a manner of taking a bow.

"But that was our idea!" Ralph said as the wogglepillar looked up from the Hungry Tiger's neckline where he rested.

"You stole it!" Cindy said with an indignant look to the skull.

"Don't worry I'll give you credit in my biography as an almost inspiration," Sean smiled before he noticed that directly in front of their path was one of his marks which meant they were going in the wrong direction.

"Great Caesar's ghost, now where do we head? My vast intellect doesn't recall any other caverns we haven't tried." Ralph said with a sigh as the Wogglepillar wished he'd just stayed in Evile's lab and spun a cocoon.

"Logically some way must exist out. It's not as if he can just disappear by magic." Cindy made a very reasonable logical assumption.

"Counterpoint by Occam's Razor sister that the simplest answer is the correct one. Evile CAN disappear by magic." Ralph said before Sita raised her paw to silence them.

"Wait I hear something…" Sita raised one of her ears to try and locate the strange sound that was undercutting their conversation.

"Beyond the bugs in my ear's arguing?" The Hungry Tiger yawned drowsily. Being hungry made him tired as well as making him more hungry.

"We're Woggleleptra!" Ralph and Cindy shouted into the Tiger's ears as Sita quite simply walked through one of the walls beside them.

"Fascinating, it must be an illusion placed here by Doctor Lackey," Michael the Arch-wizard said as he ran his hand through the wall Sita had just walked through.

The Hungry Tiger soon followed his love into the wall as he found himself on the other side of a hologram generated by a steam-powered projector. The room was about the size of a small house with nearly every inch covered in cables, glassware, and machinery set up by the mad scientist. In the back of the room was a metal ladder that led directly to a trapdoor in the ceiling that Rama suspected would bring them out of this cavern complex.

Sita was standing in the middle of the facility looking at a bunch of monitors as she sat on a uncomfortable metal stool.

"I have found where Evile is and what he is presently up to," Sita said as she looked at the picture of the warlock squeezing Ozma like a vice.

"By Poseidon's whiskers! It's a Lurline Engine! It's definately a GUMs system but he seems to have revesed it for transmigration of mystical energies rather than basic generation," Michael said as he stared at the machines all about.

"Speak Ozzish man!" The Hungry Tiger asked, the explanation the Arch-Wizard was giving was confusing enough without being on an empty stomach.

"They've stolen Lurline and her daughter's magical powers and are storing them here! Only Ozma is left with any magical ability because the machine is confused whether she is a fairy or a human," Michael said as he read a paper-print out of the machines current activity.

"Obviously we must steal the powers for our own selfish gain!" King Sean shouted as he gave his best indignant voice about the whole thing.

"You mean restore them to Lurline and her sisters along with my own abilities," Michael said dryly to the skull beside him.

"Yes of course," Sean muttered before gritting his teeth in frustration.

"Dealing with this kind of power must be done delicately lest all of Avy-Lyon suffer for one false…" Ralph the Woggleptra twin started to say before the Hungry Tiger kicked over one of the machines and started tearing out circuits with his claws. Sita soon joined in as sparks started to fly from their animal attack on the device.

"Well that works too I'd say brother." Cindy reassured him even as Michael smashed a monitor beside the two wogglepillars.

With the destruction of the Lurline Engine, Evile's image on the monitor began to grow smaller as his stolen energies departed him forever.

***

Chapter 13

King David Ozroar had invited Milo and Vorestia inside without a hesitance of a second-thought the moment he had seen them and was currently sitting them down at the massive round table he had grown just in case the slightly crazed hermit of a King ever managed to figure out how to grow a group of knights to sit at it. A jolly-looking man with a short golden beard and a slightly large belly from two many years of growing his own sweet foods without the notice of his wife, King David gladly served them his best china that he had grown and prepared a magnificent feast catered to their every taste.

"You have no idea what it's like to lack visitors for as many years as I've been trapped on this island. I swear to you if I hadn't possessed that lovely book tree out in the Forrest of Knick-Knacks I would have gone mad. As such I've managed to find myself quite a few wonderful new skills in my considerable leisure time such as horticulture, basketweaving, gourmet cooking, and how to make bird houses!" The King said gaily as he plopped down at the throne at the north side of the table across from his guests in the South.

"I'm very pleased to see you've adapted so well to your new surroundings Your Majesty..." Milo wasn't sure what exactly to say to King Ozroar whose kidnapping had until recently imperiled all of Oz.

"Adapting? Yes, but truly speaking I would do anything to return to my beloved family on Avy-Lyon. Well I wouldn't dump myself in a pool of acid or allow myself to be eaten whole or do something nasty to someone who didn't deserve it but you can understand what I mean I hope." King Ozroar said as he poured himself a drop of tea on his cup of sugar.

Milo looked at the strange figure and in a slightly awed tone "If I see a March Hare around here and a dormouse I wouldn't be surprised."

"What was that? Tea for your sugar?" King Ozroar said as he cast a magical spell with a long teakwood wand to send the cup of tea floating over the table before accidentally making a too big wave with it, spilling it's hot contents on Milo's lap.

"Uh thank you," Milo said as he removed a napkin from the table to wipe away the stain.

"Oats?" Vorestia said as she ate her meal. It was a fabulous ever-full bag of feed that she kept her head in for her section of the meal.

"I'm fine without." Milo corrected as he looked at King David and tried to figure out how to get the man, Vorestia, and himself off Edenia without too much trouble.

"So Mr. Umbrella man, do you have any family you've been exiled from by an evil wizard?" David said even as he buttered the jam on the table with his toast. Table manners you must understand are the first thing you lose when you live an extended time as a bachelor I'm sorry to say.

"As a matter of fact yes Your Highness. I have been exiled from my lady-love who is a Fairy-Princess Oz named Ozma. She is the loveliest, the gentlest, wisest, most magical woman in the world and I care for her very deeply. I hope to be able to return to her very soon as well." Milo said before lifting the lid off the mutton he was about to eat and finding a live sheep underneath. The sheep of course quickly bolted and Milo didn't stop him.

"How very curious. I have a daughter named Ozma who is the Princess of Oz." King Oz said as he looked at his steak which was too rare and pointed his wand upon it. The steak promptly was struck by enough force to light a new sun and left the pound of meat a piece of charcoal. King Ozroar gladly then started munching on the ashen brick.

"Yes I do believe they are in fact the same person sir." Milo said as he decided to forego eating for a bit.

King Ozroar pulled out a very large Stove-pipe hat from his crown, which was of course magical, followed then a pair of glasses and finally a adding machine. "Do you have a job young man?"

"I'm the spiritual leader of numerous Oz citizens and pursuing a state of ultimate enlightenment for myself and them as a whole," Milo answered quickly.

"I'll take that as a no. Do you have any prospects?" King Ozroar pushed a button on his adding machine.

The Engagement of Ozma
Book Two in the Umbrella Man of Oz series

Milo was more than mildly insulted by that one "I hope to become your daughter's husband!"

"A gold-digger eh?" King Ozroar typed that into his adding machine.

"Now look here sir!" Milo started to get up from his chair before King Ozroar pointed his wand at him and sent him flying backwards into it.

"Are you a pacifist and willing to convert to Ozranism if you marry her?" King Ozroar asked blinking as he cupped his hands.

"If you don't count umbrella whackings and I have no idea what Ozranism is!" Milo said and he was certain he had encountered every religion there was after his travels in Oz.

"Tsk Tsk Tsk Tsk," King David said. He did not consider people who performed umbrella whackings pacifists at all and furthermore while he had just made up Ozranism, it was a very dear religion to his heart.

Milo had absolutely no idea how to respond to this bizzare turn of events.

"Well I give you my blessing Mister Starling and hope you have many fascinating and wonderful years as my daughter's husband. The Nine hundred year waiting period is absolutely killer for people who don't find immortality but I suggest eating magic apples and listening on how I met my wife," King Ozroar intoned with a grin that reminded Milo very much of a shark after having been fed.

"Ooooo story!" Vorestia clapped her hands as she licked her saltlick on the table.

"Uhhhh okay. The advice of a wise man refreshes like water from a mountain spring. Go ahead." Milo said as he leaned back in his chair.

"Very well the story begins a long time ago in a gala...no sorry dimensi...no we're in the Otherworld...planet...no...Land far far FAR away." King David lept onto his chair and made dramatic gestures before leaping back down upon his posterior to continue the extravagant tale.

"Oz?" Milo ventured a guess.

"Absolutely!" King David said as Vorestia munched on her oats like popcorn.

"Oz was a much different land back then you must understand because while we were a magical land we weren't nearly as magical as many others and the situation was grim indeed for the people of it. My father King Oz the First was ruler of the tiny patch of green land in the center of the much vaster land about it surrounded by unpleasant but not especially lethal desert. Savage pygmies were to the East, Fierce Amazons to the South, Kilt wearing Bezerkers to the North, and brutal legions to the West!" King Oz looked over his shoulder as if he expected any one of the warlike proto-Ozites to jump out and devour him at any moment.

"Kilt wearing bezerkers…alright," Milo said, wondering just how much isolation and age had colored the man's memories of the entire thing.

"Aiye, which means yes. Alas my father was an old man and soon was forced to go to a better place than our humble country could provide him and built a magical boat with his court wizards to seek out new lands and eventually return to Oz to save it in it's time of greatest need. Given it's been a thousand years and the troubles Oz has had, I'm of the mind he's not coming back at this point." King David sighed and adjusted the little golden crown on his head which had an A on a golden lion emblazoned on it.

"I can imagine why," Milo said feeling sorry for Ozma's grandfather.

"Maybe he was just really busy," Vorestia suggested in hopes that nothing bad had happened to him.

"Well a thousand years is enough time to take care of most business and I think it's just carelessness he hasn't come back yet personally. In any case with my father gone, I as the eldest of the line of the founder of our land was required to become King. Unfortunately I was not very Kingly for I hated violence and immediately dissolved our army which upset my counselors greatly since they were afraid at any point we would be invaded," King Ozroar replied. He looked embarrassed and Milo nodded.

"Turning the other cheek is often misinterpreting as slapping someone else," Milo said with a nod. Pacifism was a hard act to follow. It could also be quite upsetting if you were put in charge of the people who were not.

"I certainly have no idea what you mean. In any case I much preferred to play the harp which I was extremely good at." King David removed a small fiddle and played a bit of a Kentucky jig which the pair clapped at the end of, not knowing what else to say the crazed monarch.

"The situation might have reached a very different conclusion than it did had not it been further complicated by my brother Saul discovering a giant cache of Emeralds that the Nome King had hidden underneath our castle. The Nome King knew that our father was so honest that he would never touch the emeralds that were not his and they would be safe. My brother Saul however had no such scruples and knew that with such wealth he could raise a great army and conquer the surrounding lands if he were King," King David continued his story.

"Nomes I hate em!" Vorestia stuck out her tongue and spat with distaste. Unicorns you must realize have very little in common with Nomes given the former prefer wide open forrests and sunlight while Nomes enjoy their dusty, dank, and otherwise thoroughly unpleasant caverns. A unicorn can't possibly understand why someone would look at a gem reflecting light to create a rainbow when you can get the real thing after a rainstorm.

"They were merely prideful and grouchy in my time Lady Vorrie. Then Good King Goldric and his son Silvernus were overthrown and they became a much more wicked people. In any case, I knew my brother had decided secretly to do away with me the very night I was to celebrate my first year as King." King David leaned back and thought about that particular thought, so far back that his seat tipped completely over.

"Oh my!" Milo said running over to help him up but the King seemed fine on the floor.

"I'd have thought you'd have tossed him in the moat if you'd known he'd kill you. I'd have speared him good with my horn and then stomped him for good measure," Vorestia said as Ozroar felt the empty air above her forehead sadly.

"Yes but he probably would be very cold in the moat now wouldn't he? Well I left with my trusty harp towards my favorite spot in Oz which was a meadow that was reputed to be a place where faeries dance though no one had seen any in twenty years. This was of course because faeries were not as common in Oz as they are now and even now they have plenty places to go other than one specific grotto. Twenty years is almost nothing of a time to them at all." David said even as he somersaulted up into the air and onto his feet like a trained gymnast.

"Well not when your trapped in a human girl's body...abet a very attractive human girl's body." Vorestia said looking at her reflection in the nearby well-polished table.

"In any case, I played my harp with all of my heart that night in worry for my country which I was sure would be destroyed by either my brother or the nations surrounding it. It was then Lurline the Lovely heard my beautiful song and floated down with her band to listen to it from their dance in the grove. Lurline had just been crowned High Queen of the Faeries by her mother and was lying heavily underneath the burden which had until that point been solely how to pass the time beyond her dances." King David stopped for a moment to think about what he had next to say.

Milo was really of the mind they should figure out some way off this island right now but it really was a very fascinating story and he was anxious to hear how the breathtakingly beautiful older woman had indeed been smitten by the mere mortal before him.

"Lurline was moved deeply by my music and I was glad to have such a receptive audience to my work which I loved a great deal more than ruling. Finally nearing dawn we had discussed everything under the sun in-between strummings and she asked me to come away with her to be her husband," King Ozroar sighed with a dreamy look in his eye.

"My that was a short courtship," Vorestia said, you really couldn't get to know a person in her mind in such a short time.

"Well people lived shorter lives then. Which I admit doesn't affect much immortals," Milo pointed out. Milo as anyone who read the previous chronicle will know is a great believer in love at first sight.

The Engagement of Ozma
Book Two in the Umbrella Man of Oz series

"I said unto Lurline that I could not leave my kingdom without a King even if I was a very bad one and certainly not in the shape that it was currently in. Luly, as I call her, had long loved Oz and it's surrounding lands and agreed to do something about it. Finally she decided to enchant the land slowly so that it would be more blessed than all other lands in the world, make sure the desert became impassable so no invaders from beyond could seek to destroy us, and place my brother in charge of the surrounding lands with out so much as a knife being poked." King David smiled and gave a nice twang on his fiddle.

"I thought your brother was evil," Milo commented as he scratched the top of his head with his umbrella.

"Well he was but that was eventually resolved with the aid of a forbidden fountain." King Oz smiled and chuckled to himself. Saul Ozroar had ruled a brief time as a tyrant but upon the regaining of his memory he'd been helped to bring peace to all the warring kingdoms of the square before dying a very happy man.

"That's a wonderful story though I fail to see how it applies to me. A wise man's words express deep streams of thought but this is a bit too deep of a pond for me." the Umbrella man of Oz shrugged and found a group of strawberries on the table that looked quite delicious. He reached over to them before King David tossed them out the window for looking inedible.

"Obviously he's saying that love will conquer all in the end," Vorestia explained as she looked at the flower decoration on the table and started grazing.

"So now all we do is have to figure out how to get off the island to help it do so," Milo said slightly bitterly. The Supreme master worked in mysterious ways but sometimes a bit too mysterious for people who like their toast buttered by the knife and not vice versa.

"Well there's a giant which lives on the other side of the island who blows hurricanes when's he's not nodding off to sleep. We could ask him to blow you back to Avy-Lyon." Vorestia replied inbetween her chomps on heather.

"Oooooo how lovely! I wish you'd told me years ago." King Ozroar clapped his hands and went to fetch his coat.

Charles Phipps

"Many favors are showered on those who please the king!" Milo said with a shout as he jumped in the air for joy. It was just possible he might end up with his Lady love after all.

***

Evile Lackey didn't know what was happening but he didn't like it. The Lurline Engine below being destroyed. He could no longer contain in his body the magical energies of the Fairy Queen or her daughters. One by one colored balls of mystical power flew from him into their respective daughter as their ability to work sorcery was restored. With each ball of light the Warlock grew a little smaller until at the thirteenth ball he was on the ground, all but powerless.

Ozma leapt from Evile's arms before he grew too small to hold her and once on the ground she pointed her wand directly at the Warlock and shouted the secret magical spell for disarming an Erb or warlock of his black powers forever.

This spell is usually reserved for Fairy Princesses only and when a wizard is very powerful it may not work but since I don't approve of wicked magical users I say it is high time that the spell is spread as far as it can possibly be.

The magical word is 'Zonnanamar' and if you say it right it may be possible to end a wicked person's enchanted reign of terror.

"Ahhhhh! You've destroyed all my beautiful wicked wizardry!" Evile shouted in shock. His mind had been blanked of all the potion recipes, true names, proper wand waving methods, spoken incantations, alchemical machine schematics, and of course the GUM theory. He could no more tell a crystal ball from a bowling one let alone see the future or other places with it. In some ways worse than the actual loss of his great power was the knowledge that he had possessed it once and would never so again.

"And it serves you right!" Dorothy cried with a shout. She'd not been so frightened in her life in many a year.

"Evile Lackey you shall accompany us back to Castle Eternia where you will tell us all you know about the disappearance of my father and any other terrible deeds you have done in order that they may be corrected. Then you will be forced to drink from the fountain of Oblivion and live a useful life!" Ozma of Oz ordered, she was at the very end of her patience but she still managed to be as merciful as she was kind.

"My daughters words I enforce with the full law of Fairy-Land. You cannot escape Evile Lackey!" Lurline the Just said, comming up behind her daughter even as the rest of her band gathered round.

"Ha! You'll never force me to tell you what I've done with your father and fiance!" Doctor Lackey sneared. It was theoretically possible to make an Erb feel guilty for their evil deeds and the same for a warlock but it required an exceptional amount of work. The Wicked Witch of the West's son slowly moved his feet back towards the center of the Stone circle even as Ozma stood there shocked.

"You've done something to Milo?" Ozma asked in shock. She had been so pre-occupied with her mother's tests that she hadn't even noticed he was missing. Which just goes to show you that even the absolute best person on the planet can occasionally make a mistake regarding her loved ones.

"You brute! If you've done anything I..." Dorothy couldn't think of anything nasty enough to describe what she wanted to do to the man. If nothing else Evile had achieved his goal of hurting the one who had slain his mother.

Evile pulled then off a stick pin from his lapel as he shouted "Beware! One false move and I'll drop this pin which contains a secret magical explosive I created before my powers were taken away! It's so powerful that it'll blow this island up!" This was of course hogspittle and it was an ordinary tacky pin the warlock had picked up at a faire as a consolation prize.

"Mom can I just set him on fire?" Kessily said as she fluttered up beside her Queen.

"No Kessily," Lurline said as she gazed with pity upon the base beast before her.

As Evile slowly backed he staggered a bit as just behind him the Hungry Tiger was lifting up the trap door from Evile's laboratory to the surface of Avy-Lyon. Evile's magical lighter fell out of his pocket even as the manic madman began the list of demands he had for the return of their loved ones.

Charles Phipps

"First of all I want all my magical powers restored and a complete library of powerful new magic from your stores. I also want a gigantic Roc as my personal mount with a hundred Metalurgians to be my personal slaves. I'll have you enchant me furthermore a castle with a arsenal of alchemical canons that will allow me to conquer whatever kingdom I choose to settle down in…" Evile might have went on with his list had not the Hungry Tiger picked up the magician's lighter and set fire to his overcoat.

"YAHOOoooooooooeeeeeeeeyyyyyyyyy!" Evile Lackey's licking his lips and rubbing his hand to turned to a terrible shout as he caught fire. Instead of turning into ashes instantly though Evile instead burst upwards like a bottle rocket into the air. Sailing higher and higher and higher the warlock finally exploded into a huge beautiful series of sparkles that filled the air in a kalidescope of magnificent colors. It was the nicest thing Evile had ever given the world and it was also the absolute last. The Hungry Tiger had put out the Wicked Warlock of Avy-Lyon and nevermore was anything ever heard from him again.

"Hungry Tiger that was very naughty of you!" Princess Ozma scolded before going over to embrace her companion leaving the whole.

"Oh say can you see by the dawns early light…" The Bald Eagle put his right wing over his chest and began to sing to the explosions in the sky.

Lurline's band not knowing what else to do also covered their chests and began to sing with the Eagle even as Lurline herself walked over to check on the escapees from Evile Lackey's clutches, including her very own true Court Wizard! Michael who was looking much worse for wear thanks to his experience but very grateful for his freedom, embraced his queen with a deep hug.

"My Queen Ozma, I would like you to meet my beloved fiance Sita," The Hungry Tiger gestured towards the lovely white tigress which followed him up the ladder into the bright sunlight.

"Your Royal Highness, it is so good to finally meet you in person. I am honored beyond words. I look forward to serving under you as ruler with my husband of the Tiger Kingdom," Sita said as she lowered her head towards the little ruler of Oz.

The Engagement of Ozma
Book Two in the Umbrella Man of Oz series

"It is I who am honored Lady Sita and I am anxious to hear about all your trials and tribulations. I furthermore gladly pronounce you rightful King and Queen of Tigerland which has been without a ruler since the time when the previous Maharajas were slain by the Wicked Witch of the West's son," Ozma waved her magical wand over both of them and crowns appeared upon their heads.

King Sean then plopped up from the bottom of the pit "And of course reward me with my own kingdom of fawning slaves and immeasurable wealth!"

"You will be allowed to be a paperweight on my desk King Sean if you promise to behave and not rewrite any of my words," Queen Ozma said tapping him on the head with her wand.

"Excellent! The ear of a Queen! Yes I'm moving up in the world indeed," the Skull cackled maniacally.

Queen Ozma then noticed the woggleleptra that were sitting around the Hungry Tiger's collar and said "And you young heroes, how may I reward you for your part in rescuing the Tiger Princess?"

"You can lower the height requirements for the Athletic college! It's unfair to bugs who have yet to reach their chrysalis!" Ralph the Wogglepillar said with a fierce frown.

"We're not bugs Ralph!" Cindy gave her brother a nudge with her head.

"Oh right!" Ralph winced as he realized his mistake.

"I cannot change the height requirements because that would be unfair to the other students but I will in fact make allowances for students of varying size to be allowed to compete and smaller sized learning pills prepared." Ozma tapped both of the wogglepillars lightly on the head with a smile.

"Oh how can you be so calm Ozma?" Dorothy asked as she tugged on her hair and tears nearly welled into her eyes, she was worried sick for her friend and not at all confident that she'd ever see him again.

"I am calm Dorothy because it will only be a clear and level head which restores the one who is dearest to my heart. Giving way to fear and anger merely accomplish what Evile tried to do." Ozma said with a smile as she closed her eyes gently to think on what to do in this situation.

"I'm not exactly sure but what just happened sis?" Dawn asked her sister with a blink.

"I'm not exactly sure either but logically we'll see this through." Dusk said blinking even as she struggled to put the pieces together in her head.

"Oh it just feels it'll turn out all right. With our combined winged selves...errrr...and nonwing folk we're sure to come to a happy ending!" Dawn slapped her hand against her heart with a breath of refreshing air.

"You have my full magical resources at your disposal," Tasb whispered into her ear as the dark skinned maiden kissed her sister on the cheek.

"You'd have all my magical resources as well my Lady Ozma if not for the fact that unfortunately Evile took them with himself to the place below." Michael held out his hands which could not cast even the simplest cantrip or glamour anymore and waved them in the air pitifully.

"Oh no Michael! Without you who will create the famous white ships that have served Avy-Lyon for centuries?" Oceania said with a shocked gasp.

"And who will create the fabulous magical make-up that helps me look my best?" Glitteria said in surprised terror. Glitteria was actually the plainest of Ozma's sisters and it was her self confidence and style that made her seem like such a catch to the thousands of young suitors who came for her hand.

"And who will make new forms of animals for my gardens?" Kirri said in terror even as she turned herself into a kangaroo.

"And all the toys that we give to Santa Clause for his shops!" Christine said as she thought of the many children on Earth who benefitted from her protection.

"You may all learn to do such things on your own sisters. I have kept careful notes of all my spells and journals so that my knowledge would never be lost and it is high time that I started teaching the subject to people even if I no longer practice it. Who knows? In an immortal land I may someday be able to relearn all of the many thousand of years of lore I once had," Michael said with a

The Engagement of Ozma
Book Two in the Umbrella Man of Oz series

smile even as he looked into the sky, glad his magic had done some good in the end.

"Your optimism is heartening Arch-Wizard. I only hope that together we may help our sister and mother recover those dearest without the power we once held." Morgan shook her head with a sigh, feeling a great deal of guilt for not recognizing the wickedness that was all about. Sadly she was not the type to be a queen of the faeries for she accepted all too easily things at face value and relied on her mother's advice rather than her own heart.

"No force on Earth will stop the Highest of All Royal Families! Now can I have my toupee?" The Bald Eagle cheered as he watched the last of the sparks flutter to the ground.

***

Jellia Jamb, Trot, Button Bright, and Betsy Bobbin looked out from the windows of the Emerald Palace, where the citizens had been gathered, to the site of the mountainous pile of junk that was the Illumi-nati invasion force. One hundred and fifty five thousand candle holders of various shapes and sizes were piled skyward with all about them the sights of burned building, charred emeralds, and smoke stains. It was quite possibly the biggest mess that the capital of Oz had ever seen.

"Well I'm certainly not cleaning this mess up by myself," Jellia said finally as she shook her head at the calamity.

"Don't worry, I am certain everything will find a way of working itself out. It always does somehow," Jack Pumpkinhead Oz the First said with a sigh. The King of Oz was wearing a royal technicolor coat and a tiny crown that had been carved out of his top's stem.

"Well personally I don't intend to leave the Emerald City like this for the Queen to find when she returns. It would reflect badly upon me as the Royal Wizard," The Wizard of Oz said in a huff even as he pinched his nose for the smell coming downwind.

"Not to mention the people would be rather unhappy about their homes being burned down as well," King Jack said as he raised a branch finger into the air to accentuate his point.

"We are an absolutely the worst rulers that Oz has ever seen," Trot said as she buried her head into Betsy's shoulder and Button grabbed hold of Trot's legs with a sigh.

"Not so!" A voice filled the air with a educated musical tone. Flying through one of the many windows in the hall the group stood in was Zim the Flying Sorcerer. The gigantic eight foot tall green haired man was carrying a huge Pumpkin in his hands and had a trailing scarf flying from around his neck.

"Oh hello Mr. Zim, what a pleasure to make your acquaintance with this head," Jack bowed and unfortunately his head fall off of his stick.

Toto bounced up and barked at the Grand Magician of Munchkinland before Zim removed a tiny homegrown steak for the dog that had been specially grown to delight doggy taste buds. Giving the food a toss in the air, Toto leapt up and grabbed it in his mouth before beginning his meal.

"Trust me Mr. Pumpkinhead that you do not need to recover that head. Glinda and I have been observing events from her palace in the Book of Records as they unfolded and you have all handled matters brilliantly. Sometimes we must bow before those of superior wisdom in a crisis even when they are not necessarily such at first glance. For your grand rulership Jack I present to you this Royal Pumpkin whose seeds are of superior quality to your current pumpkin brand and which shall last much longer before spoilage sets in," Zim said as the magician handed over the giant pumpkin to Jack with pride.

"Ooooo thank you!" Jack's head said on the ground before his body took the Pumpkin from Zim's hand and plopped it on. Immediately his head on the ground went silent and the faceless pumpkin made some 'mmmmp' noises.

"You probably should have waited to carve your face before you put it on," Zim conjured forth a pen-knife to begin working on Jack's new features as he talked.

"Well we weren't very good rulers of Oz while she was away but the least we can do is figure out how to fix this giant mess. Hank and I will get everyone organized to drag all these candles back to the

Illumi-nation," Betsy said nodding toward the gigantic mass of wicks and candles.

"Maybe we can instruct them to melt them all down and remake them with less iron in them. I can go down to Lake Quad and make a bucket brigade with the mushroom people who live down there to bring water for the scrubbing." Trot looked at the place and thought of some nice sea chants that would do good for swabbing the streets and walls.

"and I will order legions of young men to come forward and rebuild all that's been burned. We'll have a war with the dead trees in the Green land and get plenty of wood." Button smiled mischeviously as he swung an imaginary ax. He'd learned a few things from Nick Chopper before he'd wandered off to find other things of interest like sling-shots and building rockets.

"And I will supervise because only perfect polishing will be proper," Jellia waved her duster lightly in the air.

"Now see, look what you can accomplish when you put your efforts together towards one common purpose?" Zim said with a smile even as he backed away a few steps from the four's cross looks at him.

"In any case as the Mayor-Elect of the City of Emeralds, I give my full blessing to your recovery efforts," The Wizard of Oz said with a bow as he waved his hand merrily towards the four young people on their mission.

"Bark!" Toto said, the Dog giving a slight growl to the Wizard.

"Now listen here mutt! The recount results will be in any time now and if the Snark Snark hadn't made off with the ballot box for the Southern quarter I'd be mayor already," The Wizard said some words that he would regret later on, specifically when Toto grabbed hold of his leg in a deep bite.

As the Wizard danced around with the little dog attached to his ankle, the four nodded to each other and placed their hands together. "When Ozma returns, the city will be as good as new if not better!"

Zim the Flying Sorcerer could only chuckle as he finished the job on the Royal Pumpkinhead of Oz. The Wizard of Munchkinland could have intervened at any time to put out the huge flames but Glinda had advised him to hold his hand. The Royal Court of Oz was undergoing a very distinct change and he was interested deeply in seeing how the wonders of adulthood would effect it. Provided none of them just took the Nome King's belt and reduced themselves back to children to avoid it. Zim had always feared that was a distinct possibility with the inhabitants of the Emerald City and not necessarily bad. He'd always wondered what it might have been like to have a childhood of his own, he'd never had one because of the unique circumstances of his birth.

"Oh joy! I can talk again! I bet my father will be so proud of me for ruling her country while she's away! I bet my other father will be pleased too! Do you think my father will get along with my stepfather? If they don't I don't know whatever I should do!" Jack said with a sigh and then clapped his hands together.

"Don't worry Jack I'm sure they will get along swimmingly," Zim said, making sure that Jack had plenty of wrinkles in his pumpkin. Wrinkles after all were a major source of wisdom though few people had noticed it quite yet.

"Oooo we're going to invite them to a beach party?" Jack asked.

"Then again perhaps I didn't miss much in childhood," Zim chuckled to himself even the Wizard pried Toto off his leg.

***

Chapter 14

Milo Starling whistled the road music to a 1939 musical that he was quite fond of though for the life of him he couldn't remember its name. The travel to the location of the giant was a relatively swift one with a unicorn guide and only got them trapped in quicksand with a horde of cannibal vines once. Given I'm sure that you have no interest in a life threatening escape or the brave and heroic actions of the trio to save themselves from certain doom, I'll simply skip over that part and take you directly to their arrival at the resting place of the giant that was their ticket to rescue.

"Well this is absolutely wonderful! A plague on both our houses!" Milo cursed as he banged his umbrella against the nearby rocks to show his frustration with what he saw.

The Giant known as Rimy was the strongest of all as far as anyone could tell with lungs that indeed did blow the majority of hurricanes in the world. This was not his actual job because Hurricanes while necessary in some places are not really necessary when Rimy remembers to do his job and send small storms. Unfortunately like Maggie the urge to slack off on one's job is a considerable one so that he routinely ventured here to take naps. Milo's outburst stems from the fact that this time the huge man had covered his head with a mountain and only his mouth was visible, it would be very difficult indeed to get him to help them off Edenia.

"Now, now it's not as bad as all that. Certainly the situation looks a bit dire but so did it for Arthur facing the Saxons!" King Ozroar said with a happy grin, trudging along beside the pair.

"As I recall Arthur died fighting the Saxons and the kingdom fell to them," Milo pointed out to the monarch.

"Oh pish-posh he'll be back," King David said with a wrinkle of his nose.

"You know this reminds me of the time we were almost devoured by cannibal vines, does anyone else remember that?" Vorestia said, pulling tiny bits of the terribly hungry plant from her silvery hair.

"Yes, I seem to recall something of it to the effect of an hour ago yes," Milo said, trying to be as polite as possible with the frustration he felt to this situation. He decided just to laugh at it and sure enough all the anger that had been welling up in him died away, followed by pure and good thoughts of his love Ozma.

"Well the situation seemed hopeless then but we found away out. Okay we just followed King Oz when he climbed out on them like ropes but aside from a bit of blood loss and some horrible scars we're just peachy!" Vorestia commented with a clap of her hands in delighted pleasure.

"Your optimism gives me great hope for the future milady. I shall persevere," Milo gave the unicorn a slight kiss on the cheek before being shoved to the ground.

"Hey watch it! You're engaged buster!" Vorestia frowned down upon the Umbrella man who shook his head bewildered.

"Yes, yes I am," Milo blinked as he adjusted his tie and looked at the form of the huge stadium length man who was in front of them. His mouth shooting out huge puffs of wind into the air with each breath that he took.

"Well let's just put our heads together on this and come up with a sure fire way of finding our way off the island," King Oz then laid his head on the side of Milo's shoulder.

"Perhaps my umbrella can help!" Milo said rather desperately as Vorestia leaned her head on his other shoulder.

"You're right, it does look a bit cloudy," King Ozroar smiled and pointed to the absolutely clear sky.

"No this was a magical creation of Queen Ozma herself! Surely in it is some magical capacity for flying that will whisk us away to safety!" Milo pointed to the sky and shook the umbrella to it, trying to get it to act again.

"Oh you mean like in 'Sky-Island'? That'll work," Vorestia nodded vigorously after removing her head from Milo's shoulder.

"Unfortunately I must inform you that I do not possess the capacity for flight Sir Starling," the Umbrella then started wiggling in Milo's hand and speaking with a strong tenor voice.

The Engagement of Ozma
Book Two in the Umbrella Man of Oz series

"You can talk!" Milo said in absolute surprise for while he was fairly used to normally inanimate objects speaking around him, they usually did by the time he got to know them well.

"Well certainly I can talk! I am after all as you said a creation of Queen Ozma herself which means I am one of the most enchanted objects in Oz and certainly the most enchanted umbrella in all the Earth!" The emerald green object opened and closed itself in pride.

"Yet you can't take us into the sky? Flying is the most common magical umbrella ability in the world!" Milo said, slightly cross with his umbrella despite his best efforts not to be.

"Well you could load up a patch back at the Emerald City but it would cause everything else to stop working with me. Besides I wouldn't help you even if I could!" The Umbrella hissed back at Milo who was taken aback by the device's anger. Milo let the item go and it fluttered down to the ground where it stood up on it's tip and glowered it's handle menacingly at the trio.

"I do believe you've offended him Milo!" Vorestia said before giving a 'shame, shame, shame' rub with her fingers.

Milo blinked, wondering what he'd done. "I…uh…sir…"

"Good heavens man you've done nothing but abuse me since the beginning of our relationship! Dashing me against the ground, pulling me out during cold rainstorms to cover you while I get wet, abandoning me for long periods of time indoors with no one to talk too! I swear the only time you've even shown me the slightest bit of concern was when we were surounded by all those beasts and you said thank you. Well I need more than thank you!" The umbrella finished its rant and just stood there waiting for Milo's reply.

"I suppose I'm very sorry for my behavior towards you my small companion and I admit it has been atrocious. While I certainly don't deserve it I would very much appreciate if you would give me a second chance and allow me to make amends for all the trouble I've caused you," Milo chose his words carefully as he looked at the umbrella.

"Well I can forgive you, this time. But I warn you that if I don't see visible improvement in your behavior then I'm going to find some other potential Umbrella wizard to bide my time with and he'll be superior in every way!" The Umbrella shook itself silly before jumping back into Milo's hands.

"Right. Now we're back to the starting point of this little escapade. Patience is one of the seven virtues," Milo said before King Ozroar climbed up on top of the Giant Rimy's chest.

"Perhaps we can use the great beast's breath to fly us to Avy-Lyon! There is more force here than the cyclone which brought Dorothy to destroy the Wicked Witch of the East!" King David called back to the people still remaining on the ground below him.

"I admit it's a better plan than any we've had thus far. Do you think noble umbrella that you could carry us on the wind of the giant's breath to the land of Avy-Lyon without magical flying powers?" Milo asked the emerald green article in hopes that his kind words would persuade it to do him this favor.

"What? All three of you? The unicorn has been putting on the pounds you know!" The Umbrella angrily retorted.

"I have not!" Vorestia said scandalized. She was just curvy in her mind, that's all.

"Now look here, I'll have none of that talk even if we do desperately need your help," Milo said to the umbrella crossly, there was such a thing as common courtesy you know.

"You're right. I apologize to the robust unicorn. Very well, I will take you all as far as I can go. Just realize that there's no gaurentee you won't end up food for the whale-sharks," The Green Umbrella said even as Milo took Vorestia's hand and she took the hand of the former King of Oz.

"It's a risk they are willing to take!" King Oz said, patting Milo on the back with his free hand.

"Well on the count of three then. One…two…threeeeeeeee!" Milo screamed into the air as the trio were thrown up, up, up, and away into the sky which they soon became a part of.

"Well this isn't so bad is it?" Milo said to his companions who fluttered behind him by his hand like a kite's tail. The Sea of Immortality was a great gigantic silver mass that stretched upon endlessly with the only occasional sight of a whale-shark or one of the fabulous white ships of Avy-Lyon to break the glittering sight.

The Engagement of Ozma
Book Two in the Umbrella Man of Oz series

"Don't say that! Every time someone says that it isn't so bad then nature finds some way to make it worse!" Vorestia the unicorn pleaded, and being so close to nature as unicorns are, it was hard to refute her.

However contrary to the ideas of unicorns that the universe is out to get everyone, it actually is only out to get some people after all, nothing seemed to happen that was in any way unpleasant. In fact the plan went off without a hitch as the sight of Avy-Lyon soon came into view and the emerald umbrella began to direct them down to land upon its lovely shores.

"See? The Supreme Master rescues men from danger while letting the wicked fall into it!" Milo said happily even as the umbrella folded up and they began plummetting down to the Earth at a speed that while nowhere near close to that of light was still likely to be very painful once the ground was struck at it.

"Funny, I don't remember doing anything wicked..." King David Ozroar said as he tumbled through the sky.

"I told you that three was a bad idea!" The Green Umbrella screeched while it tumbled beside it's owner toward the waiting embrace of the world below.

"Oh well it shan't be the first time I've been dropped from an obscenely high altitude to almost certain destruction," Milo said causally as he began his evening prayers.

"You should really tell us about the other times!" Vorestia shouted at the top of her lungs before there was a lurch on all of the group and their descent was stopped.

Flutter held King David Ozroar, Morgan held Milo, Kirri held Vorestia, and Kessily waved the green umbrella around like a sword. The princesses of Avy-lyon had spotted the falling group from above and come to the rescue of them just in the nick of time. Slowly but surely the faeries then dropped them one by one on the ground next to the Great Stone Circle.

"Milo!" Ozma said as she wrapped her arms around her lover with all of her might, nearly crushing the exhausted preacher.

Dorothy was not far long to hug Milo tenderly but she waited until Ozma had finished kissing him quite a number of times to do since these sort of reunions are the stuff romances are made of.

"It was terrible Milo! It turned out Evile Lackey, Igor's father had actually replaced Michael the Court Wizard!" Dorothy explained.

"He's been sent to heights he never would have achieved on his own though now," Kessily joked before Tasb gave her a swat on the back of the head.

It was tacky to gloat over villain's defeats.

"Darnit and I was hoping to remove his mask in the end and explain everything," Milo muttered. He'd often enjoyed doing that with his friends back home.

To say that Lurline and King Oz's reuniting was anything less would be an insult to the two figures whom without the Land of Oz as we know it would not exist. Lurline and David looked upon each other much as they had when they first saw each other with deep unconditional love and while one was dressed for court and the other the rather hastily grown attire of a forest king, they nevertheless looked perfect in their bondage.

Vorestia sniffed as she felt her curse by Lurline flutter away from her like a bad mood faced with the happiest day of her life. At the very moment she became once again a beautiful white mare with a fabulous crystal horn atop of her head, a no purer or prettier figure in all the land. Of course she could become a woman again if she wished but she much perferred being able to trot like most sensible folk. "I absolutely love Happy Endings."

"It'd be even happier if I ended up as the King of Oz and everyone was my slave. Oh well, this will have to do," King Sean said before starting to make terrible crying noises.

At the Castle Eternia, the celebration for the returning triumphant King and Queen of Avy-Lyon was something that rivaled the very grandest of Oz parties with all the happiness that it entailed. Though David was a mortal man the people loved him more than anyone outside of their immediate family because of his goodness and strange sense of humor. They heralded his return with as much fanfare as they heralded Michael who while now being powerless as an Arch-Wizard was nevertheless a welcome change from the person who had been pretending to be him. Evile Lackey had not made any friends in his many years on Avy-Lyon and no one was sorry to see him gone where the goblins go.

The Engagement of Ozma
Book Two in the Umbrella Man of Oz series

It should go without saying that they stayed longer than they originally intended and when it was finally time to return to the Land of Oz, the large group of Ozites and new immigrant in King Sean were actually sorry to have to go. A magnificent fanfare was prepared with Lurline and her Band assembled with King Ozroar, whose mind had recovered handily in the company of his family, and Michael at the center of it to see the group off on the Train of Thought.

"…and no run-on sentences! This means you Ozma during your farewell speech!" The Conductor pointed to the tiny Princess of Oz as the group prepared to board.

The Queen of Oz looked offended at the conductor but looked to her fiance and her best friend with a smile and knew that no words were needed to convey the feelings they wanted to for the Lord and Lady of Avy-Lyon or their gigantic family.

"I will miss you all. Though this trip started horribly, it has been one of the most rewarding of my life. I can think of nothing that would make it more grand," Ozma said, and of course she spoke the truth.

"I can think of one thing my daughter," Lurline chuckled as Dawn and Dusk pulled out the longest scroll in Avy-Lyon history. The thing was huge beyond belief. It moved over the balcony of the Castle, down the air, and over the mountains that immediately surrounded the Castle of the Seelie fey. It was over a mile in length by the time it finally reached the end of its magical paper with every inch of it covered in the signatures of faeries across the Otherworld.

"It has been difficult indeed sister but we have gathered the names of all the faeries in the Land loyal to the Supreme Master and the cause of things good and just. Even the Mightiest of all and Mistress of everything insisted to add her own name to it to approve the union that you two embark on. You'll find it of course at the beginning and the end," Morgan gestured to the scroll as Ozma burst out laughing to the gesture.

"My thanks and I am pleased to see that you all have also signed it. Please keep it here safe until the day of the wedding in which we will surely need it as a reminder of all the people affected by our love," Ozma smiled to her sisters gave a final wave goodbye.

Charles Phipps

"I have already designed a gigantic mechanical dragon to carry to Oz on that date. It will be my next project as soon as I have outfitted the Bald Eagle with a metallic toupee of the finest feathers. I have convinced him that it will be more fashionable if his toupee also gives him an advanced sensor array," Sparksia giggled with joy at the prospective projects.

Ozma could only laugh at the possibilities as she strapped herself into the train's seat.

"I wonder what happened to Vorestia," Milo said aloud as he found himself nestled between his wife and Dorothy who was becoming very fast friends with the Lady Sita.

"My understanding is that she has gone off in search of her old love from before her exile. She has promised to visit us and attend the wedding," Ozma assured her fiance even as the Train sailed off into the Skyline and departed Avy-Lyon for a time.

The Engagement of Ozma
Book Two in the Umbrella Man of Oz series

Epilogue

The Train of Thought arrived at the Emerald City sometime around midnight when the majority of the capital dwellers had gone to sleep. The Emerald Palace was however still awake with a number of crystals glowing brightly to illuminate the glittering halls as Ozma, Milo, and Dorothy returned. Rama and Sita had asked specifically to be dropped off at the jungle nearby Tigerland so that they could make preparations for a truly grand coronation that of course the royal court would all be invited to. Tired themselves from a long vacation they decided that the first thing they would do when they reached their bedrooms was to take a nice long nap.

"One moment Milo, I'm going to go check the throne-room and see if anyone is still up," Ozma said as she pushed open the doors to the throne-room and discovered a large gathering of her friends and family. Jack Pumpkinhead was sitting on the throne with his muge larger crown adorned head, Zim the Flying Sorcerer was standing nearby him like a counsellor, the Scarecrow, Scraps, Trot, Betsy, the Wizard, Jellia, Button Bright, E. Bused, Toto, Raspy the King of Zo, Glinda, Aunt Em, Uncle Henry, and King Pastoria. Above the group was a very large sign which said 'Welcome back Your Highnesses.'

"Boy we have a lot of parties here in Oz," Ozma laughed and walked in to embrace her friends.

"Oh my! Were you waiting up here all night for us?" Dorothy said, walking into the room joyfully.

"Let's just say that we are VERY glad to see you all back," Trot said, hugging Dorothy who was her closest friend after Captain Bill and Betsy.

"So did anything of interest transpire while we were away?" Milo said as he looked at the gathered assortment of Oz's best.

"Well we got invaded by a bunch of candles, I got a new head, and they made me King!" Jack Pumpkinhead Oz the First said with a salute of his arms.

"And if you believe that, I have a bridge to sell in Brooklyn!" E. Bused smiled as he pulled out the century old deed to the property.

"We're very, very, very, very, very glad to see you Ozma," Betsy couldn't resist hugging the Little Princess of Oz for comfort.

"So who won the Mayor-ship of the Emerald City?" Ozma asked as she looked at both Toto and the Wizard, neither of them looked very happy.

"Well actually the funny thing was it seemed that everyone was so annoyed by our campaigning that they voted for the third-party candidate," The Wizard gritted his teeth, trying to look like he was being a good sport about it.

"Grrrrrrr," Toto murmured.

"Third party canidate? I voted for Toto," Dorothy blinked as she looked between Milo and Ozma.

"Well the Wizard had the experience. I voted for him," Milo said cleaning his glasses.

"Ummmm, I voted for the third party candidate too," Ozma looked sheepish.

The Wizard and Toto blinked in shock at the fairy-queen.

"Who IS the third party candidate Ozma?" Dorothy asked, not having heard of anyone else running for Mayor.

"I'd also like to know how he got a million votes!" The Wizard stamped his foot in frustration, the Emerald City has nowhere near a million people after all even counting animals.

"I think I have an idea," Milo said as he lifted up his umbrella. "Will all inanimate objects in this room please say who they voted for in this election?"

"The Public Benefactor!" there was a resounding chorus from the walls, throne, and even clothes on people.

"Well that answers that particular mystery," Milo said proudly as he put his umbrella down.

"I am grateful to you all for coming to welcome me back to Oz but it's really time for all of us to return to our beds and tomorrow I shall tell you all about the grand adventure we had while we were in Avy-Lyon," Ozma shooed off her friends and gave a kiss to her 'son' in Jack Pumpkinhead. With a plop she then positioned herself inside her throne and looked at her fiance.

The Engagement of Ozma
Book Two in the Umbrella Man of Oz series

"There's no place like Oz Milo," Ozma said joking even as her tummy rumbled a bit. She hadn't eaten since they had boarded the train of thought many hours ago.

"Oh here, take this. It's an apple leftover from Edenia that I took from your father's table," Milo handed her a golden apple that Ozma sleepily nodded towards and bit into.

Ozma blinked at the apple even as she swallowed "Milo do you realize this is one of the enchanted apples of Edenia?"

Milo looked at the apple "Oh no! Is that bad?"

"I'm not sure actually. Depending on what type of person you are they can grant long life, your secret heart's desire, or a terrible curse!" Ozma said even as she felt something very strange happening to her. With a start Ozma bolted off her throne and clutched her stomach before Milo backed away in shock at the results.

"Milo…I…I…have wings!" Ozma called as she batted the beautiful gold and green butterfly wings that now grew out of her back. A few attempts at clumsy flying followed as the tiny queen of Oz also found that she could make them disappear into her back at reappear at will. Wrapping her fiance in a kiss she said the words that we will end this book on "This was the best trip imaginable."

Ozma then passed the apple's remains to Milo, who was initially hesitant but with the Supreme Master's approval took a bite out of it. Milo thus became the only one hundred percent human, one hundred percent fairy in Oz…save when Santa Clause visited. The 150% fairy Ozma and he had many more adventures before their wedding in 2895 but those are stories for another time.

Suffice to say they lived happily ever after and Ozma also clobbered her sisters in every winged sport she challenged them too.

Which is the best place I can certainly leave this story on.

The End

Special Thanks to Melody Grandy, Dave Hardenbrook, Michael Carrow, and of course L. Frank Baum for the use of their characters and ideas.

About the Author

Charles Phipps came to Oz relatively late in his life, at least compared to those who grew up reading about L. Frank Baum's wonderful creation. Introduced to the books by a close friend, he soon grew to love every one of the wonderful things produced by the forty-one plus books produced about the world.

Producing 'The Wooing of Ozma' as a tribute to his favorite character and its hero Milo as a tribute to home state and profession, he has been anxiously working on the sequel ever since.

"I hope to continue on with this series to help develop I think Ozma as a character apart from her perfect queen persona but maintaining her integrity as a role model. There are few more lovable people in literature and I hope that fans of Ozma will agree with my interpretation of her love," Charles comments on this work.

He is currently finishing up his degree in history at Ohio University Southern Campus in Ironton, Ohio. He hopes to fill his ambitions of eventually teaching the subject as well as joining his friend Milo's profession.

"Perhaps I'll someday be whisked off to Oz too," he jokes.

Charles has also hinted he's interested in expanding beyond writing Oz into the areas of mystery and science fiction.

Printed in the United States
28670LVS00003B/246